*Sir Gawain and the Green Knight*
and the Idea of Righteousness

DUBLIN STUDIES IN MEDIEVAL AND RENAISSANCE LITERATURE

Series Editor
JOHN SCATTERGOOD
Professor of Medieval and Renaissance English
Trinity College Dublin

This series is concerned with significant aspects of medieval and renaissance literature up to the end of the seventeenth century. It will include studies of important single works, of major authors and of broad movements. It is intended to publish both monographs and collections of essays on particular topics. The research of established academics will be made available as will studies by the new generation of younger scholars. The series will include reviews and revaluations of major aspects of the literature of the period as well as original studies which break new ground or offer fresh approaches to familiar areas; but however detailed the research, it will be presented in such a way as to be accessible both to specialists and non-specialists alike.

In This Series

RICHARD A. McCABE
*The Pillars of Eternity: Time and Providence in* The Faerie Queene

GERALD MORGAN
Sir Gawain and the Green Knight *and the Idea of Righteousness*

Gerald Morgan

# *Sir Gawain and the Green Knight*
## and the
# Idea of Righteousness

IRISH ACADEMIC PRESS

The typesetting of this book was produced by
Seton Music Graphics Ltd, Bantry for
Irish Academic Press, Kill Lane, Blackrock, County Dublin.

ISBN 0-7165-2470-8

A catalogue record for this book
is available from the British Library.

Printed in Ireland by
Colour Books Ltd, Dublin

*For Samuel and Sarah*

Sicut aliqua domus est media inter scientiam artificis qui eam fecit, et scientiam illius qui ejus cognitionem ex ipsa jam facta capit (*ST*, 1a 14.8 *ad* 3).

In the same way a house mediates between the knowledge of the architect who made it and that of one who gets his knowledge of the house from the house itself once it is made (Aquinas).

My 'splendid isolation' was not without its advantages and charms. I did not have to read any publications, nor listen to any ill-informed opponents; I was not subject to influence from any quarter; there was nothing to hustle me. I learnt to restrain speculative tendencies and to follow the unforgotten advice of my master, Charcot: to look at the same things again and again until they themselves begin to speak (Freud).

> I ain't got much polish, me manners is gruff,
>   But I've got a good coat, and I keep meself smart;
> And everyone says, and I guess that's enough;
>   'You can't but like Morgan, 'e's got a good 'art.'
>
>                     (T. S. Eliot)

'Sir Gawain said he was sorry he had slain the woman. Sir Bors then proposed a resolution opposing the slaying of women, which was passed. A very large knight rode in and challenged the entire company; this was tabled for a twelvemonth. There being no further business, we adjourned' (from a cartoon in *Punch*, 21 March 1984, by Bud Handelsman)

# Contents

# Preface

A POEM IS AN ARTEFACT existing in itself, independent of both author and reader, although it is generated by the one and regenerated by the other. Its essential condition is one of anonymity, as E.M. Forster observes in his essay 'Anonymity: An Enquiry':'all literature tends towards a condition of anonymity, and that, so far as words are creative, a signature merely distracts us from their true significance.' Whether or not one subscribes to this view of literature (and the attempts to find a name for the author of *Sir Gawain* show that some scholars at least have resisted it), in practice it has to be accepted in the case of medieval romances that we are dealing with poems in the absence of any knowledge of their authors. The critical method upon which this book is based, therefore, is the simple one of reading and re-reading the text of the poem itself until its nature and meaning have gradually disclosed themselves. It is a method that is simple to characterize, but much less simple to execute. The initial impulse is to free oneself as far as possible from the values of one's own age and to enter imaginatively a world that is differently constituted. This cannot be done without an acceptance of the vulnerability implicit in the extent of one's ignorance and a willingness to remain in a state of ignorance until answers of some kind begin to emerge. If this process is pursued with sufficient rigour then an interpretation should result that is not only unforced but also fresh and independent. Whether such an end has been achieved in the present instance I must leave it to my readers to judge.

But even the closest scrutiny of a text is seldom sufficient for its complete understanding. All texts have been shaped by their historical contexts, so that at some point it is necessary to go beyond the text to the larger context of ideas that have informed it. I have gone to the context of medieval scholasticism, and especially to the thought of its most distinguished representative, Aquinas, in order to grasp the ideas that are imaginatively significant in *Sir Gawain*. I have done so because of the general historical plausibility of scholasticism as a context for a poem written at the end of the fourteenth century, and more specifically because the imaginatively central symbol of the pentangle is drawn from scholastic sources. I have supplied only so much theory as is necessary for my present purposes, and do not claim to provide the learned and comprehensive treatment of late medieval scholastic theory that is to be found in the important study of A.J. Minnis, *Medieval Theory of Authorship*, second edition (Aldershot, 1988).

As is evident from my reference to Minnis, I cannot claim to be a purely fourteenth-century reader and entirely remote from the twentieth-century scholarly world of which I am a part. I should like, therefore, to acknowledge two works of modern scholarship which have influenced and aided me greatly in my labours. The first is the second edition of *Sir Gawain and the Green Knight*, revised by N. Davis in 1967, and in particular its glossary (pp. 159–232), which is a model of its kind and has added greatly to the precision of our knowledge of the poem. The second is *A Reading of Sir Gawain and the Green Knight* by J.A. Burrow (London, 1965). I think it is fair to say that this is the first book to match the literary sophistication of the poem itself, and marks a new development in the critical discussion of the poem. In my own analysis of the poem I take issue with some of the interpretations of both of these eminent scholars, but I hope that these disagreements will in no sense be construed as a qualification of my sense of indebtedness to them.

A good deal of the matter of this book has already appeared in the form of articles. I am indebted to the editors of *The Modern Language Review* for permission to use my article 'The Significance of the Pentangle Symbolism in *Sir Gawain and the Green Knight*', *MLR*, 74 (1979), 769–90, to the editor of *The Review of English Studies* for permission to use my article 'The Validity of Gawain's Confession in *Sir Gawain and the Green Knight*, *RES*, NS, 36 (1985), 1–18, and to the editors of *Medium Aevum* for permission to use my article 'The Action of the Hunting and Bedroom Scenes in *Sir Gawain and the Green Knight*', *Medium Aevum*, 56 (1987), 200–216.

My remaining obligations contain an element of personal as well as professional indebtedness, since the writing of this book has in itself turned out to be something of a quest. My sense of obligation to the General Editor of this series, Professor John Scattergood, is much more than merely conventional. He has helped me through more than one crisis in his usual kindly and unfastidious manner, and I have always been able to rely upon his scholarly generosity. Mrs Corinna Lonergan, the Head of the Italian Department at Trinity, has been a constant source of wise advice, and her inspiring teaching of the *Inferno* has often stirred my own enthusiasm for Dante. I have profited greatly from discussions with Dr David Scott-MacNab, for his formidably precise knowledge of the practices of medieval hunting has made the argument of the poem clearer to me at a number of points. In a more general way I have gained from the literary sensitivity and balanced judgment of Miss Helen Cooney, a postgraduate student whom I had the good fortune to supervise. My greatest debt in many ways is to the students I have known at Trinity, and I have often been encouraged by their honesty, enthusiasm, critical intelligence, good humour and (not least) bad jokes. I am grateful to Miss Lee Guckian, our departmental secretary, for organizing and completing the preparation of the manuscript, and to Miss Leona Coady, her successor, who has seen the book to completion with seemingly effortless efficiency. I am also grateful to Mrs Alice Tunney, Ms Liane Goodwin, and Miss Helen McGrail of the Central Secretariat for doing much of the typing of the manuscript. I must also thank Miss Geraldine Mangan, the senior departmental secretary, for many acts of personal kindness.

I am especially indebted to Dr Sineád O'Brien, for the clarity of her thought and soundness of her judgment have been vital elements contributing to the progress of this work. I wish also to thank Miss Brenda Cornell for her support at a time when I had most need of it. Mrs Emma Bristow and Mrs Ivy Jones have inspired me by their courage, and thus greatly helped me in the writing of this book. My wife and children have always given me their support, and I am deeply indebted to them for their loyalty and generosity. Finally, I sign this preface with my full name in acknowledgment of my debt to my father.

GERALD RAYMOND MORGAN

# Abbreviations

| | |
|---|---|
| Arthur, *Medieval Sign Theory:* | R.G. Arthur, *Medieval Sign Theory and Sir Gawain and the Green Knight* (Toronto, 1987). |
| Barron: | W.R.J. Barron, *Sir Gawain and the Green Knight* (Manchester, 1974). |
| Benson, *Art and Tradition:* | L.D. Benson, *Art and Tradition in Sir Gawain and the Green Knight* (New Brunswick, New Jersey, 1965). |
| Burrow, *A Reading:* | J.A. Burrow, *A Reading of Sir Gawain and the Green Knight* (London, 1965). |
| Davenport, *The Art:* | W.A. Davenport, *The Art of the Gawain-Poet* (London, 1978). *Sir Gawain and the Green Knight*, edited by J.R.R. Tolkien and E.V. Gordon, second edition, revised by N. Davis (Oxford, 1967). |
| Davis: | |
| EETS (OS): | Early English Text Society (Original Series). |
| *JEGP:* | *Journal of English and Germanic Philology.* |
| ME: | Middle English. |
| *MED:* | H. Kurath and others, *Middle English Dictionary* (Michigan,1952– ). |
| *MLR:* | *Modern Language Review.* |
| OE: | Old English. |
| *OED:* | *The Oxford English Dictionary*, second edition, prepared by J.A. Simpson and E.S.C.Weiner, 20 vols (Oxford, 1989). |
| *RES*, NS: | *Review of English Studies*, New Series. |
| Spearing, *The Gawain-Poet:* | A.C. Spearing, *The Gawain-Poet: A Critical Study* (Cambridge, 1970). |
| *ST:* | Aquinas, *Summa Theologiae*, edited by T. Gilby and others, 61 vols (London, 1964–81). |
| *Suppl.:* | *Divi Thomae Aquinatis Summa Theologica*, second edition (Rome, 1894), Volume V, *Tertiae Partis Supplementum*, translated by Fathers of the English Dominican Province (London, 1917). |
| Waldron: | R.A. Waldron, *Sir Gawain and the Green Knight* (London, 1970). |

# CHAPTER ONE

# The Idea and the Principles of Art

## I

THE STUDY OF LITERARY works has been thrown into a ferment by the competing theories of the present generation. In the process the reader has been enhanced in status at the expense of the author. First of all we have been led to suspect an author's intention as the sole criterion of meaning in a work. The created artefact contains matter that lies beyond the author's conscious intent. Such unconscious levels are somehow accessible to the reader though not to the author. Second, since the objective criterion of the author's intention as embodied in his text has been abandoned, the importance of the subjective response of the reader has been emphasized. Every reading, no matter how ill-informed or prejudiced, has its own validity. Finally, in the mysterious and bewildering world of post-structuralism, the dissolution of the author is complete. It is the reader not the author who generates meanings in a text.

These critical ideas are often developed with great subtlety and contain truths that cannot be ignored by the interpreters of medieval literature, since they shape the assumptions and condition the judgments of the modern audience of that literature. The process of imaginative reconstruction of medieval texts becomes more difficult (or at least its results more difficult to credit) as modern literary theories gain more widespread acceptance, since the production of medieval texts is the conscious result of theories directly antithetical to those that dominate the modern literary world. Whereas modern literary theory proceeds from a position of philosophical subjectivism or scepticism, medieval theory proceeds from the objectivity of the form or idea. And the centrality of the idea in the formation of a literary work can be as baffling in its way as the ramifications of post-structuralism. Such bewilderment is expressed by a recent critic of *Sir Gawain and the Green Knight* in respect of the pentangle, the symbolic expression of that poem's idea:

> The pentangle passage in *Sir Gawain and the Green Knight* is notoriously difficult, and most readers are inclined to regard it as a learned irrelevancy or as bearing, at best, only remotely on the central concerns of the poem.[1]

---

1. A.D. Horgan, 'Gawain's Pure Pentaungle and the Virtue of Faith', *Medium Aevum*, 56 (1987), 310–16 (p. 310).

It is necessary, therefore, before we come to elucidate the particular idea of the pentangle, that we attempt to define the nature of the idea itself and its bearing upon the generation and existence of medieval works of literature. The terms that are appropriate to a work of the 1390s[2] such as *Sir Gawain* are those of medieval scholasticism, and it is in these terms that I shall seek to explain the relation of the idea to the work of art.

## II

Creation as it is understood in the Middle Ages in its strict sense is the production of things out of nothing. Only God therefore can create (*ST*, 1a 65.3):

> Creatio autem est productio alicujus rei secundum suam totam substantiam, nullo praesupposito quod sit vel increatum vel ab aliquo creatum. Unde relinquitur quod nihil potest aliquid creare nisi solus Deus, qui est prima causa.

> Creation, however, is the production of anything in the totality of its substance, presupposing nothing that is either uncreated or created by another. Whence it follows that no-one is capable of creating except God alone, who is the first cause.[3]

The production of things by nature presupposes by contrast a pre-existing matter (*ST*, 1a 45.2):

> Sed et ipsa natura causat res naturales quantum ad formam, sed praesupponit materiam.

> Even nature itself causes natural things as to their form, yet presupposes their matter.

The same is true of art, but whereas nature is an intrinsic principle of change, art is an extrinsic principle (*Commentary on Physics*, §268):

2. It has been customary to date the poem to the 1390s, but there is no compelling reason to do so. The various kinds of indirect evidence of date have been recently examined by W. G. Cooke, '*Sir Gawain and the Green Knight:* A Restored Dating', *Medium Aevum*, 58 (1989), 34–48 and the conclusion reached that the most likely period of composition is 1330–1360. The most significant single piece of evidence would seem to be the absence of any reference to a breastplate or a *peyre plates* in the description of the arming of Gawain (pp. 41–42), although it is probably not conclusive. A date of 1370 would fit well the description of Gawain's armour. In any event the invocation of the terms of Scholastic philosophy remains unaffected by any of the possible dates for the composition of the poem.

3. Reference to the *Summa Theologiae* is to the text and translation of T. Gilby and others, 61 vols (London, 1964–81).

> In nullo enim alio natura ab arte videtur differre, nisi quia natura est principium intrinsecum, et ars est principium extrinsecum.

> For nature seems to differ from art only because nature is an intrinsic principle and art is an extrinsic principle.[4]

Thus natural things and artists can be called producers or generators rather than creators if we are to use a terminology rigorously in accord with these distinctions. No derogation of nature or art is intended here, but rather the transcendent power of God is affirmed.

But medieval distinctions of this kind are not reflected in modern notions of creativity. To talk now in terms of artistic creativity is not to posit creation *ex nihilo*, but to extend the notion of creativity so as to focus on an artist's productive use of matter and fashioning of it for his own distinctive ends. Such creativity we can predicate also of the medieval poet, for nature and art are efficient causes, that is, more is involved than a mere instrumentality. It is profoundly misleading, therefore, to characterize the role of the medieval poet as no more than that of a translator[5] or 'a mediator or middleman, rather than that of a creator or inventor'.[6] Such language needs careful qualification, and is in any case hardly acceptable unless we can fix the term 'creator' in its technical medieval sense. Since we cannot do so, we must claim for medieval poets no less than for their modern successors what is their due, namely the possibility of artistic originality. The matter of modern poetry is likely to be the personal (and unique) experience of the poet, whereas that of the medieval poet is likely to be a literary source or sources. But both experience and literary sources are the necessary pre-existing materials of any poet. Originality is to be defined in the use of these materials. Simple transcripts of personal experience are no more creative than simple reproductions of literary sources.

The created universe is fashioned by God to the likeness of the idea in the divine mind (*ST*, 1a 15.1):

> . . . necesse est quod in mente divina sit forma, ad cujus similitudinem mundus est factus; et in hoc consistit ratio Ideae.

4. Reference is to *S. Thomae Aquinatis in Octo Libros Physicorum Aristotelis Expositio*, edited by P.M. Maggiòlo (Turin, 1965). The translation is that of R.J. Blackwell, R.J. Spath, and W.E. Thirlkel, *Commentary on Aristotle's Physics by St. Thomas Aquinas* (London, 1963).
5. The first section of the introduction of B.A. Windeatt's edition of *Troilus & Criseyde* (London and New York, 1984) is entitled 'The "Troilus" as translation' (pp. 3–24). Although translation is used 'in the creatively adaptive medieval sense of translation' (p. 3) the result is to focus on the origin of Chaucer's poem in its sources rather than in his art.
6. H. Specht, *Chaucer's Franklin in the Canterbury Tales* (Copenhagen, 1981), p. 22.

. . . there must be in the divine mind a form, to the likeness of which the world is made; and that is what we mean by an Idea.

God's act of creation is to produce a perfectly ordered universe, which Aquinas takes to include the existence of material beings subject to corruption (*ST*, 1a 2ae 85.6). By God we understand the creative principle of all things (*natura naturans*) and by nature we understand the whole of created being (*natura naturata*). The regularity of the universal order of things is a fundamental postulate of medieval thinkers, and the context in which all discussions of nature and art must be set. Thus we can make a fundamental distinction between the first cause that is God and the order of secondary causes or fate (*fatum*) dependent upon God, as it is expounded by Boethius (*De consolatione philosophiae*, IV.6)[7] and Aquinas following him (*ST*, 1a 116.2, and *ad* 1). Nature and art are therefore secondary causes within the order created by God, and stand in an ordered relation to one another. Nature is divine art (*Commentary on Physics*, § 268):

> Unde *patet quod natura nihil est aliud quam ratio cuiusdam artis, scilicet divinae, indita rebus, qua ipsae res moventur ad finem determinatum.*

> Hence, it is clear that nature is nothing but a certain kind of art, i.e., the divine art, impressed upon things, by which these things are moved to a determinate end.

Human art is an intellectual virtue, that is, a habit of the practical intellect (*ST*, 1a 2ae 57.3). But there is a complexity in the relationship of nature and art because man combines in his being both material and immaterial principles. He is the result of natural generation in the production of the sensitive soul (*ST*, 1a 118.1) and of immediate divine creation in the production of the rational soul (*ST*, 1a 118.2). Man is therefore a part of nature and at the same time is superior to natural things. This duality in human nature is inevitably reflected in thinking upon the relation of art and nature.

In the *Metaphysics*, VII.7 Aristotle identifies the work of art as derived from 'the form . . . in the soul of the artist'.[8] By form is understood 'the essence of each thing and its primary substance':

> Therefore it follows that in a sense health comes from health and house from house , that with matter from that without matter; 'from health',

---

7.  Chaucer translates Boethius's 'de fati serie' (IV. 6.11–12, p. 338) as 'of the ordre of destyne' (IV. 6.26–27, p. 451). Reference is to *Boethius, The Theological Tractates: The Consolation of Philosophy*, translated by H.F. Stewart and E.K. Rand, Loeb (London and Cambridge, Massachusetts, 1918) and to L.D. Benson and others, *The Riverside Chaucer*, third edition (Oxford, 1988).
8.  Reference is to the *Metaphysica*, translated by W.D. Ross, in *The Works of Aristotle*, edited by J.A. Smith and W.D. Ross, Volume VIII (Oxford, 1908).

and 'from house', for the medical art and the building art are the form of health and of the house; and 'from that without matter', for I call the essence substance without matter. Of productions and movements one part is called thinking and the other making,—that which proceeds from the starting-point and the form is thinking, and that which proceeds from the final step of the thinking is making.

Scholastic Aristotelians develop this fundamental notion in relation to God as creator. As God creates the world to the likeness of ideas or forms in the divine mind, so the artist creates the work of art to the likeness of the idea in his mind (*ST*, 1a 45.6):

> . . . Deus est causa rerum per suum intellectum et voluntatem, sicut artifex rerum artificiatarum. Artifex autem per verbum in intellectu conceptum et per amorem suae voluntatis ad aliquid relatum operatur.

> . . . God is the cause of things through his mind and will, like an artist of works of art. An artist works through an idea conceived in his mind and through love in his will bent on something.

The idea of the artist is thus all-important, for art is the intellectual virtue whereby the artist imposes his intention or idea on the pre-existing matter in the process of art. In as much as that intention is unrealised there is no art (so far are we removed from intentionalist fallacies) (*ST*, 1a 2ae 57.3 *ad* 1):

> . . . cum aliquis habens artem operatur malum artificium, hoc non est opus artis, immo est contra artem.

> When anyone endowed with art produces bad work, this is not the work of his art; but contrary to it.

The idea is the principle of the existence of the work of art, as the divine idea is of the created universe. It is here, then, that we must locate the excellence of the artist, his creative power and the source of the vitality of his work. For ideas, thus understood, are what is most real in art no less than in nature. The correspondence thus established between divine art and human art tends towards the elevation of art in respect of nature.

On the other hand nature as God's art is prior to the works of art created by man, and underlies it (*ST*, 1a 45.4 *arg*.3):

> Praeterea, illud proprie producitur per primam emanationem quod supponitur in secunda, sicut res naturalis per generationem naturalem quae supponitur in operatione artis.

Then again, to be exact, that which is produced in a primary origination is presupposed to what issues in the second place: thus a natural product underlies what is worked up by art.

The derivation of art from nature is expressed by Dante when he describes nature as a son, and art as a grandson (*Inferno*, XI. 97–105):

> 'Filosofia,' mi disse 'a chi la 'ntende,
>      nota non pur in una sola parte
>      come natura lo suo corso prende
> da divino intelletto e da sua arte;
>      e se tu ben la tua Fisica note,
>      tu troverai, non dopo molte carte,
> che l'arte vostra quella, quanto pote,
>      segue, come 'l maestro fa il discente;
>      sì che vostr'arte a Dio quasi è nepote.

'Philosophy, for one who understands,' he said to me 'notes, not in one place only, how nature takes her course from the divine mind and its art; and if thou note well thy *Physics* thou wilt find, not many pages on, that your art, as far as it can, follows nature as the pupil the master, so that your art is to God, as it were, a grandchild.[9]

The relationship of son and grandson points not only to derivation but also to likeness. Here we see in the order of creation a fundamental correspondence in the process of secondary causes, the intrinsic principle of nature and the extrinsic principle of art. Nature produces its like in an individual being, that is, it produces form in matter (universal generation) and in the same way art imposes its form in matter. Art imitates nature, therefore, both in the sense of the natural object and in the sense of the processes of nature (*Commentary on Physics*, § 171):

> Eius autem quod *ars imitatur naturam*, ratio est, quia principium opera-tionis artificialis cognitio est; omnis autem nostra cognitio est per sensus a rebus sensibilibus et naturalibus accepta: unde ad similitudinem rerum naturalium in artificialibus operamur. Ideo autem res naturales imitabiles sunt per artem, quia ab aliquo principio intellectivo tota natura ordinatur ad finem suum, ut sic opus naturae videatur esse opus intelligentiae, dum per determinata media ad certos fines procedit: quod etiam in operando ars imitatur.

9. Reference is to the text and translation of J.D. Sinclair, *The Divine Comedy of Dante Alighieri*, 3 vols (London, 1971).

The reason for saying that art imitates nature is as follows. Knowledge is the principle of operation in art. But all of our knowledge is through the senses and taken from sensible, natural things. Hence in artificial things we work to a likeness of natural things. And so imitable natural things are (i.e., are produced) through art, because all nature is ordered to its end by some intellective principle, so that the work of nature thus seems to be the work of intelligence as it proceeds to certain ends through determinate means. And this order is imitated by art in its operation.

There are possibilities here for different conceptions of the relation between art and nature, and they depend upon the definition of the idea or form which is the cause of the work of art. We need to distinguish between Platonic (or more especially neo-Platonic) and Aristotelian (or more especially Scholastic) theories of the ideas, and identify the ways in which they have influenced one another.

For Plato ideas are subsistent entities, existing in a supercelestial realm (for Plotinus and neo-Platonists as ideas in the divine mind) apart from things and from intellect. It is ideas that are properly said to exist or to possess reality; things are only copies or shadows of the ideas and such reality as they possess is a derived reality through participation in the ideas. Since things derive their meaning and existence from ideas, ideas cannot be derived from things. They are in fact innate, and come about as the result of reminiscence (*ST*, 1a 117.1). For Plato the artist can attain to no more than an imitation of things, that is, an imitation of imitations (*Republic*, X.597 E). A neo-Platonist such as Plotinus, however, not only locates the ideas in the divine mind, but also by analogy identifies a corresponding process in the mind of the artist (*Enneads*, V.8.1):

> . . . then, we must recognize that they (i.e., the arts) give no bare reproduction of the thing seen but go back to the Reason-Principles (i.e. Ideas) from which Nature itself derives.[10]

Augustine reflects this neo-Platonic conception of art in his doctrine of divine illumination, by which is possibly meant the direct infusion of ideas into the mind by God.[11] The work of art thus derived from ideas in the mind

10. Reference is to *Plotinus: The Enneads*, translated by S. MacKenna, fourth edition, revised by B.S. Page (London, 1969), pp. 422–23. I owe the reference to E. Panofsky, *Idea: A Concept in Art Theory*, translated by J.J.S. Peake (New York, 1968), p. 26.

11. The interpretation of Augustine's doctrine of divine illumination is a controversial matter. For a discussion of ontologistic and ideogenetic interpretations of that doctrine, see F. Copleston, A *History of Philosophy*, 9 vols (London, 1946–75), II, 60–67.

of the artist is derived from a principle higher than that of nature. The artist has no allegiance to nature as the source of his art, and therefore is dismissive of it. His work is ordered to a higher reality, that is, to the necessary and unchanging ideas of things, and not to contingent, changing things. The work of art as ordered to ideas understood in neo-Platonic terms will therefore be non-naturalistic, and perhaps radically antagonistic to naturalistic principles (a view of art that would in the seventeenth century be called Mannerist).

For Aristotle the ideas are not to be supposed as separate from things, but are the source of the existence and actuality of things. Neither form nor matter has a separate existence, but are united in the substances that are the independent entities of the material universe. Such substances cannot be reduced to a simple unity, but are composites made up of matter and form, the one a potentiality to the other's actuality. Matter is the principle of individuation, while the form supplies the determination of a thing as the member of a species. It is a fundamental principle of Scholastic epistemology that all knowledge is derived from the senses; in the famous sentence, *nihil in intellectu quod prius non fuerit in sensu* (compare *ST*, 1a 84.7). Therefore the ideas in the mind of the artist are there by abstraction from sensible things by means of the agent intellect, that is, there is an innate potentiality for acquiring ideas, but not innate ideas (*ST*, 1a 84.3). For the formation of ideas in the mind of the artist no more is required than the natural illumination of the intellect. The distinction between the neo-Platonic and Scholastic positions in this respect is brought out by Sidney when he writes that Plato 'attributeth unto poesy more than myself do, namely, to be a very inspiring of a divine force, far above man's wit' (*Defence of Poetry*, 109/2–4).[12]

The work of art is grounded in nature, but is not to be taken as a simple reproduction in artistic terms of the sensible object as it presents itself to the beholder. First of all, it is the form abstracted from matter which is the principle of art. Here we can note two meanings of nature supplied by Aristotle in the *Physics*, namely matter or that of which the thing is composed, and form or that by which the thing is what it is (*Physics*, II.1). The form is the higher principle or essence of the thing, and nature is in consequence most properly identified with the essence or form (*Commentary on Physics*, § 153):

> Unde forma, secundum quam aliquid est naturale in actu, est magis natura quam materia, secundum quam est aliquid naturale in potentia.

> Whence form, according to which a thing is natural in act, is nature more than matter, according to which a thing is something natural in potency.

12. Reference to *A Defence of Poetry* is to *Miscellaneous Prose of Sir Philip Sidney*, edited by K. Duncan-Jones and J. van Dorsten (Oxford, 1973), pp. 71–121.

Imitation, therefore, is of the essential nature or form of things, within things and not separate from things, but for all that mentally abstracted from individual things.

In the Scholastic view of creation there is a defect in the nature of the first man in that matter is in one respect proportioned to form, and in another respect not, although in the state of innocence this defect is allowed for by the special grace of original justice (*ST*, 1a 2ae 85.6). Matter is not regarded, as by a Plotinus, as an evil principle wholly resistant to form (*Enneads*, I.6.2), but there remains nevertheless a partial resistance. In natural objects composed of matter and form, therefore, form is never perfectly imposed upon or realised in matter, as Aquinas explains in Dante's sphere of the Sun (*Paradiso*, XIII. 76–78):

> ma la natura la dà sempre scema,
>   similemente operando all'artista
>   c'ha l'abito dell'arte e man che trema.

> but nature always gives it defectively, working like the artist who has the skill of his art and a hand that trembles.

Thus in abstracting the form from things the poet is able to grasp an idea which is free from the defectiveness of particular things. Aristotle assumes as a result that a true portrait will be more handsome than the natural object or person that is portrayed (*Poetics*, 15). Scholasticism, therefore, no less than neo-Platonism, offers a notion of art rooted in the idea in the mind of the artist and ordered immediately to it. But it is also through abstraction grounded in the actuality of nature and freed from the limitation of matter. Aristotelian principles of art will lead to the productions of works that are characterized both by a likeness to nature and by an improvement upon it. Thus poetry can have truth to nature in its essential reality and at the same time can raise the mind from the corruption of matter to the incorruptibility of ideas. As Sidney puts it, the poet 'goeth hand in hand with nature, not enclosed within the narrow warrant of her gifts, but freely ranging only within the zodiac of his own wit' (*Defence of Poetry*, 78/28–30).

Not every statement about poetry is purely neo-Platonic or Scholastic, and various elements of the two can be combined and were in fact combined. Thus it is to be noticed that Aquinas is influenced more than Aristotle by Platonic exemplarism, possibly because his Christian view of creation is characterized in these terms. Aquinas's exposition of ideas in relation to art is based on a distinction between the exemplar form that generates the work (*ST*, 1a 15.1) and the accidental form that is in the work[13] (*ST*, 1a 15.2):

13. On the forms of works of art as accidental, not substantial forms, see Aquinas,
 · *Commentary on Physics*, § 108.

> Forma enim domus in mente aedificatoris est aliquid ab eo intellectum, ad cujus similitudinem domum in materia format.

> Thus the form of a house in the mind of the architect is something understood by him, to the likeness of which he produces the form of a house in the matter.

The form in the work as the likeness of that exemplar is related to it in the following way (*ST*, 1a 18.4 *ad* 2):

> Nam alterius modi esse habet quandoque forma in exemplari et in exemplato; sicut forma domus in mente artificis habet esse immateriale et intelligibile, in domo autem quae est extra animam habet esse materiale et sensibile.

> Sometimes the form has one kind of existence in the exemplar and a different kind in the copy: for example, the form of a house in the mind of the architect has an immaterial and intelligible existence, in the actual house outside the mind a material and sense-known one.

Such a relationship between the exemplar and its likeness, both in the mind of the human artist and the divine creator (*ST*, 1a 15.1), explains why the idea is accorded a status above that of the work of art. Hence Sidney affirms that 'any understanding knoweth the skill of each artificer standeth in that *idea* or fore-conceit of the work, and not in the work itself' (*Defence of Poetry*, 79/6–8).[14] This affirmation seems on the face of it to conflict with Aristotle's view that the idea stands to the work of art as potentiality to act (*Commentary on Physics*, § 151). But Aquinas characteristically reconciles Platonic exemplarism and the Aristotelian doctrine of potentiality and act by combining the notion of the superior nature of the idea with the greater reality of the actual existence of the work of art (*ST*, 1a 18.4 *ad* 3):

> Sicut domus nobilius esse habet in mente artificis quam in materia: sed tamen verius dicitur domus quae est in materia quam quae est in mente; quia haec est domus in actu, illa autem domus in potentia.

> Similarly a house has a higher kind of existence in the mind of the architect than it has in matter; but still a 'true house' is a material one rather than one in the architect's mind; because the former is a house in the state of actuality, the latter only in the state of potentiality.

---

14. The influence of Platonic exemplarism is evident here, but we do not need to assume Mannerism in the strict sense, as does G.Shepherd, *Sir Philip Sidney: An Apology for Poetry* (Manchester, 1973), pp. 157–58, unless we are to assume that the idea is directly infused by God, a view at odds with Sidney's denial of divine inspiration (*Defence of Poetry*, 109/2–4).

Nevertheless the tendency of Aquinas's exposition is such as to emphasize the importance of the idea. In the first place the comparison of human art and divine art operates against the Aristotelian distinction of potentiality and act, since the first production of material creatures does not involve a passage from potentiality to act (*ST*, la 65.4). And in the second place Aquinas determines the truth of a work of art not in relation to things, but to the intellect of the artist on which it depends (*ST*, la 16.1):

> Unde unaquaeque res dicitur vera absolute, secundum ordinem ad intellectum a quo dependet. Et inde est quod res artificiales dicuntur verae per ordinem ad intellectum nostrum: dicitur enim domus vera quae assequitur similitudinem formae quae est in mente artificis.

> Hence every thing is said to be true in the absolute sense because of its relation to a mind on which it depends. Thus man-made things are called true in relation to our mind; a house, for instance, is 'true' if it turns out like the plan in the architect's mind.

The theory of ideas does not encourage the reader to set himself above the author in the generation of the meaning of a text, for the text bears an essential relation to the author's intellect on which it depends for its existence, and only an incidental relation to the intellect on which it does not depend (*ST*, la 16.1). Nevertheless the objectivity of the theory holds out the hope that an intellect only incidentally related to the work can come into possession of the knowledge that enabled another intellect to create it. The study of the literature of the past demands above all respect for the ideas of the past, and especially for the idea of the ideas. We do not have to accept the truth of these ideas for ourselves, but we do need to embrace them imaginatively as true. For the theory of ideas in its various manifestations is not marginal, but central to medieval literature.

We can conclude, therefore, that the criterion for medieval art is the idea, and not nature, since the object of imitation is the idea in the mind of the artist. And further, that such an idea is comprehensive, that is, it is the idea of the whole and of the parts that make up the whole (*ST*, la 15.2):

> Ratio autem alicujus totius haberi non potest, nisi habeantur propriae rationes eorum ex quibus totum constituitur; sicut aedificator speciem domus concipere non potest, nisi apud ipsum esset propria ratio cujuslibet partium ejus.

> Now a plan governing a whole necessarily involves knowing what is special to the parts which make up the whole; just as an architect cannot plan a house without knowing what is special to each part of it.

It follows that in the reading of a romance such as *Sir Gawain* the identification of the idea from which it has been derived and which has supplied
its accidental form or organizing principle is a fundamental requirement, as is
also the reference to that form of each single one of its parts. Such an
approach alone makes possible the full comprehension of its artistic unity
and the imaginative coherence of its parts. The poem does not often seem to
have been approached in this way, however, and perhaps I can begin my
exposition of it negatively by giving three examples of the way in which it
has been misunderstood because of the lack of reference to a theory of ideas.
The first two examples are simple and straightforward ones, but the third is
somewhat more complicated.

The first example comes from the poet's description of Gawain's lonely
and perilous journey that takes him from Camelot to Hautdesert in his quest
for the Green Knight and his chapel (691–762). The time of the year is hardly
conducive to travel,[15] and adds to the knight's misery. The sense of physical
isolation is matched by the coldness of the weather and the barrenness of the
scenery (729–32):

> Ner slayn wyth þe slete he sleped in his yrnes
> Mo ny3tez þen innoghe in naked rokkez,
> Þer as claterande fro þe crest þe colde borne rennez,
> And henged he3e ouer his hede in hard iisse-ikkles.[16]

Even the song of the birds echoes the harshness of the season (746–47):

> With mony bryddez vnblyþe vpon bare twyges,
> Þat pitosly þer piped for pyne of þe colde.

It is Christmas Eve (734), and all these details of weather and scenery
naturally fit such a time of the year. But in the midst of so much naturally
intelligible detail there comes a discrepant element (740):

> Bi a mounte on þe morne meryly he rydes.

The adverb *meryly* provides no problems lexically; *MED* glosses it (s.v.
*mirili* adv.) as 'cheerfully, joyfully' (1. (a)) or 'in or with spiritual joy' (1.
(c)), but places the example from *Sir Gawain* somewhat doubtfully under
sense 3. '? briskly; quickly; shortly'. This has all the appearance of a contextual gloss, as does the gloss supplied by Davis, namely 'handsomely'

---

15. See M. Stokes and J. Scattergood, 'Travelling in November: Sir Gawain, Thomas
Usk, Charles of Orleans and the *De Re Militari*', *Medium Aevum*, 53 (1984), 78–83.
16. Reference is throughout to *Sir Gawain and the Green Knight*, edited by J.R.R.
Tolkien and E.V. Gordon, second edition, revised by N. Davis (Oxford, 1967).

(p.198). Silverstein explicitly justifies his own contextual gloss of 'bravely' on the grounds that 'Sir Gawain could hardly be merry or happy at the moment'.[17] All three contextual glosses are characterized by the attempt to fit *meryly* into a pattern of natural description that seems to exclude the obvious meaning of the word. The natural description is not, however, included merely for its own sake, but is an expression of the poem's idea that is elaborated in detail in the pentangle passage (619–69). Prominent among the moral virtues symbolized by the pentangle is piety or 'pité, þat passez alle poyntez' (654), and it is to the moral virtue of piety that the adverb *meryly* has direct reference. Moral virtues are hard to achieve, and it would have been easy for Gawain to have yielded to the situation in which he found himself, and lapsed into a state of gloom. But the pious Christian is joyful at the coming of Christmas even (or especially) in the most adverse earthly circumstances. Indeed the very point of Christmas lies in the redemption of the world from the misery and wretchedness of sin.

The second example comes from that decisive moment in the poem when the lady so far imposes her will upon Gawain as to get him to accept her girdle (1859–61). And not only to accept it, but 'to lelly layne fro hir lorde' (1863). The knight promises the lady that he will grant her request (1863–65):

> . . . þe leude hym acordez
> Þat neuer wyȝe schulde hit wyt, iwysse, bot þay twayne
> for noȝte.

Unwittingly he has compromised his word in respect of the Exchange of Winnings agreement. But although we as readers can see that Gawain has fallen short in fidelity to his pledged word, we do not conclude that he is a man lacking in fidelity. On the contrary, we acknowledge that the habit of virtue cannot be destroyed by a single act any more than it can be formed by a single act (*ST*, la 2ae 71.4 *sed contra*). The fact that the habit of virtue remains intact in Gawain is at once demonstrated by the care with which he keeps his promise to the lady, for he (1874–75):

> Lays vp þe luf-lace þe lady hym raȝt,
> Hid hit ful holdely, þer he hit eft fonde.

The focus here on the moral virtue of fidelity is once again an expression of the idea of the poem, for fidelity is singled out by the poet in the word *felaȝschyp* (652) and is suggested by the word *trawþe* (626) which gives its name to the whole complex of virtues. The adverb *holdely* is rare in Middle

17. T. Silverstein, *Sir Gawain and the Green Knight: A New Critical Edition* (Chicago and London, 1984), p. 137.

English, only three examples being recorded by *MED* under the glosses 'graciously; faithfully', but the adjective *hold* is well established in its primary meaning of 'loyal, faithful' (*MED*, 1. (a), (b), and (c)), and this sense of *hold* is found as far back as *Beowulf*. But Davis glosses *holdely* as 'faithfully, carefully' (p.190) and Barron incorporates 'carefully' into his translation.[18] Attention is thereby focused on the natural act of hiding something, and away from the moral significance of that act. Once again the point of contact with the poem's informing idea is lost.

The third example concerns the status of the lady as temptress, for she is described by Barron as 'a challenger whose nature is ambiguous' (p.15). In the first of the bedroom scenes the poet discloses in the lady considerable knowledge of Gawain's situation (1283–87):

> 'Þaȝ I were burde bryȝtest', þe burde in mynde hade,
> 'Þe lasse luf in his lode for lur þat he soȝt
>         boute hone,
> Þe dunte þat schulde hym deue,
> And nedez hit most be done.'[19]

Davis concludes that if such knowledge of the impending blow is attributed to the lady 'it would be a serious flaw in the handling of the plot', since 'the story as presented has given her no opportunity to know this' (p.110). One is bound to admire the resourcefulness of modern editors in their attempts to dispose of the assumed flaw. Davis himself confines the lady's utterance to the first half of line 1283, and so produces a reflection on her part that is elliptical to the point of non-existence: '"Even if I were the most beautiful of ladies", the lady thought (still he would resist)' (p.110). Other editors go further, and emend *I* to *ho* and the second *burde* to *burne*. The emendation was first proposed by Morris in 1864, sanctioned by Gollancz, and generally followed in modern editions such as those by Waldron,[20] Barron (pp. 175–76),

18. W.R.J. Barron, *Sir Gawain and the Green Knight* (Manchester, 1974), p. 127.
19. I am deliberately setting aside editorial punctuation at this point in favour of my own. The matter that follows first appeared in my article 'The Action of the Hunting and Bedroom Scenes in *Sir Gawain and the Green Knight*', *Medium Aevum*, 56 (1987), 200–216 (pp. 201–5).
20. See R. Morris, *Sir Gawayne and the Green Knight*, EETS (OS) 4 (London, 1864), p. 83, I. Gollancz, *Sir Gawain and the Green Knight*, EETS (OS) 210 (London, 1940), p. 114, and R.A. Waldron,*Sir Gawain and the Green Knight* (London, 1970), p. 85. W.A. Davenport, *The Art of the Gawain-Poet* (London, 1978) comes independently to a similar conclusion to my own when he comments that 'all attempts to punctuate this (i.e. 1283–87) so that the Lady is not aware of the nature of Gawain's quest have been artificial and implausible' (p. 166) and observes that 'knowledge that the Lady is playing a part and is not a genuinely love-lorn woman is, in any case, implicit in the style the poet developed for her, and this knowledge, together with hints of an ulterior motive, focus attention on the strategy itself, its variety and subtlety, rather

and Silverstein (p. 148). Thus, for example, Waldron offers the following translation of lines 1283–85: 'Though she was the loveliest lady the warrior had ever known, he had brought with him so much the less love because of the penalty he was going to meet forthwith' (p. 85). All these interpretations destroy to a greater or lesser degree the true source of the poem's unity in the idea of the pentangle, by making either the poet himself or Gawain violate the moral imperatives of the code symbolized by the pentangle, a code that includes *clannes* (653) or chastity. And chastity is a sufficient motive in itself for a rejection of the lady's overtures, irrespective of the impending doom of the beheading.

It is necessary that we reject here the notion of an artistic flaw, and see that far from removing a flaw modern editors have created one. A medieval romance is not a work of art constructed in accordance with the naturalism that demands the revelation of such knowledge.[21] It is built upon an abstract principle or idea that is guaranteed by a doctrine of philosophical realism, and co-ordinated in terms of its idea. It is this poetic co-ordination that has been destroyed by the editorial interference with the text or likely meaning of the text. Since there is no requirement of naturalism, the poet is under no obligation to explain to his audience the means by which the lady obtained the knowledge that she so evidently possesses. But it is important that as readers we should know that she does possess this knowledge. In this way the poet removes any ambiguity and establishes that the host's wife is a temptress. This fact is vital to our understanding of the poet's delineation of the moral situation. We might otherwise imagine the lady actually to be in love with Gawain. It is by no means a theoretical impossibility, and it would create a moral situation of a very different kind, one in which the lady might attract some legitimate sympathy from the reader.[22] But it is all a cunning pretence (1281):

> And ay þe lady let lyk as hym loued mych.

than the Lady's nature and feelings' (p. 167). I cannot agree with him, however, in his assumption that 'the poet has allowed his character's voice to merge into the narrator's' (p. 166).

21. Indeed characters are commonly credited in romances with knowledge that they cannot possibly possess. Thus Malory's Gawain has a knowledge of the time of his death when he composes his letter of repentance to Lancelot (1232/6–8):

> And the date of thys lettir was wrytten but two owrys and an halff afore my dethe, wrytten with myne owne honde and subscrybed with parte of my harte blood.

Reference is to E. Vinaver, *The Works of Sir Thomas Malory*, second edition, reprinted with corrections and additions, 3 vols (Oxford, 1973).

22. The same point is made independently by C. Dean, 'The Temptation Scenes in *Sir*

The poet's disclosure is part of a process designed to sustain the moral balance of the argument of his poem, a poem in which Gawain is the innocent victim (or intended victim) of the lady's wiles.

The very cleverness of the lady is in its turn designed to obscure the moral reality of a situation in which she has invaded the privacy of the bedroom and in so doing offended against the rights of her guest. The entrance of the lady is shown from Gawain's point of view, and Gawain is still, as the poet reminds us, 'þe god mon' (1179). The adjective is not chosen merely for its alliterating convenience, but is a significant marker of the poet's moral sympathies. The Gawain of the bedroom scenes remains the man 'for gode knawen, and as golde pured,/Voyded of vche vylany' (633–34). And in Gawain's own reactions the lady's impropriety is revealed. As the lady approaches his bed, 'þe burne schamed' (1189); he can make nothing of her conduct in terms of normal courtesies, try as he will (1195–97):

> Þe lede lay lurked a ful longe quyle,
> Compast in his concience to quat þat cace myȝt
> Meue oþer amount—to meruayle hym þoȝt.

Neither the medieval books of courtesy, nor their modern equivalents for that matter, are likely to recommend fitting behaviour for such an occasion, simply because the occasion itself is improper. It is a situation that is at all costs to be avoided.

The lady, of course, construes the situation quite differently. She represents her own presence in Gawain's bedroom as an entirely natural fact. The fault is that of Gawain for being 'a sleper vnslyȝe' (1209). Here the lady reveals the cunning that is necessary for one in pursuit of a deer, for the deer is a

*Gawain and the Green Knight'*, *Leeds Studies in English*, 5 (1971), 1–12 (p. 8): '. . . if the audience believed that the lady was genuinely in love with Gawain, the relationship between the two of them would be significantly altered. The woman would deservedly attract some sympathy from the poem's readers, so that although Gawain's rejection of her would still be morally correct, it would be much harder for the readers to approve of it emotionally. A situation not unlike that between Sir Launcelot and the Fair Maid of Astolat would result and in that episode it is the Maid who wins everyone's sympathy.' A persuasively sympathetic reading of the lady's conduct is proposed by C.B. Folks, 'Chaucer's "Wife of Bath's Tale", "Sir Gawain and the Green Knight", and the English Romance Tradition' (unpublished Ph.D. dissertation, Indiana University, 1989), pp. 110–18. Folks argues that moral guilt is fixed not upon the lady but upon Morgan le Fay as the instigator of the temptation. The implication is that the lady is acting immediately out of obedience to her husband's will in tempting Gawain, so that she is to be compared to such Chaucerian heroines as Griselda and Dorigen. The lady's ultimate moral innocence 'makes Gawain's humiliation even more bitter than if she had been either truly in love with him or borne him actual malice' (p. 116).

wise animal.[23] Such is the cunning used by the poacher at the beginning of *The Parlement of the Thre Ages* (40–42):

> I *waitted wiesly* the wynde by *waggynge* of leues,        watched;
>                                                       carefully; stirring
> Stalkede full *stilly* no *stikkes* to breke,              quietly; twigs
> And crepite to a *crabtre* and *couerede* me ther-vndere.[24]
>                                                     crab-apple tree; concealed

The *Gawain*-poet has forestalled the lady's cunning misrepresentation of the facts by assuring us that Gawain 'sleȝly ... herde/ A littel dyn at his dor' (1182–83), even though he is in a deep sleep, 'as in slomeryng he slode' (1182),[25] exhausted by the exertions of his quest and the Christmas festivities. The analogy of the deer, which are moved by 'þe fyrst quethe of þe quest' (ll50), draws attention to the matching quickness of sense in Gawain. Once more the poet exploits an expectation first aroused in the pentangle passage, for Gawain is 'fautlez in his fyue wyttez' (640). Gawain is cautious on that first morning in the bedroom, and thus he 'waytez warly þiderwarde quat hit be myȝt' (1186).

Moreover, even in the depth of his sleep he shows no lack of wisdom, for he is entitled to feel secure in the protection of his host. Similarly, in *The Parlement of the Thre Ages* the hart when asleep is protected by the vigilance of the soar (that is, a buck in its fourth year) which accompanies it (34–37):

> Bot there sewet hym a sowre þat seruet hym full *ȝerne*,        followed;
>                                                          faithfully
> That *woke* & warned hym when the wynde faylede,              kept watch
> That none so *sleghe* in his slepe with sleghte scholde hym *dere*,
>                                                          cunning; harm
> And went the *wayes* hym by-fore when any *wothe tyde*.        paths;
>                                                          danger; befall

23. On the wisdom of the deer, see Edward, Second Duke of York, *The Master of Game*, edited by W.A. and F. Baillie-Grohman (London, 1909), pp. 30–31 and 34–35.
24. Reference is to M.Y. Offord, *The Parlement of the Thre Ages*, EETS (OS) 246 (London, 1959).
25. Davis glosses the phrase (p. 213, s.v. *slyde*) as 'slept softly on', but such a gloss does not obviously apply to one in Gawain's physical condition. The use of a corresponding phrase in *Patience*, 186, 'Slypped vpon a sloumbe-selepe, and sloberande he routes', must refer to a heavy sleep, for the compound *sloumbe-selepe* translates 'sopore gravi' in Jonah 1.5. Compare also *Patience*, 466: 'He slydeȝ on a sloumbe-slep sloghe vnder leues': see *Patience*, edited by J.J. Anderson (Manchester, 1969), pp. 59 and 103.

Gawain as an honoured guest places his trust in his host and hostess. When that trust is broken he is rendered vulnerable, and the lady as temptress exploits that vulnerability to the full. It is indeed of the nature of temptation that it should be directed to the point of utmost vulnerability.[26]

How different all these things can appear if we take them out of the moral context in which the poet has set them. The scene is reduced to that of a social comedy, and it is the lady (a cunning temptress) rather than Gawain (an honourable guest) who is seen as the victim. Such a false impression is confirmed for many modern readers by the poet's use of the verb *lurken* of Gawain (1195):

> Þe lede lay lurked a ful longe quyle,

and especially when an editor of the authority of Davis glosses the past participle by the present, 'lurking' (p. 197). But the neutral gloss 'hidden' involves no grammatical dislocation and is no less lexically acceptable, as we may see from the examples supplied by *MED*, s.v. *lurken* v. (a) 'to hide, be in hiding, lie hidden'. Indeed, good things as well as bad are sometimes concealed from view. Thus *MED* cites *The Wars of Alexander*, 3991: 'Þe prowis & Þe prouidens ... Þat lurkis with-in Þis lede, full litill he kennes'. The *Gawain*-poet supplies a comparable example (1179–80):

> And Gawayn Þe god mon in gay bed lygez,
> Lurkkez quyl Þe dayly3t lemed on Þe wowes.

There is no need for *MED* to provide here as a contextual gloss the otherwise unrecorded sense (d) 'to lie comfortably', corresponding to Davis's 'to lie snug' (p. 197), when the central sense of the word is so obviously apt. The verb *lurken* is used of Gawain here with no implication of idleness or furtiveness, but rather to draw attention to the fact that, like the deer, he is being hunted. *MED* supplies an example of its use in this context in its illustration of the gerund *lurkinge*, citing Trevisa, *Barth.* 246 a/b: 'in woode . . .

---

26. This is the significance of the unprotected part of the Valley of Princes in *Purg.*, VIII. 97–99:

> Da quella parte onde non ha riparo
> la picciola vallea, era una biscia,
> forse qual diede ad Eva il cibo amaro.

At that part where the little valley has no rampart was a snake, such, perhaps, as gave to Eve the bitter food.

N. Sapegno, *La Divina Commedia*, second edition, 3 vols (Florence, 1968), II, 90 explains that 'la tentazione colpisce l'anima, dove essa è più debole e meno difesa' ('the temptation strikes the soul, where it is most weak and least protected').

wilde bestes beþ y-hunted, and wacches and deceytes arrayed and y-sette of
houndes and of hunters there place of hydynge and of lurkynge.'

It is Gawain who is sometimes held to be cunning (as distinct from prudent)
in feigning sleep when he becomes aware of the lady's presence (1200–1203):

> Þen he wakenede, and wroth, and to hir warde torned,
> And vnlouked his y3e-lyddez, and let as hym wondered,
> And sayned hym, as bi his sa3e þe sauer to worthe,
>       with hande.

What is a temptress to do when faced with moral artfulness of this kind? But
Gawain pretends to be nothing other than he in fact is. Were he not to show
surprise to the lady he would certainly be guilty of revealing an expectation
of discourtesy on her part: the lady's presence in his bedroom is shameful,
and Gawain shows the lady that he does not expect shameful conduct of her.
Thus, even in so compromised a situation, he behaves with the courtesy that
a hostess could rightly expect of such a guest.

On the second day, Gawain is submitted to a public test of the lady's
impropriety, and again his own sense of courtesy is equal to it, in that he is
prepared to allow the appearance of blame to fall upon himself (1658–63).
On this first occasion Gawain makes clear to the lady his own understanding
of the moral realities by crossing himself, although no discourtesy is involved
since such an act is entirely appropriate to the pious Christian on first awaking
from sleep. According to Barron we feel a sense of shock that Gawain
'should use the sign of the cross as part of his play-acting'.[27] But it is the act
of piety of one who puts his faith in God and not in himself. There is a good
reason why ladies should not enter the bedrooms of their guests, for no man
could in such provocative circumstances be sure of remaining continent.
Gawain is in moral peril, and by crossing himself he publicly acknowledges
the fact. Only in this way can the lady's purpose be ultimately defeated; in
the same way, in the *Psychomachia* of Prudentius, Sobrietas overcomes
Luxuria by holding up a cross.[28]

Gawain's faith and piety are thus revealed to the lady, but not discour-
teously. As the lady responds to all Gawain's defensive strategies by a counter-
attack (compare, for example, 'In god fayth', 1241 and 1248), so she attacks
his faith at the point at which she first of all pretends to take her leave. Once
again she chooses the time of maximum vulnerability: that is, when the
knight is momentarily unguarded by relief at the prospect of coming through

27. W.R.J. Barron, *Trawthe and Treason: the Sin of Gawain Reconsidered* (Manchester,
1980), p. 22.
28. I owe this point to the excellent discussion of C. Van Dyke, *The Fiction of Truth:
Structures of Meaning in Narrative and Dramatic Allegory* (Ithaca and London,
1985), pp. 52–53.

his ordeal unscathed. The lady suddenly reverses her position (logically for a temptress, but hard otherwise to understand) and launches an attack on Gawain's reputation in the light of his present conduct (1290–93). At Gawain's anxious response (1294–95) the lady blesses him: 'Bot þe burde hym blessed' (1296). She has more concern for the knight's spiritual and moral well-being than Gawain himself.

Much of the amusement at Gawain's expense which a number of modern readers[29] derive from these interchanges arises from some more general considerations. First of all, there is a ready acceptance of virtue on Gawain's part which denies the reality of virtue as issuing from internal conflict and as involving the willing of the difficult good against the easy and so very desirable evil. Secondly, there is the assumption of fault on Gawain's part in sleeping while the lord is hunting. There is certainly historical support for a general contrast between the health and vigour of the life of hunting out of doors and the lustfulness and idleness of the life within doors, for it is made in the prologue to *The Master of Game*.[30] The medieval audience's familiarity with such a contrast is exploited by the *Gawain*-poet — not, however, to convict Gawain of the sin of sloth, but to create an expectation of moral testing. Historical commonplaces are not to be preferred to the particularities of a single poetic text. Thus Gawain is exhausted by his arduous journey to Bertilak's castle (691–739) and by the revelling proper for a guest to participate in during the Christmas season (1020–28). These are points to which the lord makes explicit reference in elaborating the terms of the Exchange of Winnings agreement (1093–95). Gawain is in need of the wholesome refreshment of sleep (just as is the dreamer in Chaucer's *Book of the Duchess*, 1–27 and 270–75). He is sleeping in accordance with the terms of the agreement laid down by his host (1096–1102), for it is clear that he has not overslept and so missed attendance at mass. The pattern of action imposed by the Exchange of Winnings agreement is broken only by the lady's invasion of Gawain's privacy. Thus the fitness of sleep on the following two days is also noted by the poet. On Day 2 'oure luflych lede lys in his bedde,/Gawayn grayþely at home' (1469–70),[31] and on Day 3 'þe hende knyȝt at home holsumly slepes' (1731), even though this is the 'drowping depe' (1748) and the 'dreȝ droupyng of dreme' (1750) of which we subsequently hear. We may

29.  Such a reader is Barron; see *Trawthe and Treason*, p. 12.
30.  Compare *The Master of Game*, p. 5. For an interesting development of this argument (albeit erroneous in its application of such sinfulness to Gawain himself), see V.J. Scattergood, '*Sir Gawain and the Green Knight* and the Sins of the Flesh', *Traditio*, 37 (1981), 347–71.
31.  Davis (p. 185) glosses *grayþely*, 1470, as 'pleasantly', but the gloss 'duly, as was right' is more fitting. This is the gloss that Davis supplies for line 2292: 'Gawayn grayþely hit bydez, and glent with no membre', that is, for the corresponding second blow of the axe.

note the contrast on New Year's Day, when Gawain has to present himself for the return blow: 'Deliuerly he dressed vp, er þe day sprenged' (2009).

In addition to these two general considerations it may be felt, thirdly, that Gawain should not have participated in the Exchange of Winnings agreement at all. But the only possible reason for not doing so would be if participation in the new agreement were to prejudice the prior moral obligations incurred in the Beheading Game. It is therefore established from the beginning that Gawain will not put at risk his assignment with the Green Knight by remaining with his host (1042–82). Once this fact has been established, it is unthinkable that Gawain should not fall in with the plans of his host in so far as they involve no obvious impropriety (1088–92). The obligations of a guest can be perceived by boys as well as men, if Leo Colston's response to Marcus Maudsley in L.P. Hartley's *The Go-Between* is in any way representative:

> I sighed. It was to be a French conversation. French was one of the few school subjects which Marcus was better at than I was. He had had a French governess who had given him a good accent; he had also, unlike me, been abroad and there picked up words and phrases his governess would not have taught him. And he had an annoying habit, when one mispronounced a word, of repeating it with the right pronunciation. But he was not a prig, and had allowed his real French to be overlaid by a smattering of the pidgin French we all sometimes talked. I was his guest, with a guest's obligation to comply.[32]

Above all, the Exchange of Winnings agreement has to be seen as a part of the interlocking structure of the poem as a whole. It is in itself an interlocking structure which repeats that of the pentangle and expresses the poem's co-ordinating idea of *trawþe* in its full medieval and Aristotelian sense.[33] Gawain's participation in the Exchange of Winnings agreement, therefore, is a further expression of his moral excellence or righteousness, and hence he is described at the point of his acceptance of the terms of that agreement as 'Gawayn þe gode' (1110).

## III

Thus the argument of *Sir Gawain* is to be understood ultimately not in relation to natural principles but to an abstract idea. It is set within a structure that is clear, well-ordered, and regular. Such a structure is based on two

---

32. L.P. Hartley, *The Go-Between* (London, 1953), p. 197.
33. For an explanation of this sense of *trawþe*, see chapter 4: 'The Pentangle as the Symbolic Expression of the Poem's Idea'.

principles, firstly that of parallelism, for there are three hunts and three temptation scenes, and three blows of the Green Knight's axe, and secondly, that of enclosure, for the bedroom scenes are framed by the hunts, and the Exchange of Winnings agreement is framed by the Beheading Game, the outcome of the one being made dependent on the outcome of the other. The principle of enclosure is the dominant principle in *Sir Gawain* because the idea of the poem is the idea of the pentangle, that is, a unity made up of interrelated parts. Aristotle says that the virtues are interrelated, and the enclosed pattern of *Sir Gawain* is the structural analogue of this moral and symbolic idea. We have, therefore, a conception of formal beauty that corresponds to or is the very expression of the poem's unifying idea.

The work of art is to be seen not so much as a living organism, but as a completed whole. Aristotle, it is true, compares the unity of a work of art to the organic unity of living creatures in the *Poetics* (23), but his purpose is not that of suggesting a principle of growth or movement, but that of the functional relation of parts. The work of art is static, not dynamic. Hence Aristotle's most frequent example of the artist and the work of art is that of the architect and the house. It is the illustration of art in consequence that is familiar to us in Aquinas's exposition. In the same way Geoffrey of Vinsauf in his *Poetria Nova* begins with the illustration of the architect when he wishes to set forth the initial stages of the production of a work of art (43–49):

> Si quis habet fundare domum, non currit ad actum
> Impetuosa manus: intrinseca linea cordis
> Praemetitur opus, seriemque sub ordine certo
> Interior praescribit homo, totamque figurat
> Ante manus cordis quam corporis; et status ejus
> Est prius archetypus quam sensilis. Ipsa poesis
> Spectet in hoc speculo quae lex sit danda poetis.

> If a man has a house to build, his impetuous hand does not rush into action. The measuring line of his mind first lays out the work, and he mentally outlines the successive steps in a definite order. The mind's hand shapes the entire house before the body's hand builds it. Its mode of being is archetypal before it is actual. Poetic art may see in this analogy the law to be given to poets.[34]

Chaucer has used this example, as is well known, when he wishes to set before us the cunning machinations of Pandarus (*Troilus and Criseyde*, I.1065–69).

34.   Reference is to E. Faral, *Les Arts poétiques du xii<sup>e</sup> et du xiii<sup>e</sup> siècle* (Paris, 1924), p. 198, and to the translation of M.F. Nims, *Poetria Nova of Geoffrey of Vinsauf* (Toronto, 1967), pp. 16–17.

The end of art lies not so much in the excitation of passions as in the contemplation of beauty. And here we may note that the Middle Ages has inherited two conceptions of beauty. The first is the classical conception, which defines beauty in terms of fitness of proportions and pleasing colour, and which is given classic expression by Cicero, *Tusculan Disputations*, IV.31:

> . . . quaedam apta figura membrorum cum coloris quadam suavitate eaque dicitur pulcritudo.

> . . . a certain symmetrical shape of the limbs combined with a certain charm of colouring is described as beauty.[35]

The second is neo-Platonic, and is defined by Plotinus in terms of the radiance of the divine ideas illuminating matter (*Enneads*, I.6.3). For Plotinus beauty consists in indivisibility and unity, and so he denies the notion of proportionality of parts as a principle of beauty precisely because the very fact of parts presupposes a composite object (*Enneads*, I.6.1). The Plotinian objection is lucidly stated in the late fifteenth century (1469) by Ficino in his commentary on Plato's *Symposium*, V.3:

> Sunt autem nonnulli, qui certam membrorum omnium positionem, siue, ut eorum uerbis utamur, commensurationem & proportionem cum quadam colorum suauitate, esse pulchritudinem opinentur. Quorum nos opinionem, propterea non admittimus, quia cum huiusmodi partium dispositio in solis rebus compositis, nulla essent simplicia speciosa.

> But there are some who think that beauty consists in a disposition of parts, or, to use their own language, size and proportion together with a certain agreeableness of colors. We do not agree with their opinion because, since this kind of disposition of parts would exist in composite things only, there could be no such thing as a beautiful simplicity.[36]

These ideas are central and pervasive throughout the Middle Ages, and are combined by Aquinas in his definition of beauty at *ST*, 2a 2ae 145.2 (the authority of the pseudo-Dionysius shows that the neo-Platonist conception of *splendor* or *claritas* and not merely the Ciceronian conception of pleasing or harmonious colours is being drawn upon):

35. Reference is to *Cicero: Tusculan Disputations*, translated by J.E. King, Loeb (London and New York, 1927).
36. Reference is to M. Ficino, *In Convivium Platonis de amore commentarium*, V.3, in *Opera*, second edition, 2 vols (Basle, 1576), II, 1336, and to the translation of S.R. Jayne, *Ficino: Commentary on Plato's Symposium*, University of Missouri Studies (Columbia, 1944), p. 168.

Dicendum quod, sicut accipi potest ex verbis Dionysii, ad rationem pulchri sive decori concurrit et claritas et debita proportio. Dicit enim quod Deus dicitur *pulcher*, sicut *universorum consonantiae, et claritatis causa.*

As may be gathered from Dionysius, beauty or handsomeness arises when fine proportions and brightness run together; he says that God is named Beautiful because he is *the cause of the consonance and clarity of the universe.*[37]

The illumination of the divine idea in matter is expressed by Dante in the sphere of the Sun in words appropriately put into the mouth of Aquinas and thus revealing the co-ordination of Platonic and Aristotelian conceptions in the work of the most famous of all the medieval followers of Aristotle (*Par.*, XIII., 52–54):

> Ciò che non more e ciò che può morire
> non è se non splendor di quella idea
> che partorisce, amando, il nostro sire.

That which dies not and that which can die are nothing but the splendour of that Idea which our Sire, in Loving, begets.

Aquinas adds a third criterion of beauty, namely 'integritas, sive perfectio, quae enim diminuta sunt, hoc ipso turpia sunt' ('integrity or completeness— since things that lack something are thereby ugly') (*ST*, la 39.8). There is surely no difficulty in accepting the notion that an incomplete work or a ruin falls short of the beauty of the whole complete in its parts. Thus we may say that *The Canterbury Tales* falls short of the beauty of *Troilus and Criseyde*, and *The Faerie Queene* falls short of the beauty of the *Commedia* and also (in this respect at least) of *Sir Gawain and the Green Knight*.

37. Compare *ST*, la 39.8 where *claritas* as one of three elements of beauty is elaborated as follows:

> Quantum vero ad tertium, convenit cum proprio Filii inquantum est Verbum, quod quidem *lux est et splendor intellectus*, ut Damascenus dicit.

> Brightness coincides with what is proper to the Son as he is the Word, *the light and splendour of the mind*, in Damascene's description.

CHAPTER TWO

# The Reputation of Camelot

I

THE POET'S PURPOSE at the very beginning of his poem is to establish the nobility of Arthur and Camelot by linking it to the nobility of Troy. The method of his opening description is characteristically logical in accordance with rhetorical precept and admirably clear in its order of development. Thus we proceed from the nobility of Aeneas and his lineage, 'Ennias þe athel, and his highe kynde' (5), to the nobility of Brutus, the great-grandson of Aeneas, 'þis burn rych' (20), and to Arthur, the noblest of the kings of Britain (26):

> Ay watz Arthur þe hendest, as I haf herde telle.

The logical arrangement is apparent too in the geographical progression of the founding of the kingdoms, from Rome (8–10), to Tuscany (11), to Lombardy (12), and to Britain (13–19). The *Gawain*-poet is drawing upon a well established tradition, and the significance of his own poetic argument is reinforced by the vitality of that tradition. Thus *Wynnere and Wastoure* (1352–70) also begins with a reference to the founding of Britain and the treachery of Troy (1–4):

| Sythen that Bretayne was *biggede* and Bruyttus it *aughte* | founded; possessed |
| Thurgh the takynge of Troye with tresone withinn | |
| There hathe *selcouthes* bene sene in *seere* kynges tymes | wonders; many |
| Bot neuer so many as nowe by the *nyne dele*.[1] | ninth; part |

In the case of the alliterative *Morte Arthure*, a work possibly contemporaneous with *Sir Gawain*, the reference to the descent from Troy comes at the end. The author of the *Morte* refers to Hector and Priam rather than Aeneas, and so avoids the potential ambiguity that has bedevilled interpretation of the opening lines of *Sir Gawain* (4342–46):

---

1.  Reference is to *Wynnere and Wastoure*, edited by S. Trigg, EETS (OS), 297 (Oxford, 1990). In dating the poem 1352-70 I follow the broad limits proposed by Trigg, rather than the specific date of 1352-53 established by Gollancz; see Trigg, pp. xxii-xxvii.

> Thus endis Kyng Arthure, as auctors *alegges,*                    declare
> That was of Ectores blude, the kynge son of Troye,
> And of Sir *Pryamous* the prynce, praysede in erthe;              Priam
> Fro *thythen* broghte the Bretons all his bolde *eldyrs*          thence;
>                                                                   ancestors
> Into *Bretayne the Brode*, as þe *Bruytte* tellys.[2]    Britain; chronicle

The tradition is no less meaningful for Spenser writing the national epic of England in 1590. When Britomart, the Knight of Chastity, hears Paridell's account of the sack of Troy (III.9.38):

> She was *empassiond* at that piteous act,                      deeply moved
> With zelous *enuy* of Greekes cruell *fact,*             hostile feeling; deed
> Against that nation, from whose race of old
> She heard, that she was lineally *extract*:                     descended
> For noble *Britons* sprong from *Troians* bold,
> And *Troynouant* was built of old *Troyes* ashes cold.[3]      New Troy
>                                                                  (London)

Spenser's poem helps us retrospectively to explain the title *Felix* that accompanies Brutus in *Sir Gawain* (13), for in the chronicle of British kings that forms the matter of canto 10 of the Legend of Temperance we learn that (II.10.13):

> Thus *Brute* this Realme vnto his rule subdewd,
>    And raigned long in great felicitie.

But the clarity of the *Gawain*-poet's purpose and of his execution of that purpose has been called into question by those modern commentators who identify Aeneas himself as the traitor referred to in the opening lines (3–4):

> Þe tulk þat þe trammes of tresoun þer wroȝt
> Watz tried for his tricherie, þe trewest on erthe.

One of their number is no less an authority than Davis. In a lengthy note (p.70) he sets out the medieval tradition of Aeneas's treachery, singling out the influence of the *Historia destructionis Troiae* of Guido de Columnis, and concluding imperturbably that 'the legend of Aeneas' treachery did not embarrass writers in English who wished to trace the descent of the Britons

2.   Reference is to *The Alliterative Morte Arthure: A Critical Edition*, edited by V. Krishna (New York, 1976).
3.   Reference is to *Edmund Spenser: The Faerie Qveene*, edited by A. C. Hamilton (London and New York, 1977).

from him, through Brutus'. But the fact is that the notion of a treacherous Aeneas is an embarrassment to the argument of the nobility of the descent from Troy. Moreover, the moral and imaginative coherence of *Sir Gawain* is such as to set it apart from all other medieval romances. It is not difficult to suppose, therefore, that the author of *Sir Gawain* would be sensitive to the ambiguities and contradictions implicit in the treachery of Aeneas even though many lesser writers may have been relatively undisturbed by them. The fact of a medieval tradition associating Aeneas with the treachery of Troy cannot, of course, be denied. But over against it has to be set the Virgilian tradition in which Aeneas is celebrated for his public virtues as the founder of the Roman Empire. Which of the two traditions is relevant to the *Gawain*-poet? Both cannot be. The literary problem is to set the poem in the one context that makes sense. There is no value in evoking a tradition that is at odds with the sympathies of the poem.

There is no doubting the centrality of the Virgilian tradition in the Middle Ages. Dante's reverence for Virgil, 'lo mio maestro e 'l mio autore' ('my master and my author') (*Inf.*, I.85) is evident from the *Commedia*; Virgil stands in the allegory as the voice of human reason, and guides the fictional Dante through hell and purgatory to the Earthly Paradise on the summit of the mountain of purgatory. Chaucer provides a summary of the *Aeneid* in varying levels of detail in his *House of Fame* (I. 143–465) and draws upon the *Aeneid* for the Legend of Dido (*LGW*, III.924–1367). Indeed he shows a reverence for Virgil not unlike that of Dante in invoking his name at the end of *Troilus and Criseyde* (V.1792) and at the beginning of the Legend of Dido (*LGW*.III.924–26):

> Glorye and honour, Virgil Mantoan,
> Be to thy name! and I shal, as I can,
> Folwe thy lanterne, as thow gost byforn.

There is no reason, then, to deny the availability of the Virgilian tradition to the poet of *Sir Gawain*. And it is to be noted that Virgil has set out to eliminate the possible attribution of treachery to Aeneas. This is a point that has been observed and explicitly stated by Tasso in his *Discorsi del poema eroico* (Book III):

> Ma con l'artificiosa narrazione de la rovina e de l'incendio di Troia rimosse Virgilio da gli animi quella suspizione che s'ebbe d'Enea: perché egli fu sospetto di tradimento, come dice Servio; . . . mutò gli avvenimenti e l'ordine de le battaglie per accrescer la gloria d'Enea e terminar con un fine più perfetto il suo nobilissimo poema. A queste finzioni fu molto favorevole l'antichità de' tempi.

Still, with his artistic narrative of the devastation and burning of Troy Virgil removed the suspicion about Aeneas, because he was suspected of treason, as Servius says . . . He . . . changed the order and incidents of battles so as to increase the glory of Aeneas and bring his noble poem to a more perfect ending. The antiquity of the times involved greatly favoured these inventions.[4]

The sophistication of the *Gawain*-poet's introduction of the idea of the treachery that led to the destruction of Troy is evident in his play upon the seemingly opposed notions of *tricherie* and *trewest* (4), for treachery is nothing if it is not untrue. There is no such verbal play in the opening lines of *Wynnere and Wastoure*, and the contrast enables us to see the attention that the *Gawain*-poet has brought to bear upon the fact of treachery, and perhaps also to discern its real significance. Truth, as Aquinas explains, is the conformity of intellect to thing (*ST*, la. 16.2):

Et propter hoc per conformitatem intellectus et rei veritas definitur. Unde conformitatem cognoscere est cognoscere veritatem.

Accordingly truth is defined as conformity between intellect and thing. Hence to know that conformity is to know truth.

Treachery lies in the lack of conformity of intellect and thing; the truest treachery, therefore, will be that in which there is the greatest lack of conformity. The poet's method here depends upon the certainty of our identification of the traitor, for the traitor is no ordinary traitor among traitors. He must be someone of the status of a Judas or a Ganelon. In the case of Aeneas there cannot by definition be any such certainty . But there is a Trojan traitor who fits the poet's description, and that is Antenor. So well known is he that he has given his name to the second zone of the traitors in Cocytus in the ninth circle of Dante's hell, that is, Antenora (*Inf.*, XXXII.88), the zone of the traitors to their country. Chaucer refers to Antenor as 'the traytor that betraysed Troye' in *The Book of the Duchess* (1120) and elaborates on the irony of his exchange for Criseyde as follows (*TC*, IV.202–5):

This folk desiren now deliveraunce
Of Antenor, that brought hem to meschaunce,

4.    Reference is to E. Mazzali, *Torquato Tasso: Scritti sull' arte poetica*, 2 vols (Turin, 1977), II, 218-19 and to M. Cavalchini and I. Samuel, *Torquato Tasso: Discourses on the Heroic Poem* (Oxford, 1973), p. 59.

> For he was *after* traitour to the town afterwards
> Of Troye. Allas, they *quytte hym out to rathe*![5] ransomed him
> too soon

The power of poetry depends upon the effectiveness of allusion, and so differs from philosophy which aims at the explicitness of logical discourse. But the impact of a poem can be entirely lost when the point of an allusion is missed, or muffled when it is shrouded in uncertainty. Hence it is necessary to insist that only of Antenor can it be said that his treachery was ' þe trewest on erthe' (4). Such an identification enables the poet to develop a contrast between Antenor and the nobility of Aeneas and his kindred as founders of the kingdoms in the west (5):

> Hit watz Ennias þe athel, and his highe kynde.

Davis claims that *athel* 'means "of noble birth" without implication of honourable character'(p.70), but elsewhere the poet uses the adjective with primary reference to nobility of character, as of the astonished courtiers, 'mony aþel freke' (241), at the appearance of the Green Knight, and of Arthur himself, 'aþel Arthure þe hende' (904). Indeed Dante proves in the *Convivio* that nobility is predicated in the first place of individuals and only secondarily of families (IV.20.5):

> . . . 'l divino seme non cade in ischiatta, cioè in istirpe, ma cade ne le singulari persone, e . . . la stirpe non fa le singulari persone nobili, ma le singulari persone fanno nobile la stirpe.

> . . . the divine seed falls not upon the race, that is the stock, but falls upon the several persons, and . . . the stock does not ennoble the several persons, but the several persons ennoble the stock.[6]

Sordello goes so far as to say that virtue is rarely transmitted within families (*Purg.*, VII. 121–23):

5. These clear references outweigh the linking of the names of Antenor and Aeneas in *Troilus and Criseyde*, II. 1474, although Fyler may be right (note to *House of Fame*, 240-382, p. 980) in seeing in it an implication of 'Aeneas's reputation as one of the betrayers of Troy'. But in so far as Chaucer knows Aeneas as a traitor, it is as a traitor to Dido; see, for example, *HF*, 265-68 and 293-99, and *LGW*, F 1232-39, 1285-89, and 1325-29. In stressing the falseness of Aeneas to Dido Chaucer has been influenced by Ovid's account in *Heroides*, 7.
6. Reference is to G. Busnelli and G. Vandelli, *Il Convivio*, second edition, 2 vols (Florence, 1964), and to the translation of P.H. Wicksteed, *The Convivio of Dante Alighieri* (London, 1903), p. 326.

Rade volte risurge per li rami
l'umana probitate; e questo vole
quei che la dà, perchè da lui si chiami.

Rarely does human worth rise through the branches, and
this He wills who gives it, that it may be sought from Him.[7]

This emphasis on individual virtue is expressed by Sordello on the lower slopes of purgatory (Ante-Purgatory) in the Valley of Princes, and fittingly so, for kings and princes especially have to learn that their true virtue is not in their birth.

*Sir Gawain* is a poem that is above all concerned with the reality of virtue, but the poet is simultaneously aware of the presence of sin. The co-existence of the two, both within the individual and within society, explains why the poet should begin by setting the treachery of Antenor beside the nobility of Aeneas. The act of treachery leads not only to the destruction of Troy but also to the exile from Troy of those who through their virtuous exploits found the kingdoms of western Europe. By a parallel we shall see that the treachery or rather malignancy of Morgan le Fay (2456–62) leads to the testing of Camelot and so to its vindication in the virtuous conduct of Gawain.[8] Such are the ways of Providence, for man's virtue is made evident through the medium of sin: *o felix culpa*! The opening lines of the poem are thus not only logical and clear, but also reveal a complexity that we shall find to be characteristic of the poet's moral thinking in general.

7. Genealogical trees were once drawn to be read from the bottom upwards; hence *risurge*.
8. The treacherousness of Morgan le Fay towards Arthur is a central element in Malory's *Tale of King Arthur*, and is chiefly expressed in the story of Arthur and Accolon; see Vinaver, *Works of Sir Thomas Malory*, pp. 133-52. The author of the *Perlesvaus*, a continuation of the *Roman de Perceval* of Chrétien de Troyes, underlines the fact that Arthur himself was conceived in sin; edited by W.A. Nitze and T.A. Jenkins, *Le Haut Livre du Graal: Perlesvaus*, 2 vols (Chicago, 1932 and 1937; reprinted New York, 1972), 6605-8, and translated by N. Bryant, *The High Book of the Grail* (Cambridge and Totowa, New Jersey, 1978), p. 181:

   Sire, fait li provoires, li rois Uter l'ocist (i.e. Goloé) l'endemain qu'il ot jeü a sa feme la nuit; tantost si esposa la roïne Ugerne; e d'itant com je vos di fu li rois Artus concheü en pechié, qui est ore li mieldre roi dou monde.

   'Sire,' replied the priest, 'King Uter killed him (i.e. Gorlois) the day after he had spent the night with his wife, whereupon he married Queen Ugerne; and so, as I told you, King Arthur, who is now the finest king in the world, was conceived in sin.'

The description of Camelot that now follows (37–59) certainly lives up to the expectations that have been aroused by the account of its Trojan ancestry. The poet focuses on the nobility of the court in a series of varied phrases: 'mony luflych lorde' (38), 'alle þo rich breþer' (39) and ' þise gentyle kniȝtes' (42), and defines that nobility in terms of courtesy, courage or strength, and fame. Courtesy is behaviour that is proper to a court, and it finds its natural expression in jousting, dancing, and composing songs (42–43, and 47):

> Justed ful jolilé þise gentyle kniȝtes,
> Syþen kayred to þe court caroles to make.
>
> Dere dyn vpon day, daunsyng on nyȝtes.

One might compare the description of singing and dancing (*karolyng*, 754) in the garden of Mirth or delight in *The Romaunt of the Rose* (729–92); the young man, who is still not yet 'twenty yer of age' (21), is invited by *Curtesie* (796) to join the dance (793–811). The same associations are found together in another young man of twenty years of age, namely Chaucer's Squire (*CT*, A 95–96):

> He koude songes make and wel endite,
> Juste and eek daunce, and weel purtreye and write.

Courtesy is the virtue called by Aquinas *modestia*, and the essence of it is decorum or propriety, that is, a fitness in relation first to the person and second to the company and occasion (*ST*, 2a 2ae 168.1). Thus the merriment shown by the court is appropriate both to its age (the sanguine age of adolescence)[9] and also to the occasion, and the poet signifies its fitness by the use of the adverb *oryȝt* (40):

> With rych reuel oryȝt and rechles merþes. [10]

There is no sense here of 'dissipation, debauchery' (*MED*, 1.(a)) that is suggested by Youth's use of the noun *ryotte* in the account of the life he leads that he gives in *The Parlement of the Thre Ages* (253):

---

9.  See J.A. Burrow, *The Ages of Man: A Study in Medieval Writing and Thought* (Oxford, 1986), p. 33.
10. The adjective *rechles* is glossed by *MED*, s.v. *recheles* adj. 3. as 'carefree, untroubled by care', and by Davis as 'care-free, joyous' (p. 206). The meaning does not seem doubtful, and I can see no advantage in arguing for the ambiguous presence of the sense 'heedless, imprudent' (*MED*, 1.(a)), as does J.A. Burrow, *A Reading of Sir Gawain and the Green Knight* (London, 1965), pp. 7-8.

With renkes in ryotte to reuelle in haulle.

Youth specifies no occasion, for it is revelry for its own sake that attracts him. The fitness of merriment at Christmas, on the other hand, is deeply ingrained, and George Eliot describes it some five centuries later in her account of Squire Cass's New Year's Eve's dance in *Silas Marner*, albeit significantly in respect of different age-groups (Part I, ch.11):

> It was not thought of as an unbecoming levity for the old and middle-aged people to dance a little before sitting down to cards, but rather as part of their social duties. For what were these if not to be merry at appropriate times, interchanging visits and poultry with due frequency, paying each other old-established compliments in sound traditional phrases, passing well-tried personal jokes, urging your guests to eat and drink too much out of hospitality, and eating and drinking too much in your neighbour's house to show that you liked your cheer? And the parson naturally set an example in these social duties. For it would not have been possible for the Raveloe mind, without a peculiar revelation, to know that a clergyman should be a pale-faced memento of solemnities, instead of a reasonably faulty man . . . [11]

The second quality that the poet singles out is that of courage or strength, and he does so first of all in reference to jousting, for (42):

> Justed ful jolilé þise gentyle kniȝtes.

Davis glosses *jolilé* as 'gallantly' (p.192), but *MED* ((b)) is surely right in identifying the sense 'vigorously, stoutly'. In jousting the young men of the court display their strength and agility, and in these respects they again resemble Chaucer's Squire, for he is 'wonderly delyvere, and of greet strengthe' (*CT*, A 84). Spenser's Red Cross Knight is a young knight who has yet to prove himself, and he too is presented initially in terms of his strength (*FQ*, I.1.1):

> Full iolly knight he seemd, and faire did sitt,
>    As one for knightly giusts and fierce encounters fitt.

The courage of the knights in Camelot is summed up by the *Gawain*-poet in the last two lines of the wheel in the stanza describing them (58–59):

> Hit were now gret nye to neuen
> So hardy a here on hille.

11. Reference is to George Eliot, *Silas Marner* (London, 1906), p. 139.

The third quality that the poet focuses upon is that of fame, for the knights are 'ledez of þe best' (38). The fact is immediately reinforced by the reference to the Round Table (39), for it is that institution of knighthood that the poet clearly has in mind. When it comes to the actual seating arrangements at the feast which is later described (107–15) it emerges that these presuppose a hierarchy based on long tables. The fame of the institution of the Round Table is familiar enough to readers of Arthurian romance, and it is invoked by the poet of the alliterative *Morte Arthure*, who proposes to tell a tale (17–18):

| | |
|---|---|
| Off the *ryeall renkys* of the Rownnde Table, | noble; knights |
| That *chefe* ware of *cheualrye* and cheftans nobyll. | best; knighthood |

The knights in Camelot are fittingly (*rekenly*, 39) members of the honourable institution of the Round Table, that is, they belong to it by merit of their virtues. The *Gawain*-poet returns to the matter of their fame in an explicit formulation of the idea (51):

Þe most kyd kny3tez vnder Krystes seluen.

The combination of courtesy, courage, and fame is a classic combination, and can be illustrated from the works of Chrétien de Troyes in the twelfth century to those of Spenser in the sixteenth century. Chrétien sets out these qualities in the portrait of Erec at the beginning of *Erec et Enide* (81–92):

Aprés les siust a esperon
uns chevaliers, Erec a non;
de la Table Reonde estoit,
an la cort molt grant los avoit;
de tant com il i ot esté,
n'i ot chevalier si loé,
et fu tant biax qu'an nule terre
n'estovoit plus bel de lui querre.
Molt estoit biax et preuz et genz
et n'avoit pas. XXV. anz;
onques nus hom de son aage
ne fu de si grant vaselage.

After them there swiftly followed a knight, named Erec, who belonged to the Round Table, and had great fame at the court. Of all the knights that ever were there, never one received such praise; and he was so fair that nowhere in the world need one seek a fairer knight than he. He was very fair, brave, and courteous, though not yet twenty-five years old. Never was there a man of his age of greater knighthood.[12]

These qualities are subsequently illustrated in the adventure of the sparrow-hawk. Spenser's Calidore is indeed the Knight of Courtesy, but to courtesy are added courage and fame (*FQ*,VI.1.2):

> But mongst them all was none more courteous Knight,
>     Then *Calidore*, beloued ouer all,
>     In whom it seemes, that gentlenesse of spright
>     And manners mylde were planted naturall;
>     To which he adding comely guize withall,
>     And gracious speach, did steale mens hearts away.
>     Nathlesse thereto he was full stout and tall,
>     And well approu'd in batteilous affray,
> That him did much renowme, and far his fame display.

Erec is twenty-five and, as we have seen, other literary figures that bear comparison with the knights of Camelot, like Chaucer's Squire, are only twenty. And it is in relation to details such as these that we may begin to see the significance of the *Gawain*-poet's characterisation of the court as in its 'first age' (54). This is a phrase with precise implications, but it has not been properly understood, partly because of the multiplicity of age-schemes that were available in the Middle Ages, partly because the associations of the medieval age-names are very different from modern ones, and partly because the age-limits of the terms are subject to considerable variation. Thus the key term *juventus* stands for the period of man's perfection and maturity; in the *Isagoge* of Johannitius and the *Canon* of Avicenna it is the period from thirty to thirty-five or forty,[13] in the *Convivio* of Dante it is the period from twenty-five to forty-five (*Convivio*, IV.24 3–4), and in Aquinas's commentary on the *Sentences* it is the period from twenty-five to fifty.[14] These examples are all drawn from the four-age scheme of the medical or physiological tradition, which had by the late fourteenth century been absorbed within the vernacular writings.[15] It seems likely that the *Gawain*-poet's use of the phrase 'first age' has reference to the first age of the four-age scheme, namely that of *adolescentia*. Fortunately this is a term that has a good deal of stability, although there are some variations in its usage and some complexity in its range. For

12. Reference is to M. Roques, *Erec et Enide*, CFMA (Paris, 1970), and to the translation of W.W. Comfort, *Chrétien de Troyes: Arthurian Romances*, with introduction and notes by D.D.R. Owen (London and New York, 1975), p. 2.
13. See Burrow, *Ages of Man*, pp. 22-23.
14. Cited by Busnelli and Vandelli, *Il Convivio*, II, 304.
15. See Burrow, *Ages of Man*, pp. 12-36.

Aquinas and Dante *adolescentia* is the period up to twenty-five, for Johannitius up to twenty-five or thirty, and for Avicenna up to thirty. *Adolescentia* comprehends in fact three distinct periods of a man's early existence, as Aquinas observes in his exposition on the *Sentences*:

> Variantur enim in homine aetates secundum diversas notabiles varietates in statu ipsius: unde prima aetas dicitur infantia usque ad septimum annum; secunda pueritia usque ad quartum decimum; tertia adolescentia usque ad vigesimum quintum; quae tres aetates computantur quandoque pro una.

> For the ages in man are diversified according to different notable changes in his condition: whence the first age is called infancy up to the seventh year; the second boyhood up to the fourteenth; the third adolescence up to the twenty-fifth; which three ages are reckoned sometimes as one.

This identification of the *Gawain*-poet's 'first age' is due to the work of M. Dove, who in an illuminating discussion associates it with the age-name *first youthe*, used by Trevisa for his translation of *adolescentia* in Higden's Polychronicon.[16] On this basis she rules out the glosses 'the flower of their youth' (Davis, p.161), and 'early adulthood' (*MED*, 1.b(b)), since 'the former is blurred by a suggestion of "the best age" and the latter inclines too much towards the second part of youth, and away from early adolescence' (p.136).[17] She fixes the boundaries of the first age as at one end the boyish exuberance of childhood, and at the other the strength of the second part of youth (p.137). The importance of the element of boyishness in the first age is signified by the fact that *pueritia* rather than *adolescentia* is used as the general term for that age, as by Albertus Magnus in his *De aetate*, tractatus 1, chapter 2:

16. M. Dove, *The Perfect Age of Man's Life* (Cambridge, 1986), p. 136. The adolescence of Gawain and Camelot is expressed in terms of an initiatory myth by C. Wrigley, '*Sir Gawain and the Green Knight*: the Underlying Myth', in *Studies in Medieval English Romances: Some New Approaches*, edited by D. Brewer (Woodbridge and Rochester, New York, 1988), pp. 113-28: 'It has always been recognised in a general way that the romance heroes progress from innocence to experience . . . Romance is in fact about adolescence . . . If Gawain becomes a man in the course of the story he must have begun it as a child; and it is very clear that children are what he and all the folk of Camelot are, at least metaphorically . . . There is no warrant for taking the first age to be mature if young adulthood, . . . '(p. 117).
17. I must as a consequence of Dove's analysis acknowledge the incorrectness of my own description of the court as being 'in the full vigour of its youth, that is, the period of its greatest perfection' in my article, 'The Significance of the Pentangle Symbolism in *Sir Gawain and the Green Knight*', *MLR*, 74 (1979), 769-90 (p. 782).

Aetas autem in omnibus aetate participantibus in quatuor aetates dividitur . . . Hae autem in homine magis notae sunt; et ideo in homine nomina specialia receperunt; quoniam prima vocata est pueritia; secunda autem iuventus, sive virilis, rectius autem vocatur virilis quam iuventus, quia iuventus ad pueritiam videtur pertinere. Tertia vero vocata est senectus; et quarta et ultima senium, sive aetas decrepita.

But age in all things participating in age is divided into four ages . . . These are, however, more completely known in man; and so in man they have received particular names; because the first was called boyhood; the second indeed youth, or manhood, more properly however it is called manhood than youth, because youth seems to relate to boyhood. The third indeed was called old age; and the fourth and last decline, or the age of decrepitude.[18]

The linking by Albertus of *pueritia* and *iuventus* shows to some extent how uncertain the boundary was between the two, and may prepare us for some blurring of the distinction. Indeed we have seen that the period between twenty-five and thirty is assigned by some authorities to *adolescentia*, and to *iuventus* by others.[19] Thus reference is made by the *Gawain*-poet to Arthur's *joyfnes* or youth, and then immediately after to his boyishness, for he is described as 'sumquat childgered'(86). In fact the whole description of Arthur at this point (85–89) is a concentrated account of boyish energy or youthful vitality, a celebration of the period of adolescence in the king himself. The adjective *joly* (86) which is applied to Arthur's youth does not have to mean 'merry, cheerful, glad', although that sense is well attested by *MED* (1.(a)) and supported by Davis's gloss 'gay' (p.192). Such a meaning fits the wider context of Christmas festivities and of Arthur's participation in them (106). But the immediate emphasis on Arthur's strength (which excludes neither courtesy nor merriment) is also appropriate. The required sense is that of 'vigorous, strong, youthful' (*MED*, 2.(a)) and takes up the reference to *jolilé* (42). The translation 'lively in his youthfulness' (Waldron, p.33) would seem preferable to 'youthfully light-hearted' (Barron, p.33). The doubtful word *childgered* is glossed by *MED* as 'boyish, light-hearted' (s.v. *child*, n. 13. (d)), and these values are reflected in Davis's glosses 'boyish, merry' (p.171). In a note Davis observes that 'the general sense of boyish conduct can be deduced from a few occurrences of the related noun' (p.75). What this means for Dove is not boyish light-heartedness, but boyish changeability and restlessness

18. Cited by Busnelli and Vandelli, *Il Convivio*, II, 290-91.
19. Such an overlap between *adolescentia* and *juventus* may enable us to accommodate the list of qualities predicated of Gawain in the pentangle passage (640-55), for these would seem to belong to the period of youth rather than adolescence, certainly at least as Dante defines them (*Convivio*, IV. 26.2).

(p.137, and n.11, p.164). The word is carefully qualified by the poet—*sumquat childgered* (86)—so as to ensure that the king's conduct cannot be taken to exceed the bounds proper to adolescence. The phrase suggests boyish energy rather than merriment. The pejorative force of Modern English 'childish' is certainly ruled out by the context. These meanings are reinforced by the adjective *ly3t* in the following line, for once again the required sense is 'energetic, brisk, active' (*MED*, 5. (a)), rather than 'cheerful, merry, joyful' (*MED*, 7. (a)), the sense adopted by Davis (p.195). Thus Waldron's translation, 'he loved an active life' (p.33), which is also followed by Barron (p.33), is what best suits the immediate as distinct from the wider context. Finally the adjective *wylde* as applied to Arthur's brain (89) is aptly glossed by Davis as 'restless' (p.227), and again there is no pejorative implication. The word is commonly used in Middle English in reference to the passionate activity of youth, as of Alison in *The Miller's Tale* (*CT*, A 3225):

> For she was wylde and yong, and he was old.

Criseyde rejects the suggestion of Pandarus that she abandon the pleasures of reading for those of dancing, since she does not think dancing fitting for the life of a widow (*TC*, II. 116–19):

> 'Ye ben so wylde, it semeth as ye rave.
> It satte me wel bet ay in a cave
> To bidde and rede on holy seyntes lyves;
> Lat maydens gon to daunce, and yonge wyves.'

In the person of Arthur are summed up the values of the court, that is, fame and courtesy as well as courage, for a court centres on a king, and the values of Camelot radiate outwards from Arthur himself. Hence we learn of the king's nobility and fame (25–26) before we learn of that of the court over which he presides. Subsequently we learn of his courtesy in the observation of the custom of not eating before an adventure on a noble festival (90–102), in making merry at Christmas (106), and in his gracious conversation before the meal (108):

> Talkkande bifore þe hy3e table of trifles ful hende.

Further, the poet makes clear that boyish energy in Arthur also extends to youthful courage, for he returns to this theme in the wheel that concludes the stanza which begins with the account of that boyishness (103–5):

Þerfore of face so fere
He sti3tlez stif in stalle,
Ful 3ep in þat Nw 3ere,

and reiterates it at the beginning of the following stanza (107):

Thus þer stondes in stale þe stif kyng hisseluen.

The presentation of Camelot is of an ideal court, but it contains some surprising elements along with the familiar ones. The reason is, as Dove has pointed out (p.137), that it is of an ideal at a certain stage of life, namely that of adolescence. But it is possible to recognise that Camelot is an ideal, even though Arthur's boyishness may be puzzling, simply from the stylistic features of the text, for the poet is writing within the tradition of epideictic rhetoric. This is the rhetoric of praise or censure in which the aim is consistency in emotional appeal, such as the eliciting of admiration from the reader in the case of praise. The author of the *Rhetorica ad Herennium* explains the concerns of epideictic rhetoric as follows (III.10):

Quoniam haec causa dividitur in laudem et vituperationem, quibus ex rebus laudem constituerimus, ex contrariis rebus erit vituperatio con-parata. Laus igitur potest esse rerum externarum, corporis, animi.

Since epideictic includes Praise and Censure, the topics on which praise is founded will, by their contraries, serve us as the bases for censure. The following, then, can be subject to praise: External Circum-stances, Physical Attributes, and Qualities of Character. [20]

One obvious feature of such a style is the use of superlative language, and the *Gawain*-poet does not fall short in this respect in the praise in which Arthur and the court are interlinked (51–53):

Þe most kyd kny3tez vnder Krystes seluen,
And þe louelokkest ladies þat euer lif haden,
And he þe comlokest kyng þat þe court haldes.

Such unqualified praise is characteristic of romance, and makes an appeal to universal or objective standards of excellence rather than to their individual realisation. A similar consideration lies behind a second stylistic feature,

20. Reference is to [*Cicero*] *Ad C. Herennium de ratione dicendi* (*Rhetorica ad Herennium*), translated by H. Caplan, Loeb (Cambridge, Massachusetts and London, 1954).

namely the use of qualitative description such as 'good', 'fair', or 'noble'. We might observe here the poet's use of the fixed evaluative epithet *gode* (109) with which he introduces Gawain to us, and which is repeated at significant moments during his quest, for example, just before the fateful meeting with the Green Knight when Gawain announces himself as 'gode Gawayn' (2214). A clever and emphatic variation on the usual phrase, 'Gawayn þe god mon' (1179), is used by the poet as a preface to the first bedroom scene. The test of such stylistic devices is not vividness, but propriety, and the consequent establishment of a series of moral points of reference.[21] The use of qualitative description is by no means an exercise in redundance. Chaucer's repetition of the evaluative adjective *worthy* in the portrait of the Knight (*CT*, A 43, 47, 64, and 68) together with the related noun *worthynesse* (*CT*, A 50) has not been proof against the interpretation of the portrait as a satire upon the corruption of chivalric values in the late fourteenth century.[22]

The poet's representation of Arthur's conduct in the rest of the narrative of Fitt I is entirely accounted for in terms of the ideal that has been established at its beginning. Thus courtesy and courage are combined in equal measure in Arthur's greeting of the Green Knight (251):

> And rekenly hym reuerenced, for rad was he neuer.

The subsequent anger that Arthur shows (316–27) is not to be interpreted as a falling-off in courtesy. The virtue of courtesy is essentially one of fitness. And this meaning of courtesy is to be taken strictly; courtesy is a matter of fit words and not fair words. To be pleasant when the occasion requires harsh rebukes is to degenerate into the vice of obsequiousness or even flattery, as illustrated by Spenser in the unfittingly fair words of Blandina (*FQ*, VI.6.41–42). There is more than one kind of anger as Chaucer's Parson explains (*CT*, I 538–40):

> But ye shal understonde that Ire is in two maneres; that oon of hem is good, and that oother is wikked.
> The goode Ire is by jalousie of goodnesse, thurgh which a man is wrooth with wikkednesse and agayns wikkednesse; and therfore seith a wys man that Ire is bet than pley.
> This Ire is with debonairetee, and it is wrooth withouten bitternesse; nat wrooth agayns the man, but wrooth with the mysdede of the man, as seith the prophete David, "*Irascimini et nolite peccare.*"

---

21. On the use of superlatives and qualitative description in romance, see M. Lambert, *Malory: Style and Vision in Le Morte Darthur* (New Haven and London, 1975), pp. 24–33.
22. By T. Jones, *Chaucer's Knight: the Portrait of a Medieval Mercenary* (London, 1980).

It is righteous anger of this kind that Christ himself displayed in driving the money-changers out of the temple (John, 2.13–17), and after Christ's example Chaucer's Parson too (*CT*, A 521–23). Arthur is also right to be angry, for he and his court have been grossly insulted by the arrogant and disdainful words of the Green Knight (307–15). Such anger is not to be condemned, but praised, as Aquinas observes (*ST*, 2a 2ae 158.1):

> Si autem aliquis irascitur secundum rationem rectam, tunc irasci est laudabile.

> All the same, to be angry in accord with right reason is praiseworthy.

Moreover, Arthur is not so moved by anger as to have lost possession of himself, for in taking upon himself the Green Knight's challenge (328):

> Lyȝtly lepez he hym to, and laȝt at his honde,

that is, he behaves strictly in accordance with the rules of the game laid down by the challenger (291–92):

> If any freke be so felle to fonde þat I telle,
> Lepe lyȝtly me to, and lach þis weppen.

The court is enabled by this kingly example to meet at least the first part of the Green Knight's test, and by the end of the first fitt it has regained its composure (467–86), despite the gruesome beheading (421–43) and the violently menacing departure (444–59) of the adversary. Fittingly it is Arthur himself who restores this courtly equilibrium, while at the same time concealing his own astonishment (467–69). Thus he finds the right words with which to comfort the Queen (470–73):

> 'Dere dame, to-day demay yow neuer;
> Wel bycommes such craft vpon Cristmasse,
> Laykyng of enterludez, to laȝe and to syng,
> Among þise kynde caroles of knyȝtez and ladyez,'

and also to hearten the knight who has maintained the court's honour (476–77):

> He glent vpon Sir Gawen, and gaynly he sayde,
> 'Now sir, heng vp þyn ax, þat hatz innogh hewen'.

Finally, indeed, we turn to the emergence of Sir Gawain as the knight who takes up the Green Knight's challenge. There is, as Burrow has shown (*A*

*Reading*, pp. 8–12), no sense of the special election of Gawain, although we may well gather from his place at table (109) the distinction he possesses even in so distinguished a company. By contrast in Malory's version of *The Tale of the Sankgreal* only one knight can sit in the Siege Perilous (860/8–17) and draw the sword from the stone (862/23–863/1). Galahad's assurance of his own destiny is revealed in the reply to Arthur's words of the marvel of the sword in the stone, which has resisted the efforts of many good knights to draw it forth (862/29–30):

> 'Sir', seyde sir Galahad, 'hit ys no mervayle, for thys adventure ys nat theyrs but myne.'

He then proceeds without difficulty to draw the sword from the stone (862/33–34). The special election of Galahad is accompanied by a sharp distinction made by the Cistercian author of the original *Queste del Saint Graal* between Grail Knights and Sinful Knights, allegorized in Gawain's dream of the three white bulls and one hundred and forty-seven black bulls (942/3–19) and interpreted by the hermit Nacien (946/4–947/3). Such neo-Platonic absolutism is not acceptable to the author of the Vulgate *Mort Artu* nor to Malory himself. Malory's *Morte Darthur* as a whole is built on the recognition that no man is free from sin, and of sinful knights it is Lancelot who is the best. Since in *Sir Gawain* there is no special election, there is consequently no division of white bulls and black bulls. Gawain is one of an undivided company of knights of the Round Table (109–11), and expresses the chivalry of that institution in courteously taking upon himself the challenge of the Green Knight (339–61). We are not to be surprised if Gawain's excellence as the representative of such an institution is measured by the extent of his imperfection (even though the values of the court have been presented initially in superlative terms). At the same time Gawain is the best of sinful knights. In representing Gawain in this way the poet is drawing upon authentic traditions, different from those familiar to readers of Malory and deriving from the romances of Chrétien de Troyes. According to the hierarchy of knights of the Round Table as set forth in *Erec et Enide* (1667–84), Gawain occupies the first position, followed by Erec; Lancelot as yet has the distinction only of third position. These relative values are subsequently suggested by the *Gawain*-poet in his own catalogue of knights (550–55). The ideas and values of the poem are placed in a false perspective if the character of Gawain is interpreted in the light of its representation as degenerate in the traditions that lie behind Malory's *Morte Darthur*. There is no necessity to assume that these traditions are relevant to a poem such as *Sir Gawain*. No poet is under any obligation to reconcile variant traditions. He is responsible only for the coherence of his own work, and in the interest of his own poetic argument he can exercise the freedom (as Virgil does in the *Aeneid*) to alter traditional accounts for the sake of that work. In the end it is the uniqueness of the created artefact that counts. Gawain is indeed a representative figure, but only of the values of Camelot as they are set out by the poet. Moreover, he is the best among the best; hence it is fitting that he rather than Ywain, or Eric (551) or (in this poem a lesser knight than either of those two) Lancelot (553) should take up the Green Knight's challenge. The fact is implicitly acknowledged by the Green Knight when he discovers the identity of his adversary (390–91):

> 'Bigog,' quoþ þe grene kny3t, 'Sir Gawan, me lykes
> Þat I schal fange at þy fust þat I haf frayst here.'

The poet offers no criticism of Camelot in this first fitt (although there are not a few who have professed to find it). And the reason for the laudatory description is not far to seek, for it is the virtue and renown of the Round Table that explains the appearance of the Green Knight at Camelot. It is his purpose to put that reputation to the test (258–64):

> Bot for þe los of þe, lede, is lyft vp so hy3e,
> And þy bur3 and þy burnes best ar holden,
> Stifest vnder stel-gere on stedes to ryde,
> Þe wy3test and þe worþyest of þe worldes kynde,
> Preue for to play wyth in oþer pure laykez,
> And here is kydde cortaysye, as I haf herd carp,
> And þat hatz wayned me hider, iwyis, at þis tyme.

The way in which that reputation is put to the test by means of the Christmas game is also fitting to the period of adolescence to which the court belongs. The Green Knight refuses to engage in armed combat those who are only 'berdlez chylder' (280). This is, of course, a calculated insult, but it is not only an insult, for it underlines once again the fact of the youthfulness of the knights. And it is fitting too that young knights should be put to the test, for they have still to some extent to prove themselves.

We are to understand, therefore, from Fitt I that the poem as a whole will consist in the testing of the values of Camelot as represented by Gawain. These matters are not meant to be obscure, and they are further clarified by the Green Knight's explanations at the end of the poem. Morgan le Fay, he tells Gawain, (2456–58):

> . . . wayned me vpon þis wyse to your wynne halle
> For to assay þe surquidré, 3if hit soth were
> Þat rennes of þe grete renoun of þe Rounde Table.

The immediate object of temptation or testing is knowledge, as Aquinas explains (*ST*, 1a 114.2)

> Dicendum quod tentare est proprie experimentum sumere de aliquo. Experimentum autem sumitur de aliquo, ut sciatur aliquid circa ipsum; et ideo proximus finis cujuslibet tentantis est scientia.

> Properly speaking, to tempt is to put someone to the test. Now we put someone to the test so as to find out something about him. Hence the immediate goal of any tempter is knowledge.

The tests around which *Sir Gawain* is constructed, that is to say, the Exchange of Winnings agreement as well as the Beheading Game, are designed to reveal to us a knowledge of human virtue and its limitation. And what we learn (to anticipate somewhat) is that Gawain deserves his reputation as the best, but that even the best remain fallible and imperfect. In the process we shall be led to see what it means to be the best, and how excellence can be reconciled or combined with imperfection.

# CHAPTER THREE

# The Handsomeness
# of the Green Knight

## I

MUCH OF THE PLEASURE in *Sir Gawain* derives from the representation of the Green Knight himself. He is a source of energy in the poem and an endless fascination for readers who are unable to determine his essential meaning. As Burrow puts it, 'the account of his appearance and actions does indeed bristle with suggestions' (*A Reading*, p. 3). But it has to be said that the ready acceptance of such critical uncertainty is especially congenial to modern readers for whom ambiguity is one of the great virtues of poetry. Aristotle, however, lists ambiguity among the errors of style in his *Rhetoric* (III.5):

> The third (foundation of good style) is to avoid ambiguities; unless, indeed, you definitely desire to be ambiguous, as those do who have nothing to say but are pretending to mean something.[1]

I have no doubt that this view of ambiguity is closer to that of the *Gawain*-poet himself, as is the corresponding assumption of clarity as one of the stylistic virtues (*Rhetoric*, III.2):

> Style to be good must be clear, as is proved by the fact that speech which fails to convey a plain meaning will fail to do just what speech has to do.

I wish to argue in this chapter, therefore, that the portrait of the Green Knight is distinguished not for its ambiguity but for its clarity. In particular I shall call in question Benson's judgment that 'the portrait as a whole is significantly blurred, and it is impossible to visualize a coherent figure of the challenger'.[2] Such a judgment is not only at odds with medieval rhetorical principles of description, but also involves a failure to grasp the poet's aim and achievement.

1.   Reference to the *Rhetorica* is to the translation of W.R. Roberts, in *The Works of Aristotle*, edited by W.D. Ross, Volume XI (Oxford, 1924).
2.   L.D. Benson, *Art and Tradition in Sir Gawain and the Green Knight* (New Brunswick, New Jersey, 1965), p. 61. It seems to be universally held that the portrait

The element of the marvellous in the character of the Green Knight was referred by some earlier critics of the poem to a supposed background in vegetation myth. Speirs in particular has insisted on the relationship between the Green Knight and the Green Man:

> The Green Knight whose head is chopped off at his own request and who is yet as miraculously or magically alive as ever, bears an unmistakable relation to the Green Man — the Jack in the Green or the Wild Man of the village festivals of England and Europe. He *is* in fact no other than a recrudescence in poetry of the Green Man.[3]

There are some features of the portrait of the Green Knight that do indeed invite such a comparison. In the first place, there is the undeniable fact of his greenness itself; he is 'oueral enker-grene' (150), that is, bright green all over, and this greenness is subsequently compared to the colour of grass: 'grene as þe gres and grener hit semed' (235). Secondly, he has a beard that is compared to a bush (182):

> A much berd as a busk ouer his brest henges.

And thirdly he carries in his one hand a holly branch (206–7):

> Bot in his on honde he hade a holyn bobbe,
> Þat is grattest in grene when greuez ar bare.

of the Green Knight is intended by the poet to be and in fact is ambiguous. A.C. Spearing, *The Gawain-Poet* (Cambridge, 1970) concludes his study by underlining the ambiguity of the Green Knight (p.236): 'Everything about him is ambiguous, from his opening appearance as a creature half-man and half-giant, half-knightly and half-brutish, . . . to the final disclosure that he is two apparently different people, both the terrifying challenger and the jovial host.' Davenport, *The Art of the Gawain-Poet,* draws a comparison between ambiguity and abstraction in the poet's creation of the Green Knight (p.205): 'In *Sir Gawain* the voice of authority is completely equivocal, since in the Green Knight the poet created an ambiguous, shifting figure who is never allowed to simplify into an abstraction.' The assumption of ambiguity has hardened into dogma, and certainly needs to be challenged, for it obscures the poet's conception of his work. The detailed realisation of the Green Knight in Fitt I looks forward to his final role in the judgmental scene of Fitt IV, since it invests him with the authoritativeness for such a role. In other words the voice of authority is not equivocal.

3.   J. Speirs, 'Sir Gawain and the Green Knight', *Scrutiny,* 16 (1949), 274-90, and in *Twentieth Century Interpretations of Sir Gawain and the Green Knight,* edited by D. Fox (Englewood Cliffs, New Jersey, 1968), pp. 79-94 (p. 83).

These details do not constitute an impressive list when one considers the wealth of detail in the poet's description of the Green Knight as a whole. But they are not entirely negligible, and the greenness is on any view the most outstanding of all the details. Speirs has certainly made the most of them, but it would seem that he has accomplished all that is now possible in such a critical approach to the poem.

We may perhaps grant the fact of the ultimate mythological origin of these details. Even so the question would still remain as to whether they possess any present literary significance. We may take as a comparison to the Green Knight the hero whose strength increases until noon and declines after it. There are two examples of this phenomenon in the *Morte Darthur*. The first is Sir Ironside, the Red Knight of the Red Lands, in *The Tale of Sir Gareth* (320/30–321/3):

> And also there was faste by a sygamoure tre, and thereon hynge an horne, the grettyst that ever they sye, of an olyvauntes bone, and this Knyght of the Rede Launde hath honged hit up there to this entente, that yf there com ony arraunte knyghte he muste blowe that horne and than woll he make hym redy and com to hym to do batayle.
>
> 'But, sir, pray you,' seyde the damesell, 'blow ye nat the horne tyll hit be hygh none, for now hit is aboute pryme, and now encresyth his myght, that as men say he hath seven mennys strength.'

The second and more famous example is that of Sir Gawain himself (the Malorian Gawain), and it is recorded in the account of his disastrous combat against Lancelot in *The Tale of the Morte Arthur* (1216/31–1217/1):

> Than had sir Gawayne suche a grace and gyffte that an holy man had gyvyn hym, that every day in the yere, frome undern tyll hyghe noone, hys myght encresed tho three owres as much as thryse hys strength. And that caused sir Gawayne to wynne grete honoure.

A solar myth seems quite likely as the explanation of the waxing and waning of knightly strength after this manner. But it is not an explanation that tells us much of significance about the narratives in which such knightly strength is exercised. The increasing might of Sir Ironside is a means whereby the reader may measure the magnanimity of Sir Gareth (321/4–8):

> 'A! fy for shame, fayre damesell! Sey ye nevir so more to me, for and he were as good a knyght as ever was ony I shall never fayle hym in his moste myght, for other I woll wynne worshyp worshypfully othir dye knyghtly in the felde.'

Later Malory is concerned to demonstrate Lancelot's fortitude in enduring the worst that Gawain can offer him (1217/10–28). The pattern of events is substantially repeated in the second fight between the two (1219/27–1221/13) and in the process Lancelot's superiority is doubly affirmed (1220/5–24).

As C.S. Lewis observes,[4] the solar myth is remote from the central imaginative concerns of Malory's work. And in the same way the vegetation myth is remote from what is imaginatively significant about the Green Knight. Speirs is right to advocate the abandonment of the study of sources and analogues for the study of the poem itself (pp. 80–82). But the discussion of the Green Knight in terms of vegetation myth is yet another extra-textual pursuit of very limited value for the understanding of the poem. Indeed, in so far as it leads to an opposition between courtly sophistication and natural vigour (Speirs, pp. 87–88), it falsifies the relationship between the court and the Green Knight by overlooking the youthful vitality of the one and the courtly appearance of the other. The imaginative impact of the Green Knight is due not to his presumed mythical origin, but to the art with which the poet introduces him into the poem. The poet arouses and fulfils the reader's expectation with an inevitability that is possible only for one who is the master of his art.

Almost everything that we experience in the poem is experienced in the superlative degree, and in the person of the Green Knight the poet has produced a marvel to match. Britain is a land noted for marvels (23–24), but the marvel to be unfolded is marvellous even by these standards; it is 'an outtrage awenture of Arthurez wonderez' (29). Arthur's custom of awaiting a marvel before taking food at a high festival (90–102) is decidedly a literary phenomenon. Malory supplies an excellent example of the custom in matter very probably of his own invention in *The Tale of Sir Gareth* (293/7–12):

> So evir the kynge had a custom that at the feste of Pentecoste in especiall afore other festys in the yere, he wolde nat go that day to mete unto that he had herde other sawe of a grete mervayle. And for that custom all maner of strange adventures com byfore Arthure, as at that feste before all other festes.

The setting of Pentecost makes clear the origin of this custom and the associated marvels, for it recalls the coming of the Holy Ghost to the apostles and the bestowal upon them of the gift of tongues (Acts, 2.1–7). Now the appearance of the Green Knight is accommodated to this literary pattern. The poet not only tells us of Arthur's noble custom, but immediately prefaces the entry of the Green Knight by reminding us of it (132–33):

4. C.S. Lewis, 'De Audiendis Poetis', in *Studies in Medieval and Renaissance Literature* (Cambridge, 1966), pp. 1-17 (pp. 9-10).

> An oþer noyse ful newe neȝed biliue,
> Þat þe lude myȝt haf leue liflode to cach.

And as the first fitt is neatly drawn to its conclusion, Arthur is made to observe (474–75):

> Neuer þe lece to my mete I may me wel dres,
> For I haf sen a selly, I may not forsake.

The dramatic effect of the disclosure of the Green Knight's greenness is also the product of poetic art, for it comes at the end of the wheel and is the carefully calculated result of metrical artifice (149–50):

> He ferde as freke were fade,
> And oueral enker-grene.

The wonder is further emphasised by the astonished silence to which it reduces the court (232–45). The impact of the greenness of the Green Knight owes almost everything to art, and almost nothing to myth. His appearance in the poem at once puts the courage and courtesy of Camelot to the test, and it is these virtues that are the central objects of the poet's interest.

The presence of the marvellous in a romance does not in any event require the justification of myth, for it is what the literary kind itself requires. Aristotle has observed that the marvellous is proper to the epic and tragic kinds, and so a source of the pleasure that such works give (*Poetics*, 24):

> The marvellous is certainly required in Tragedy. The Epic, however, affords more opening for the improbable, the chief factor in the marvellous, because in it the agents are not visibly before one . . . The marvellous, however, is a cause of pleasure, as is shown by the fact that we all tell a story with additions, in the belief that we are doing our hearers a pleasure.[5]

But not any character or incident outside of the order of nature is allowable into a poem in the guise of the marvellous. For, as Tasso explains, the marvellous, like any other object of imitation, must satisfy the criterion of verisimilitude (*Discorsi*, II, 191–92, and p.38):

> Ma benché io stringa il poeta epico ad un obligo perpetuo di servare il verisimile, non però escludo da lui l'altra parte, cioè il maraviglioso:

---

5.    Reference to the *De poetica* is to the translation of I. Bywater, in *The Works of Aristotle*, edited by W.D. Ross, Volume XI (Oxford, 1924).

anzi giudico che un'azione medesima possa essere e maravigliosa e verisimile.

Still, though I hold the epic poet to a perpetual obligation to preserve verisimilitude, I do not therefore deprive him of the other part, the marvellous. Rather I judge that one same action can be marvellous and verisimilar.

What this means in the first place is that if marvels are to be imaginatively credible they must be conformed to the pattern of belief upheld by the work of art as a whole. The pagan gods are acceptable in a classical poem because they are supported by the religious beliefs of pagan writers, and act in accordance with those beliefs. But in a Christian poem the pagan gods would be an absurdity (*Discorsi*, II, 189, and p. 36). This is a principle that Chaucer has recognized in his own practice, for at the end of *Troilus and Criseyde* he refers disparagingly to the pagan gods as 'swich rascaille' (V.1853). And Chaucer further capitalizes upon it by contrasting the credibility of an appeal to the one Christian God (as by a Criseyde in Book II or a Dorigen) with the lack of credibility of an appeal to pagan gods (as by a Pandarus in Book II or an Aurelius). By his conception of the Green Knight the *Gawain*-poet has shown that he also has grasped this principle. Nothing is more natural to a romance than Black Knights, Green Knights, Red Knights, and Blue Knights (as, for example, in Malory's *Tale of Sir Gareth*), and so the *Gawain*-poet has himself produced a Green Knight as his hero's adversary (albeit a Green Knight of marvellous greenness). The marvel is conformed to a Christian world order, for the Green Knight himself naturally acknowledges the power of the Christian God (256–57):

'Nay, as help me,' quoþ þe haþel, 'he þat on hyȝe syttes,
To wone any quyle in þis won, hit watz not myn ernde.'

Moreover, the poet has conceived for the Green Knight a role which is entirely appropriate to a knight. Although, as we shall see, the description of the Green Knight is clear and not ambiguous, the representation of his intentions does contain a calculated ambivalence. The Green Knight's dress (160 and 203–5) and the holly branch that he bears in his one hand (206–7) suggest that his intentions are peaceful. And yet the axe that he carries in his other hand is designed for grim business (208–13). And the Green Knight's own explanation of his peaceful dress (265–71) is hardly reassuring in the note of defiance that it strikes. The conduct of the Green Knight, indeed, answers the decorum of the hostile challenger. He offers no greeting (223) and addresses Arthur in the familiar singular form (258–74). This is not the clownishness of an untutored Perceval but a studied discourtesy. It is the offensiveness of one who knows well enough the kind of behaviour that is designed to please and to offend. The conduct of the Green Knight fits the pattern established by Meleagant in Chrétien's *Chevalier de la charrete* (43–60), as Burrow has convincingly shown (*A Reading*, pp. 17–20). Even in his hostile gestures the Green Knight does not step outside the decorum of his role, for he is not merely hostile, he is impressive. Hence the poet stresses his lofty unconcern at the impending blow (334–38). The poet does not intend to diminish Arthur (whose own courage in the face of so awesome a figure ought not to be questioned), but to impress upon us the rude dignity of the challenger. The challenge that he offers, expressed with due legal solemnity (291–98), is not lightly either to be set aside or confronted.

The action in which the marvellous occurs must be presented convincingly, and indeed Aristotle goes so far as to say that a convincing impossibility is preferable to an unconvincing possibility (*Poetics*, 24). The action must therefore continue to obey the laws of cause and effect in such a way as to suggest the reality of what has taken place. Aristotle puts it as follows in the *Poetics* (24):

> Whenever, if A is or happens, a consequent, B, is or happens, men's notion is that, if the B is, the A also is — but that is a false conclusion. Accordingly, if A is untrue, but there is something else, B, that on the assumption of its truth follows as its consequent, the right thing then is to add on the B. Just because we know the truth of the consequent, we are in our own minds led on to the erroneous inference of the truth of the antecedent.[6]

There can be no doubt that the Green Knight is just such a convincing impossibility. His presence would reduce the noblest of courts to silence in wonder and dismay (232–49); his calculated rudeness would provoke the high-spirited king to anger (316–27); his severed head would be kicked away by those whose fears had given way to a sickening sense of distaste (427–28); and the lifting of the tension at his departure would arouse a mixture of joy and relief in Arthur and Gawain (463–66). These are the vivid and realistic touches that convince us imaginatively of the poetic reality of the Green Knight's presence. And it is in the light of this testimony of the poet's art that we turn to the description of the Green Knight itself (136–202).

6.   In the *Rhetoric*, III.7 Aristotle discusses the representation of convincing fallacies in terms of propriety of language.

Benson claims of the portrait of the Green Knight that at lines 136–40 'we see him as a monster' and at lines 181–86 'as a grotesquely bearded churl' (p.61). These claims are not self-evidently correct, and on close inspection they turn out to be false.

The first phrase used of the Green Knight, namely 'an aghlich mayster' (136), may by an historical accident induce in a modern scholar an assumption of monstrosity. The adjective *aghlich*, derived from ON *agi* and OE *-lic* and corresponding to OE *egeslic*, means 'terrible' (Davis) or 'inspiring awe or respect' (*MED*, s.v.*aueli* adj. (a)), but may suggest to some readers OE *aglæca*, used by the *Beowulf*-poet of the monster Grendel (although also of the heroes Sigemund and Beowulf himself). Perhaps too the idea of monster is reinforced by the very shape of the word *mayster*. The *MED* (s.v. *maister*, n. 5. (c)) glosses *maister-man* as 'monstrous man, giant' but supplies only two examples of its use, both describing the giant of St Michael's Mount. The first is from the alliterative *Morte Arthure* (986–92):

> Thane answers Sir Arthure to þat alde wyf,
> 'I am comyn fra þe Conquerour, curtaise and gentill,
> As one of þe *hathelest* of Arthur knyghtez,      noblest
> Messenger to þis *myx*, for *mendemente* of þe pople,      excrement;
>      deliverance
> To *mele* with this maister man that here this mounte *ȝemez*;
>      negotiate; governs
> To trete with this tyraunt for tresour of landez,
> And take *trew* for a tym, to bettyr may *worthe*.'      truce; be

The immediate context, in which the key ideas are of negotiation and government, favours the sense 'chief, leader, lord' for *maister man*, and these are the glosses provided by Krishna.[7] The second example is from Malory's *Tale of Arthur and Lucius* (200/14–15):

> ' . . . for I woll seche this seynte be myself alone and speke wyth this maystir-man that kepys this mountayne.'

Malory is here following in close verbal detail the alliterative *Morte Arthure* (937–38):

> 'Fore I will seke this seynte by my selfe one,
> And mell with this mayster mane þat this monte ȝemez.'

---

7.   See also her note to line 938 on pp. 177-78, and *MED*, s.v. *maister*, n.1.(a).

Thus to translate 'aghlich mayster' as 'terrible giant or monster' would be to do so on poor lexical grounds, and on the basis of a prejudgment of its meaning. The word *mayster* in the general range of its meanings suggests rather authority and superiority. Thus it can mean 'conqueror, victor' (*MED*, 1. (e)), and is so used in *Cleanness* (1740):

Þe Medes schal be maysteres here, and þou of menske schowued,[8]

or 'social superior, patron' (*MED*, 2. (c)), as in *Sir Gawain* itself (2089–90):

Þe burne þat rod hym by
Bede his mayster abide,

or 'learned man, scholar, sage' (*MED*, 3. (b)), as in *The Canterbury Tales* (A 576–77):

Of maistres hadde he mo than thries ten,
That weren of lawe expert and curious.

The phrase 'aghlich mayster', then, means 'awesome lord'. It points to a formidable adversary, but certainly not one who is monstrous or uncouth. The commanding presence of the Green Knight is further impressed upon us later in the description by the fact that he has his powerful and mettlesome horse completely under his control (175–78).[9]

We may now observe by way of contrast the manner in which romancers introduce a wild man into their poems. In Chrétien's *Chevalier au lion* Calogrenant describes the wild man whom he encounters in the forest of Broceliande as (288–91 and p.183):

Un vilain, qui ressanbloit mor,
Grant et hideus a desmesure,
(Einsi tres leide creature,
Qu'an ne porroit dire de boche).

8. Reference is to *Cleanness*, edited by J.J. Anderson (Manchester, 1977).
9. We might compare the way in which Gerald Crich controls, steadily and relentlessly, his red Arab mare, terrified by the noise of the approaching steam train in D.H. Lawrence's *Women in Love*, edited by D. Farmer, L. Vasey and J. Worthen (Cambridge, 1987), IX, p.110:

   She began to wince away, as if hurt by the unknown noise. But Gerald pulled her back and held her head to the gate. The sharp blasts of the chuffing engine broke with more and more force on her. The repeated sharp blows of unknown, terrifying noise struck through her till she was rocking with terror. She recoiled like a spring let go. But a glistening, half-smiling look came into Gerald's face. He brought her back again, inevitably.

> . . . a rustic lout, as black as a mulberry, indescribably big and
> hideous; indeed, so passing ugly was the creature that no word of
> mouth could do him justice.[10]

This is adapted by the author of the Middle English version of Chrétien's
romance as follows (*Ywain and Gawain*, 244–48):

> I saw sone whare a man sat
> On a *lawnd*, þe fowlest wight           glade
> Þat euer ȝit man saw in syght.
> He was a lathly creature,
> For fowl he was out of mesure.[11]

Chrétien announces the fact that he is describing a churl in the opening
words of his portrait, whereas the poet of *Ywain and Gawain* (an inferior
poet) does not do so explicitly until a little later on in his account (*YG*, 268).
But Spenser, like Chrétien, comes directly to the point in his description of a
wild man in *The Faerie Queene* (IV.7.5):

> It was to weet a wilde and saluage man.

We are not meant to mistake the identity of a wild man; the distinction
between the brutish and the civilised is too important to allow of such confusion. The Green Knight is a powerful and dominating figure. That cannot
be denied; nor should we wish to deny it. But grotesqueness or monstrous
size is to be denied.

Benson has artificially divided the physical description of the Green
Knight at line 140. But the movement of the verse does not slacken, and carries
us naturally forward to ' þe myriest in his muckel' (142); the Green Knight,
that is to say, is large, but also well proportioned and handsome (140–42):

> Half etayn in erde I hope þat he were,
> Bot mon most I algate mynn hym to bene,
> And þat þe myriest in his muckel þat myȝt ride.

It is the fitness of the Green Knight's proportions that is accordingly
emphasised in the lines that follow (144–46):

10. Reference is to *Chrestien de Troyes: Yvain (Le Chevalier au lion)*, edited by T.B.W.
Reid (Manchester, 1942), and to the translation of Comfort (1975), pp. 180-269.
11. Reference is to *Ywain and Gawain*, edited by A.B. Friedman and N.T. Harrington,
EETS (OS) 254 (London, 1964).

> Both his wombe and his wast were worthily smale,
> And alle his fetures folʒande, in forme þat he hade,
>                         ful clene.

It is clear, therefore, that *myriest* must mean 'fairest, most handsome' (*MED*, s.v. *miri(e)* adj. 6. (a)), and is so used in *Cleanness* in a suggestive phrase (781–83):

> His *sondes* into *Sodamas* watʒ sende in þat tyme,       embassy; Sodom
> In þat ilk euentyde, by aungels tweyne,
> *Meuande* mekely togeder as myry men ʒonge.[12]                     walking

But against all the weight of the lexical evidence *MED* assigns *myriest* at line 142 to a poorly attested and somewhat speculative sense 7. (b) '? strong; lusty; sturdy'. Such a gloss in the present context can only be the result (once again) of a prior conception.

The comparison of the Green Knight to a giant is simply a figurative way of impressing upon us his great size. It is a common enough hyperbole for Thomas Wilson in his *Arte of Rhetorique* to illustrate the figure by reference to it (365/11–18):

> Therfore in this speache, wee must understande there is a mountyng, called of the Grecians *hyperbole*: we use this figure muche in English. As thus. He is as swift as a swallowe, he hath a belly as bigge as a barrell, he is a giaunt in makyng. The whole Temmese is litle enough to serve hym, for wasshyng his handes. In all whiche speaches wee mounte evermore a great deale, and not meane so as the wordes are spoken. [13]

The *Gawain*-poet does not 'meane so as the wordes are spoken'. In fact the description of the knight as 'half etayn' is immediately qualified into full humanity in the following line. Moreover, in the phrase 'half etayn' itself there is a suggestiveness of an arithmetical precision that prompts us to look more closely into the question of the measurements of giant-like stature. The size of the giants attacked by Yder in the romance of that name is fifty feet or even more (*Yder*, 5500–5503):

12. See *MED,* s.v. *mekli* adv. 3. (a) 'quietly', to which *Cleanness,* 783 is referred, although *MED,* 2. (a) 'courteously, graciously' is not altogether inappropriate. Anderson suggests 'nimbly, briskly' (note to line 783, p. 81), but is unable to offer any convincing lexical support. The gloss 'briskly' presumably arises from the identification of youth with vitality rather than courtesy.
13. Reference is to *Arte of Rhetorique by Thomas Wilson,* edited by T.J. Derrick (New York and London, 1982).

Il vient sus el palais, si troeve
Coste a coste les dous jaians;
Cinquante piez ot li mains grans
De longor, o cinquante o plus.

He went up into the palace and found the two giants side by side; the smaller of the two was fifty feet tall, fifty or more.[14]

Dante's description of the giants immersed in the pit of hell from the navel downward (*Inf.*, XXXI.31–33) is even more precise. Nimrod's face is the size of the bronze pine-cone in front of St Peter's at Rome, that is, 7.5 feet high (XXXI.58–59); in proportion to it (XXXI.60), from the collar-bone (XXXI.66) to the waist, his body is thirty great spans, that is, 30 x 9 inches = 270 inches or 22.5 feet high, more than the combined height of three Frieslanders at, let us suppose, 7 feet each in height (XXXI.61–64). Nimrod is thus 30 feet from head to waist. This is precisely half of his total size (XXXI.43–44), which is accordingly 60 feet.[15] This is inhuman size. He therefore babbles (XXXI.67–69) and is incommunicable in his stupidity (XXXI.70–81). Ephialtes, the second giant, is yet much larger still: 'l'altro assai più fero e maggio' (XXXI.84). The sheer bulk of Briareus is beyond measure: *smisurato* (XXXI.98). Antaeus is five full ells above the ground, excluding the head (XXXI.113–14). An English ell is 45 inches, so that five ells would amount to 225 inches; the head is presumably in proportion, that is, it is one-third of the body from the collar-bone to the wrist, and so would amount to 75 inches. This is a total of 300 inches or 25 feet for half his size, and hence 50 feet in all. Sapegno (I, 346) estimates that according to Florentine measures five ells would be equivalent to thirty spans, and that therefore Antaeus is the same size as Nimrod. But there is no equality in the size of the giants. Antaeus is less presumptuous than the others in that he both speaks and is unfettered (XXXI.100–102). It is appropriate, therefore, that he should be of a lesser bulk.

The grotesqueness of Dante's giants is entirely a matter of deformity of scale, and fully justifies the persistent comparisons of them with towers. In the case of the giant of St Michael's Mount in the alliterative *Morte Arthure* the physical deformity of rough arms, misshapen legs, and ugly appearance accompanies the disproportion of size (1094–1103):

---

14. Reference is to *The Romance of Yder*, edited and translated by A. Adams (Woodbridge and Totowa, New Jersey, 1983), pp. 200-201.
15. Some estimate him at 70 feet; see P. Toynbee, *A Dictionary of Proper Names and Notable Matters in the Works of Dante,* revised by C.S. Singleton (Oxford, 1968), pp. 463-64.

Bulle-nekkyde was þat *bierne* and brade in the scholders,

                                                   creature

*Brok-brestede* as a *brawne*, with brustils full large,         with a

                       chest striped like a badger; boar

*Ruyd* armes as an *ake* with *rusclede* sydes,        rough; oak; gnarled

Lym and *leskes* full *lothyn,* leue ȝe forsothe.        loins; shaggy

*Schouell-foted* was þat schalke, and *schaylande* hym semyde,

            having feet shaped like shovels; stumbling

With schankez *vnschaply, schowand* togedyrs;       misshapen;

                                     knocking

Thykke *theese* as a *thursse,* and thikkere in þe hanche,  thighs;

                                      monster

*Greesse* growen as a *galte,* full gry(s)lych he lukez.    fat; swine

Who þe *lenghe* of þe lede *lelly* accountes,     height; carefully

Fro þe face to þe fote was *fyfe fadom* lange.     five fathoms

                                    (thirty feet)

There is nothing disproportionate about the Green Knight. Although he is big, he is well proportioned and so handsome. And indeed, even in the matter of his great size, he does not exceed the human scale of values. Thus when Arthur takes up his challenge the poet can draw a comparison between the Green Knight's height and that of the rest of the court (332–33):

> Þe stif mon hym bifore stod vpon hyȝt,
> Herre þen ani in þe hous by þe hede and more.

He is without doubt a daunting and intimidating figure, and dominates the scene about him, even in the passive act of receiving a blow. And for this role he needs to be tall. We should imagine him to be a man well over six feet tall, perhaps as tall as seven feet, but certainly not as tall as thirty feet (to take as a measure the comparatively moderate giant-like stature of the giant of St Michael's Mount) or fifteen feet, if we are to take the phrase 'half etayn' with perfect literalness. The combination of great size and handsomeness that is found in the Green Knight is found also in Malory's description of Gareth (293/13–17, and 27–31):

> And so sir Gawayne, a lytyll tofore the none of the day of Pentecoste, aspyed at a wyndowe three men uppon horsebak and a dwarfe uppon foote. And so the three men alyght, and the dwarff kepte their horsis, and one of the men was hyghar than the tothir tweyne by a foote and an half . . .
> Ryght so com into the halle two men well besayne and rychely, and uppon their sholdyrs there lened the goodlyest yonge man and the

fayreste that ever they all sawe. And he was large and longe and brode
in the shuldyrs, well-vysaged, and the largyste and the fayreste handis
that ever man sye.

What distinguishes the Green Knight from Gareth is not monstrosity, but
simply greenness.

Benson's description of the Green Knight as 'a grotesquely bearded churl'
is much less easy to justify than the attribution to him of monstrous size; it is
indeed nothing less than a misrepresentation of the facts of the poet's own
description. Of the Green Knight's hair the poet says (181–86):

> Fayre fannand fax vmbefoldes his schulderes;
> A much berd as a busk ouer his brest henges,
> Þat wyth his hiȝlich here þat of his hed reches
> Watz euesed al vmbetorne abof his elbowes,
> Þat half his armes þer-vnder were halched in þe wyse
> Of a kyngez capados þat closes his swyre.

The dominant idea here is not the churlish but the noble. The hair is *fayre*
(181) and *hiȝlich* (183); the total effect is like that of a king's cape (185–86).[16]
If the analogy of the bush (182) reminds us of Nature, it can only be of Nature
methodized. So much is already clear from the first line of the description,
for *fannand* has the sense 'spreading out like a fan' (see *MED*, s.v. *fannen* v.
2.(c)). The comparison of hair to a fan is made by Chaucer in *The Miller's
Tale*, and in a context not merely of elegance but of foppishness; hence we
know what to expect in the subsequent conduct of 'joly Absolon' (*CT, A*
3314–16):

> *Crul* was his heer, and as the gold it shoon,                    curly
> And *strouted* as a fanne large and brode;                   spread out
> Ful streight and *evene* lay his *joly shode*.         straight; fine; parting

The Green Knight's hair does not suggest the luxuriant growth of nature un-
adorned, but nature as refashioned by art; topiary rather than a tangled under-
growth is the idea to have in mind. And when we come to the first beheading

---

16. Puttenham notes the decorum of long hair as worn by lords: 'The Lacedemonians
    bearing long bushes of haire, finely kept & curled vp, vsed this ciuill argument to
    maintaine that custome. Haire (say they) is the very ornament of nature appointed for
    the head, which therfore to vse in his most sumptuous degree is comely, specially for
    them that be Lordes, Maisters of men, and of a free life, hauing abilitie & leasure
    inough to keepe it cleane, and so for a signe of seignorie, riches and libertie, the mas-
    ters of the Lacedemonians vsed long haire.' See *The Arte of English Poesie by George
    Puttenham*, edited by G.D. Willcock and A. Walker (Cambridge, 1936), pp. 286-87.

scene the poet can tell us again of the Green Knight's 'longe louelych lokkez' (419).

How far all of this is removed from the world of the wild man is only too apparent. The hair of Chrétien's wild man is not flowing but in tufts (*Chevalier au lion*, 297–98 and p.183):

> Chevos meschiez et front pelé,
> S'ot plus de deus espanz de le.
>
> . . . his hair was in tufts, leaving his forehead bare for a width of more than two spans.

The hair of the giant of St Michael's Mount is matted (*MA*, 1078–79):

> His *fax* and his *foretoppe* was *filterede* togeders,      hair; forelock; matted
>
> And owte of his face *come* ane halfe fote *large*.      stood out; as much as

And Spenser's hairy wild man, too, is more likely to terrify than please by his appearance (*FQ*, IV.7.5):

> All ouergrowne with haire, that could *awhape*      terrify
> An hardy hart.

The fit proportions and flowing hair of the Green Knight are complemented by the richness and elegance of his dress. The very detail of the poet's description (151–67) is designed to make that point repeatedly. The Green Knight's mantle is *meré* (153), that is, 'fair', and its fur edging 'ful clene' (154), that is, 'very elegant'. The birds and butterflies embroidered on his clothing are a fine ornamentation ('gay gaudi', 167), so that the total effect is one of elegance ('aray clene', 163). And not elegance merely, but also richness. The elegance of the Green Knight's dress is such that it can only be the product of a courtly environment, and so the poet stresses also its richness and costliness. The spurs are fastened over silk bands 'barred ful ryche' (159), and the bars adorning the belt and other bright gems are 'richely rayled' (163).

The habitual attire of the wild man could hardly form a sharper contrast. The dress of Chrétien's *vilain* is strange and outlandish, and so in keeping with the rest of his appearance (*Chevalier au lion*, 308–13 and p.184):

> Apoiiez fu sor sa maçue,
> Vestuz de robe si estrange,
> Qu'il n'i avoit ne lin ne lange,
> Ainz ot a son col atachiez
> Deus cuirs de novel escorchiez
> De deus toriaus ou de deus bués.

There he stood, leaning upon his club and accoutred in a strange garb, consisting not of cotton or wool, but rather of the hides recently flayed from two bulls or two beeves: these he wore hanging from his neck.

The author of *Ywain and Gawain* describes it as a *wonder-wede* (267). Of the dress of his wild man Spenser says but little, for there is in truth but little to say (*FQ*, IV. 7.7):

> His wast was with a wreath of yuie greene
> > Engirt about, ne other garment wore:
> > For all his haire was like a garment seene.

The descriptions of the Green Knight's horse and trappings (168–78 and 187–95) and of the cunning workmanship of his axe (210–20) serve still further to emphasise a world that in its courtesy and sophistication is remote from that of the wild man. The wild man is not to be sought on horseback — in *Ywain and Gawain* he 'sat/On a lawnd' (244–45) — and his weapon is the club and not the axe — 'A wonder mace' (*YG*, 249), 'a tall young oake . . . / Whose knottie snags were sharpned all afore' (*FQ*, IV.7.7).

The true grotesqueness of the wild man and the giant can be appreciated at leisure in the lengthy descriptions in *Le Chevalier au lion, Ywain and Gawain,* the alliterative *Morte Arthure*, and *The Faerie Queene*. It is evident from each example, and from the examples taken together as constituting a type, that the Green Knight is not of their number, either essentially or incidentally. Burrow (*A Reading*, p. 20) is right, therefore, to call in question the relevance to the portrait of the Green Knight of the conventional representation of the wild man in medieval romance.


## IV

At the same time as stressing the might and elegance of the Green Knight, the poet stresses also the brightness of his appearance. This is largely but not entirely an expression of his greenness. The poet's manner, as usual, is to emphasise the central significance of his description by the repetition of the key idea.

The fur edging of the mantle is made of 'blyþe blaunner ful bry3t' (155);[17] the spurs are of 'bry3t golde' (159); the band on the horse's tail and forelock is of 'a bry3t grene' (192); and the bells hanging from the intricate knot at the end of the lace which binds fast the band on the horse's tail (such is the intricacy of the poet's own account) are 'ful bry3t of brende golde' (195). A synonym for *bry3t* is *blyþe,* which is used to describe the fur edging (155) as well as the gems that adorn the Green Knight's clothing (162). Yet another synonym is *clene*, describing both the spurs (158) and the green dress — 'clene verdure' (161). The cumulative effect of these words is unmistakable, and the poet is able to conclude of the Green Knight that (199):

He loked as layt so ly3t.

The poet's repeated use of an adjective such as *clene* may result in some slight ambiguity on its own account, for as we have seen *clene* can mean both 'bright, shining' *(MED,* s.v. *clene* adj. 4. (b)) and 'splendid, elegant' *(MED,* 5.(a)). Thus at lines 145–46 it is possible to take the poet's words as referring not to the Green Knight's elegant proportions, but to his greenness; 'fol3ande in forme' (145) might then be translated as 'matching in outward appearance, (colour)'.[18] If this interpretation were accepted, then *clene* (146) should perhaps be glossed as 'bright'. A case could also be made for glossing *clene* as 'bright' at lines 154 and 163. What is true of *clene* is true also of the other descriptive adjectives. *Bry3t* itself means not only 'luminous, shining' *(MED,* s.v. *bright* adj. 1. (d)) and 'vivid, brilliant' *(MED,* 2. (a)), but also 'beautiful' *(MED,* 2. (b)). *Blyþe* is glossed by *MED* (s.v. *blithe* adj. 3) as 'bright, shining; beautiful, fair'. And the adjective *gai* has a range of meanings that admirably suits the present context. In reference to things it can mean 'sumptuous, showy, rich, ornate; . . . elegant, fine, beautiful' *(MED,* s.v. *gai* adj. 2. (b)), and to persons 'dressed up, handsomely or richly attired' *(MED,* 2. (c)). And at the same time it includes the senses 'shining, glittering, gleaming, bright' *(MED,* 2. (a)).

It becomes evident that we are not ultimately invited by the poet to choose between brightness and handsomeness. We are close here to that Plotinian conception of beauty as the splendour of the divine idea irradiating matter, a conception sufficiently influential as we have seen to influence the thought of Aquinas *(ST,* 2a 2ae 145.2). For the *Gawain*-poet too the ideas of brightness

17. Davis glosses *bry3t* here as 'pure white' (p.169), taking up the etymological implication of *blaunner,* although it seems that the fur also is green: 'al grayþed in grene þis gome and his wedes' (151).

18. Such a possibility is suggested by M. Andrew and R. Waldron, *The Poems of the Pearl Manuscript,* York Medieval Texts, second series (London, 1978), p.213. As Andrew and Waldron also point out, such a meaning makes the use of the conjunction *For* (147) readily intelligible.

and handsomeness are at one; hence the special fitness of the phrase 'þe fayre grene' (189), used by the poet in reference to the horse's mane.

It is not only necessary to deny monstrosity of the Green Knight, but it is necessary also to insist upon his handsomeness. Among other reasons for the poet's focus upon the beautiful, flowing hair of the Green Knight — his 'fayre fannand fax' (181) — is the fact that long hair is a traditional mark of beauty. The reason why Chaucer assigns the name of Absolon to the parish clerk of *The Miller's Tale* (*CT*, A 3312–13) is that he wishes us to recall the beauty of the biblical Absalom, the son of David. Thus it is written in II Samuel 14.25–26:

> Porro sicut Absalom, vir non erat pulcher in omni Israel, et decorus nimis: a vestigio pedis usque ad verticem non erat in eo ulla macula.
> Et quando tondebat capillum (semel autem in anno tondebatur, quia gravabat eum caesaries) ponderabat capillos capitis sui ducentis siclis, pondere publico.

> But in all Israel there was not a man so comely, and so exceedingly beautiful as Absalom: from the sole of the foot to the crown of his head there was no blemish in him.
> And when he polled his hair (now he was polled once a year, because his hair was burdensome to him) he weighed the hair of his head at two hundred sicles, according to the common weight.[19]

When the poet writes of the Green Knight, therefore, that (179):

> Wel gay watz þis gome gered in grene,

it would seem that he has his beauty in mind.[20] Later he is to describe Gawain himself as 'þe gayest into Grece' (2023), that is, 'the handsomest (from here) to Greece'. The handsomeness of the Green Knight is recalled by the poet even in the fearful and ugly moment of the beheading, for after he has been beheaded by Gawain, the Green Knight (433):

> Laȝt to his lufly hed, and lyft hit vp sone.

The powerful and handsome figure of the Green Knight belongs to the context of the court and of youth. It is true that his dominating presence and disdainful attitude towards the court suggest the superiority of youth or

19. Reference is to the *Biblia sacra iuxta vulgatam Clementinam*, edited by A. Colunga and L. Turrado, fourth edition (Madrid, 1965). The translation is that of the Douay version.
20. See *MED*, s.v. *gai* adj. 3.(a), where the glosses 'excellent, noble; beautiful' are supplied.

manhood over adolescence.[21] But the lack of an absolute and clear-cut differentiation between these two age-groups enables the poet to exploit the common elements between the two so as to produce an even texture. Thus it is in the world of courtly youth that we shall find the meaning of the phrase 'myriest in his muckel' (142). Mirth, the lord of the garden of the rose, is both strong and well proportioned (*The Romaunt of the Rose*, 825–26):

> His shuldris of a large *brede,*                                    breadth
> And *smalish* in the *girdilstede.*                         slender; waist

Youth in *The Parlement of the Thre Ages*, who is thirty years of age (*PTA*, 133), is tall, strong, and well proportioned (*PTA*, 112–15):

> He was *balghe* in the breste and brode in the scholdirs,       rounded
> His *axles* and his armes were *i-liche* longe,          shoulders; in like
>                                                                            manner
> And in the *medill* als a mayden *menskfully* schapen;          waist;
>                                                                          gracefully
> Longe legges and *large,* and *lele* for to *schewe.*         sturdy;
>                                                                    handsome; see

    Associations of this kind are reinforced at every point by the details of the Green Knight's dress. The embroidery of birds and butterflies (165–66) recalls the dress of the God of Love in *The Romaunt of the Rose* (890–95):

> For nought clad in silk was he,
> But all in floures and in *flourettes,*                            buds
> Ypaynted al with *amorettes,*                                 love knots
> And with *losenges* and *scochouns,*           lozenges; escutcheons
> With briddes, *lybardes,* and lyouns,                          leopards
> And other beestis wrought ful well.

21. It would seem that Sir Bertilak de Hautdesert, a knight-householder rather than a knight-errant, is a man of more mature years. Burrow describes him as 'a powerful image of the middle age' (*Ages of Man*, p. 174) and takes his reddish-brown beard as establishing that 'high eld' (844) refers 'to that age in which a man stands at the top of life's arch, not to an older age, as has been suggested' (p. 175). Dove on the other hand refers 'hyghe eldee' to old age, but such a description is still compatible with the full exercise of one's powers; she comments that 'the Green Knight's *hyghe eldee* . . . carries with it the twin ideas of full manhood and old age — but if old age, not withered decrepitude; rather, an old age of "undiminished vigour", like Philosophia's' (*The Perfect Age*, p. 139). In either case there seems no reason to identify the age of Bertilak with that of the Green Knight; a discontinuity of age in a marvel requires no more explanation than a discontinuity of colour.

The embroidery of flowers is also made much of by Chaucer in the portrait of the Squire (*CT*, A 89–90):

> *Embrouded* was he, as it were a *meede*        embroidered; meadow
> Al ful of fresshe floures, whyte and reede.

Moreover, the *Gawain*-poet does not only emphasise the greenness of the Green Knight; he points with hardly less insistence to the combination of green and gold in his array (165–67):

> Þat were to tor for to telle of tryfles þe halue
> Þat were enbrauded abof, wyth bryddes and flyȝes,
> With gay gaudi of grene, þe golde ay inmyddes.

The same emphasis is apparent in the description of the horse's mane, tail, and forelock (187–95). And its importance is such as to bear repetition when the poet later describes the reaction of the court (233–36). This is the final confirmation, were it to be needed, that the Green Knight, for all his marvellous appearance, belongs to the world of the court. Green and gold in combination are the colours of courtly youth, as Burrow has convincingly demonstrated (*A Reading*, pp.14–16). Thus Youth in *The Parlement of the Thre Ages* (122):

> . . . was *gerede* alle in grene, alle with golde *by-weuede*.
>                                                        attired; interwoven

It is noteworthy also that the poet of *The Parlement of the Thre Ages* can refer to Youth simply as a man dressed in green (169):

> Now this gome alle in grene so gayly attyrede.

How close this description comes to that of the Green Knight two examples will suffice to show (151 and 179):

> Ande al grayþed in grene þis gome and his wedes.

> Wel gay watz þis gome gered in grene.

The descriptions of Youth and the Green Knight in this respect are simply interchangeable.

The courtly image of the Green Knight is emphatically depicted by the *Gawain*-poet in the manner that is characteristic of romance. Green and gold (or red and gold, or blue) are the primary colours in which such descriptions are decked. We should not willingly surrender these for the greys of a duller and more ambiguous convention.

## V

The significance of the portrait of the Green Knight lies in its very homogeneity, and it is the uniformity of detail which the poet in consequence stresses.

The elements of the Green Knight's appearance and dress are all in accord. The parts of his body are in due proportion or matching in outward appearance — 'alle his fetures folȝande, in forme' (145) — and he is bright green all over — 'oueral enker-grene' (150). The man and his dress alike are 'al grayþ ed in grene' (151). His neat, tightly drawn hose are 'of þat same' (157) and 'alle his vesture uerayly' (161) was bright green. The trappings of the horse are also in perfect correspondence; all the metal fittings 'anamayld was þenne' (169) — the use of the adverb þenne pointing to the series of like details — the stirrups are 'stayned of þe same' (170) and the saddle-bows are 'al after' (171), that is, entirely after the same fashion. Horse and rider are a perfect match for one another. The 'grene hors' (175) is 'fyn of þat ilke' (173), that is, completely of the same colour. The hair of the Green Knight 'of his hors swete' (180), that is, matches that of his horse, and the mane of the horse matches the hair of the Green Knight — 'much to hit lyke' (187). The horse itself has the same uniformly elegant appearance; the tail and the forelock are 'twynnen of a sute' (191), that is, plaited to match, and not only each other but also the mane that has been curled and combed (187–90).

The uniformity of the description is its most salient feature, and we may be inclined to think that the poet has if anything laboured it to the point of tedium. But uniformity is in fact difficult to achieve, and the *Gawain*-poet is right to insist upon it. On the evidence of Benson's analysis he has failed to convince at least one of his modern readers, and no doubt there are many more besides who remain unconvinced.

Such uniformity in description is the logical result of the methods of epideictic rhetoric and the poetic values associated with it. These are also Chaucer's methods in the *General Prologue*, as is evident not least in the portrait of the Knight.[22] Here a medieval poet is at his furthest remove from the modern reader who prizes ambiguity in poetry. There should be no great difficulty in theory in allowing to the medieval poet his clarity, while at the same time granting to the modern poet his ambiguity. But in practice such sophistication is seldom found, and the requirement of ambiguity is consequently imposed on medieval poetry. But it is vital for us in such respects to recognize the limitations of our own age. For what is involved is not merely a misrepresentation of the portraits themselves, but the deformity of the works in which they appear.

22. See my article, 'Rhetorical Perspectives in the *General Prologue* to the *Canterbury Tales*', *English Studies*, 62 (1981), 411-22 (pp. 416-17).

# CHAPTER FOUR

# The Pentangle as the Symbolic Expression of the Poem's Idea

## I

THE POET GIVES A long and detailed description of the device of the pentangle on Gawain's shield and coat-armour (619–65). It is a classic piece of rhetorical amplification, and of its nature suggests its poetic importance. But the poet does not rely on implication alone; he states explicitly the importance of what he is about to describe (623–24):

> And quy þe pentangel apendez to þat prynce noble
> I am in tent yow to telle, þof tary hyt me schulde.

He is entirely justified in so doing, for here we have reached the poem's pervasive idea or fore-conceit.

The description is characteristically organized in a logical structure. First of all, the poet establishes the perfect relevance of the device to Gawain by binding symbol and knight together in the form of a syllogistic argument. It is not a straightforward syllogism, however, since in it the conclusion anticipates the minor premise. Thus:

1. Major premise: the pentangle is a symbol of *trawþe* (625–26).

2. Minor premise: Gawain is *faythful,* that is, *trwe* (632).

3. Conclusion: therefore the pentangle befits Gawain (631).

The syllogistic argument has been well observed by Burrow (*A Reading*, pp. 42, and 44), but its effect can hardly be overstated, since it proposes an identity between the symbol and the knight who wears it. But what is implied by that identity or, to put it another way, what the symbolic import of the pentangle in fact is, has often been misunderstood. Secondly, the logical procedure evident in the use of the syllogism is seen on a larger scale in the organization of the two stanzas that compose the account of the pentangle. The first of the stanzas on the pentangle presents its general nature as a device, whilst in the second of the stanzas the poet turns from the general to the particular in specifying the constituent parts of the device. Such a systematic organization is, as we have seen, characteristic of the poet's descriptive technique. Dante's organization of the heavenly paradise into its general form and particular parts follows the same method, although Dante has made that method explicit in his own practice (*Par.*, XXXI. 52–54):

> La forma general di paradiso
> già tutta mïo sguardo avea compresa,
> in nulla parte ancor fermato fiso.

> Already my glance had taken in the whole general form of Paradise but had not yet dwelt on any part of it.

The general form is the white rose with its golden centre and petals likened to tiers in an amphitheatre (*Par.*, XXX. 100–138), and the particular parts are the arrangement of the elect (*Par.*, XXXII. 1–84).[1] It would have been well, perhaps, if the *Gawain*-poet had been no less explicit, for the failure to recognize the overall method of organization has often resulted in a misinterpretation both of the general significance of the pentangle, that is, by assigning the specific meaning of 'fidelity' to *trawþe* (626), and also of its detailed significance, that is, by the assignment of a wide range of meanings to *clannes* and *cortaysye* (653).

The poet focuses on the inherent fitness of the pentangle to possess a given meaning, that is, it is a whole made up of interrelated parts. This is stated clearly in the general definition of the pentangle (626–29), but it is of such importance that the poet elaborates upon it rhetorically at the end of his statement of the detailed parts (656–61). The idea is important, but it is not obscure, for it is an easily recognisable expression of the wholeness of virtue. The ethical opinion that the virtues are interconnected is at least as old as Aristotle, and Aquinas supplies an impressive list of authorities in support of it (*ST*, 1a 2ae 65.1 *sed contra*):

> Sed contra est quod Ambrosius dicit, *Connexae sibi sunt concatenataeque virtutes, ut qui unam habet, plures habere videatur.* Augustinus etiam dicit, quod *virtutes quae sunt in animo humano, nullo modo separantur ab invicem.* Et Gregorius dicit quod *una virtus sine aliis aut omnino nulla est, aut imperfecta.* Et Tullius dicit, *Si unam virtutem confessus es te non habere, nullam necesse est te habiturum.*

> On the other hand Ambrose says, *The virtues are connected and linked together, so that whoever has one would seem to have many.*

---

1.   See Toynbee, *Dante Dictionary*, revised by Singleton, Plate II, p. 707.

> Likewise, Augustine says that *the virtues that reside in the human soul are quite inseparable from one another*. And Gregory says that *one virtue without the other is either negligible or very imperfect*. So, too, Cicero, *If you admit to not having one particular virtue, it must needs be that you will have none at all*.

Such an interconnection of virtues is a commonplace of romance. Chaucer's Knight is defined not by a single virtue, but by a combination of virtues (*CT*, A 45–46), and at his death Arcite draws upon a list of virtues that motivate the knightly lover (*CT*, A 2786–95). The principle itself is explicitly invoked by Spenser at the beginning of the ninth canto of the Legend of Holiness (*FQ*,I.9.1):

> O Goodly golden chaine, wherewith yfere
> The vertues linked are in louely wize.

In *Sir Gawain* itself there is a linking of 'fraunchyse and felaȝschyp' (652) and 'clannes and . . . cortaysye' (653). The first pair looks forward to the Exchange of Winnings agreement which emerges from the fellowship (and hence fidelity) of host and guest, and which will be carried out (on Gawain's part at least) in a spirit not merely of fidelity but also of generosity. The second pair anticipates the bedroom scenes in which Gawain will be required to be not only chaste in resisting his hostess's advances, but also considerate of her status and honour by rejecting her gracefully.

At the same time the idea of hierarchy is deeply embedded in the medieval view of the universe and of man's place within it. Thus in Chaucer's *Parliament of Fowls* the four orders of birds under Nature are set out in respect of their class (*PF*, 323–29), and in the same way the three tercel eagles of the highest class are distinguished by rank (*PF*, 390–99, 449–50, and 463). The Canterbury pilgrims are also differentiated by class and rank, although the fact seems not often to have been noticed, and is still denied.[2] In *Sir Gawain* itself the seating arrangements, both at Camelot (109–15) and at Hautdesert (1001–5), observe the order of rank. It is the same with respect to the moral virtues. The notion of the interconnection of the virtues is entirely compatible with the sense of hierarchy. Generosity and fidelity belong to justice which is higher than the virtues of temperance such as chastity and courtesy (*ST*, 1a 2ae 66.4). Generosity may be set above fidelity, since generosity carries with it little of the notion of moral debt, whereas fidelity or truth is a moral debt necessary to the virtuous life (*ST*, 2a 2ae 80).[3] The dilemma of contradictory

---

2.  See my article, 'The Design of the *General Prologue* to the *Canterbury Tales*', *English Studies*, 59 (1978), 481-98.
3.  Aquinas does not make clear the relative status of generosity and truth; see *ST*, 2a 2ae 117.6.

pledges in *The Franklin's Tale* cannot be resolved by an appeal to fidelity, since on the surface at least there are conflicting, valid claims, but only by an act of generosity and the acts of emulation that it inspires. Chastity and courtesy are both parts of temperance, but whereas chastity is a species of temperance, courtesy (or modesty) is only a potential or secondary part of temperance in which the full power of the virtue is not exercised.[4] Hence chastity is to be set above courtesy, and Gawain himself does so when he sees that the lady has succeeded in bringing them to the point of conflict (1773–74). Among the moral virtues, piety or the virtue of religion, that is, the virtue by which one gives due honour to God (*ST*, 2a 2ae 81.4), is the highest of the virtues under justice and thus occupies the supreme place (*ST*, 2a 2ae 81.6):

> Et ideo religio praeeminet inter alias virtutes morales.

> Hence, religion excels the other moral virtues.

The *Gawain*-poet recognizes this both in the climactic place he gives to *pité* (654) as the fifth and final virtue of the fifth and final group of virtues, and in the language he uses of it as the virtue 'þat passez alle poyntez'.


## II

It now remains to give a more complete definition of the pentangle in its general and particular senses. And first we must turn to the key-word *trawþe* (626). Narrow and broad senses of the word *trawþe* are lexically possible, and we can choose between 'fidelity' or 'loyalty' on the one hand (*OED*, s.v. *truth*, sb. I.1, and *troth*, sb. I.l) and 'righteousness' or 'integrity' on the other (*OED*, s.v. *truth*, I.4). This distinction of meanings has appeared less evident than it might have done, since the *OED* does not formally isolate the senses of 'righteousness' and 'integrity',[5] but it seems characteristic of the moral vocabulary of chivalry for such narrow and broad senses to be developed side by side. Thus *gentillesse* can have the narrow sense of 'generosity' and the broad sense of 'nobility of character', distinct senses not formally distinguished either by the *OED* or the *MED* (2(a)), and *cortaysye* can have the narrow sense of 'politeness' (*MED*, s.v. *courteisie* n.2(a)) and the broad sense of 'the complex of courtly ideals' (*MED*, 1).[6]

4.    On the definition of potential parts, see *ST*, 2a 2ae 48, and on its application to the
      virtues of temperance, see *ST*, 2a 2ae 143.
5.    Burrow, *A Reading*, p.43 is certainly right in questioning its failure to do so.
6.    I develop this point in greater detail in my article, 'The Significance of the Pentangle
      Symbolism in *Sir Gawain and the Green Knight*', *MLR*, 74 (1979), 769-90 (pp. 771-72).

*Trawþe* at line 626 is glossed by Davis in its narrow sense of 'fidelity' (p. 220), but such a gloss is unsatisfactory from a number of points of view. First of all, it overlooks the division of general and particular on which the two pentangle stanzas are based. Secondly, it is not clear how 'fidelity' can possess an inherent fitness to mean a whole made up of interrelated parts. Of course, one can simultaneously owe fidelity to two or several persons (a situation in which Gawain eventually finds himself to his moral disadvantage), but the concept of fidelity in each case is single and indivisible. And thirdly, the colour of fidelity is blue, not gold. The symbolic value of blue is explicit in the account of the pen that Canacee makes for the deserted falcon in *The Squire's Tale*, for she 'covered it with veluettes blewe,/In signe of trouthe that is in wommen sene' (*CT*, F 644–45), and implicit in the fact that Gawain makes the exchange on the third day dressed in 'a bleaunt of blwe' (1928). Our surest approach to the meaning of *trawþe* in respect of the pentangle is indeed through the poet's use of colour symbolism. The poet prepares us to appreciate its significance with his customary skill and foresight. Our first image of Gawain's armour is of the gold equipment spread upon the red carpet (568–69):

> Fyrst a tulé tapit ty3t ouer þe flet,
> And miche watz þe gyld gere þat glent þeralofte.

The combination reappears in the description of his horse, where the golden nails are set on a red background (603–4):

> And al watz rayled on red ryche golde naylez,
> Þat al glytered and glent as glem of þe sunne.

When we come to the device of the pentangle itself, the first thing that we learn about it is that it is of gold on a red background (619–20):

> Then þay schewed hym þe schelde, þat was of schyr goulez
> Wyth þe pentangel depaynt of pure golde hwez.

It is also the last thing that we are told in the formal description of the pentangle (662–63):

> Þerfore on his schene schelde schapen watz þe knot
> Ryally wyth red golde vpon rede gowlez.[7]

---

7.  The combination of red and gold in the armour of Gawain has an heraldic as well as a symbolic fitness, for these are colours suitable to a prince. Hence Christine de Pisan states that 'the auncient lawes dyde ordeyne that no man shulde bere gold/ but that he were a prynce . . . noone shuld were red that betokneth hyghnesse/but onely þe prynces'.   See J. Finlayson, 'The Expectations of Romance in *Sir Gawain and the Green Knight*', *Genre* 12 (1979), 1-24 (p. 9, and n. 21).

It is impossible to overlook the importance of colour symbolism in the account of the pentangle, and the only conclusion that we can derive from it is that it is a direct and uncomplicated index of the pentangle's meaning. The undoubted meaning to which the colour symbolism of the pentangle points is that of righteousness, as we may observe from a comparison with Langland, *Piers Plowman*, B XIX.87–88:

> The seconde kyng siththe soothliche offrede
> Rightwisnesse under reed gold, Resones felawe.[8]

It is noteworthy that red and gold are merged together to form a single reference both in *Piers Plowman* (B XIX.88) and in *Sir Gawain* (663)[9]. In the same way gold can be used independently as a marker of Gawain's goodness (633):

> Gawan watz for gode knawen, and as golde pured.

It is an explicit reinforcement of the habitual description of Gawain as 'gode Gawan' (109), and therefore adds an element of continuity. The significance of gold by itself in this general sense is also well established; indeed it still exists in common speech in the proverbial formulation 'as good as gold'. Burrow has noted its biblical associations (*A Reading*, p.40), and Keen has drawn attention to its meaning of *noblesse* in chivalric literature.[10] Now this general meaning of *trawþe* is exactly what is required by the poet's natural identification of the device as a whole with related parts, for *trawþe* stands as the totality of virtue (and indeed also of qualities beside virtue) and it is made up of the particular qualities that are specified in the second of the pentangle stanzas. In other words the pentangle is especially fit to represent the value of integrity or righteousness, and Burrow is right in concluding (*A Reading*,

8.  Reference is to *William Langland: The Vision of Piers Plowman*, edited by A.V.C. Schmidt (London and New York, 1978).
9.  On red gold, see also *Sir Orfeo*, 149-50, edited by A.J. Bliss, second edition (Oxford, 1966):

> þe king hadde a croun on hed;
> It nas of siluer, no of gold red,

and also *Piers Plowman*, B II.15-16:

> Hire robe was ful riche, of reed scarlet engreyned,
> With ribanes of reed gold and of riche stones.

*MED*, s.v. *red* adj. 1f. (a) notes that the use of *red* with reference to the metal gold signifies that the metal is 'pure (as shown through becoming red when heated . . .)'. Hence in *Sir Gawain*, 663 the use of *red* in the phrase 'red golde' signifies 'of the color of pure or reddish gold' (1f. (b)).
10. M. Keen, *Chivalry* (New Haven and London, 1984), p. 131.

p.44) that *trawþe* at line 626 has this inclusive sense. Righteousness is perhaps more suitable than integrity, since it signifies the distinctive religious orientation of the pentangle ideal, embracing as it does faith in Christ (642–43), courage derived from the Virgin Mary (644–50), and the supreme moral virtue of piety (654).

The poet's use of colour symbolism in the description of the pentangle makes evident his desire to avoid any possible obscurity in his exposition. In the same way he sets out to eliminate any eccentricity in the use of the device. He insists, therefore, that the symbol is not of his own devising, and that it is well known to his audience. The symbol in fact was devised by Solomon (625), it is known in popular tradition as ' þe endeles knot' (630) and in more learned circles as ' þe pure pentaungel' (664). The claim by a recent critic that the symbol of the pentangle is possibly the poet's invention is simply a contradiction of the text:

> It is not inconceivable that the symbolism antedates the poem, and that the author has introduced it in order to illustrate it by means of his fiction; but, in that case, one might expect to find some trace of it else-where. No such evidence has so far come to light; and one must therefore consider the possibility that the symbolism of the pentangle, as it appears in the poem, is the author's own invention.[11]

We shall do well instead to rest our case on the poet's own assurances, and since the word that the poet uses most frequently for the symbol is that of the *pentangel* itself (620, 623, 636, and 664) it is to the learned tradition that we must look to explain its use. This tradition is that of Scholastic Aristotelianism, and indeed the pentangle as a symbol, implicit or explicit, for the rational soul is to be found in the central texts of this tradition. The origin of the analogy between the nature of the soul and the geometrical figure would seem to be Aristotle's *De anima* (II.3), although the figure of the pentangle itself is not mentioned:

> Similiter autem se habent ei, quod de figuris est, et quae secundum animam sunt. Semper enim in eo quod est consequenter, est in potentia quod prius est, et in figuris, et in animatis; ut in tetragono quidem trigonum est, in sensitivo autem vegetativum.

> There is indeed an analogy between what holds of figures and what holds of the soul. For in that which is consequent there is always potential that which is primary, both in figures and in animate beings.

---

11.  Horgan, p.310. I set out to document the evidence to which Horgan refers in my article, 'The Significance of the Pentangle Symbolism', pp. 772-73.

As the triangle is contained in the square, so is the vegetative in the sensitive.[12]

Aquinas draws out the full detail of Aristotle's analogy in his character-istically systematic way in the *Summa Theologiae* (la 76.3):

> Et in *De Anima* comparat diversas animas speciebus figurarum, quarum una continet aliam, sicut pentagonum continet tetragonum, et excedit. Sic igitur anima intellectiva continet in sua virtute quidquid habet anima sensitiva brutorum et nutritiva plantarum. Sicut ergo superficies quae habet figuram pentagonum non per aliam figuram est tetragona et per aliam pentagona, quia superflueret figura tetragona ex quo in pentagona continetur, ita nec per aliam animam Socrates est homo et per aliam animal, sed per unam et eandem.

> . . . and in the *De Anima* he compares the different kinds of souls to geometrical figures, where one includes another and has something over, as a pentagon includes a quadrilateral. In this way the intellective soul has among its capacities everything the sense-soul of animals and the nutritive soul of plants have. Thus as a pentagon-shaped surface can supply us with a quadrilateral without being reshaped in order to do so, since a quadrilateral is contained in any pentagonal figure, so Socrates is not constituted a man by one soul and an animal by another, but both man and animal by the one soul.

Aquinas uses the word *pentagonum* in his exposition, whereas Dante uses the Italian word *pentangulo* that directly corresponds to the *pentangel* of the medieval English poet in his account of the same ideas in the *Convivio* (IV.7.14 –15):

> Chè, sì come dice lo Filosofo nel secondo de l'Anima, le potenze de l'anima stanno sopra sè come la figura de lo quadrangulo sta sopra lo triangulo, e lo pentangulo, cioè la figura che ha cinque canti, sta sopra lo quadrangulo: e così la sensitiva sta sopra la vegetativa, e la intellettiva sta sopra la sensitiva. Dunque, come levando l'ultimo canto del pent-angulo rimane quadrangulo e non più pentangulo, così levando l'ultima potenza de l'anima, cioè la ragione, non rimane più uomo, ma cosa con anima sensitiva solamente, cioè animale bruto.

12. Reference is to A.M. Pirotta, *Sancti Thomae Aquinatis in Aristotelis librum de anima commentarium*, sixth edition (Turin, 1959), p. 73, and to *Aristotle's De Anima in the Version of William of Moerbeke and the Commentary of St Thomas Aquinas*, translated by K. Foster and S. Humphries (London, 1951), p. 197.

For, as says the Philosopher in the second *Of the Soul*, the powers of the soul are graded, as the figure of the quadrangle is of higher grade than the triangle and the pentagon of higher grade than the quadrangle, thus the sensitive is of higher grade than the vegetative, and the intellectual of higher grade than the sensitive; and so, just as if you withdraw the last side of a pentagon you have a quadrangle left, but no longer a pentagon, so if you withdraw the last power of the soul, that is the reason, the man is no longer left, but something with a sensitive soul only; that is, a brute animal.

What is important here is the centrality and pervasiveness of these ideas. We cannot say that the *Gawain*-poet had a first-hand knowledge of Aquinas or Dante (although neither proposition would be inconceivable), but he did have direct access to the system of ideas disseminated by them. Thus in relation to the pentangle we can establish that the following ideas constitute a common body of knowledge among learned men of the *Gawain*-poet's generation. The conception of being is hierarchical, and among living organisms we can observe a hierarchy of vegetative, sensitive, and rational powers. Each has its corresponding geometrical symbol: the triangle, the quadrangle, and the pentangle. The pentangle is therefore established as a symbol of human excellence or perfection. The general term that the *Gawain*-poet uses to describe such perfection is *trawþe*, whereas the terms that Dante uses are *gentilezza* or *nobilitade*.

The connection between the pentangle and human perfection or nobility is emphasised by the *Gawain*-poet at the end of his description by his reference to 'þe *pure* pentaungel' (664). What Dante has to say of nobility in the *Convivio* clarifies further the meaning of the pentangle in *Sir Gawain*, as well as being of more general interest to English readers as the source of Chaucer's *gentillesse* in *The Wife of Bath's Tale* (D 1109–76). Nobility, Dante observes, is a term that can be applied without impropriety to any number of different objects; there are, for example, noble stones, noble plants, noble horses, and noble falcons as well as noble men *(Convivio,* IV.16.5). By the use of this term we indicate the perfection in each thing of the nature peculiar to it (IV. 16.4):

Dico adunque che, se volemo riguardo avere de la comune consuetudine di parlare, per questo vocabulo 'nobilitade' s'intende perfezione di propria natura in ciascuna cosa.

I say, then, that if we would have regard to the common custom of speech, this word 'nobleness' means the perfection in each thing of its proper nature.

When we talk of the nobility of the man we must first of all, therefore, determine what kind of being man is. Here Dante would propose a distinction between the order of nature and that of reason (IV.9.4):

> E a vedere li termini de le nostre operazioni, è da sapere che solo quelle sono nostre operazioni che subiacciono a la ragione e a la volontade; che se in noi è l'operazione digestiva, questa non è umana, ma naturale.

> And to perceive the limits of our operations, be it known that those only are operations of ours which are subject to the reason and to the will; for albeit there are digestive operations in us, these are not human, but natural.

That which is distinctive of man is the habit of choice. The authentic and distinctively human activity is moral activity, the product of free will (IV.9.7):

> Sono anche operazioni che la nostra [ragione] considera ne l'atto de la volontade, sì come offendere e giovare, sì come star fermo e fuggire a la battaglia, sì come stare casto e lussuriare, e queste del tutto soggiacciono a la nostra volontade; e però semo detti da loro buoni e rei perch'elle sono proprie nostre del tutto, perchè, quanto la nostra volontade ottenere puote, tanto le nostre operazioni si stendono.

> There are also operations which our reason considers as they exist in the act of will, such as attacking and succouring, standing ground or fleeing in battle, abiding chaste or wantoning; and these are entirely subject to our will, and therefore we are considered good or bad on their account, because they are properly ours in their entirety; for, so far as our will can have its way, so far do operations that are really ours extend.

Nobility is not, however, to be identified with moral virtue, but is a more comprehensive term; its relationship to virtue is as cause to effect (IV.18.2). Thus nobility includes not only moral virtues but also natural dispositions, laudable passions, and bodily graces (IV.19.5):

> Riluce in essa le intellettuali e le morali virtudi; riluce in essa le buone disposizioni da natura date, cioè pietade e religione, e le laudabili passioni, cioè vergogna e misericordia e altre molte; riluce in essa le corporali bontadi, cioè bellezza, fortezza e quasi perpetua valitudine.

> . . . the intellectual and the moral virtues shine in it; good dispositions given by nature shine in it, to wit tenderness and religion, and the praiseworthy emotions, to wit shame and compassion, and many

others. There shine in it the excellencies of the body, to wit beauty, strength, and, so to speak, unbroken health.

The comprehensiveness of nobility answers that of the pentangle, since the rational soul comprehends sensitive and vegetative functions. The point is made at once in the specification of the constituent parts of the pentangle, since the first of the pentangle's groups of five is that of the five senses (640). This echoes Dante's view that nobility is made manifest in the whole man, and not merely the rational part of the soul (IV.23.3):

> Germoglia dunque per la vegetativa, per la sensitiva e per la razionale; e dibrancasi per le vertuti di quelle tutte, dirizzando quelle tutte a le loro perfezioni.

> It buds, then, in the vegetative, in the sensitive and in the rational, and branches out through the virtues of all of these, directing them to their perfections.

It cannot be said that the five senses occupy a significant place in the poet's narrative, but neither are they given much weight in the pentangle passage itself. On the other hand the acuteness of Gawain's sense of hearing plays a small but important part in the drama of the first bedroom scene (1182–86).[13] The second group of five is the five fingers, and these occupy a similarly limited part in the exposition of the particular detail of the pentangle. The interpretation of them has proved especially problematic, and there seems to be the danger of giving them too little weight or too much. Thus Burrow has expressed the view (with which I have some sympathy) that this second group of five has been necessitated by the poet's scheme and not by his moral exposition (*A Reading*, p. 46). On the other hand R.H. Green has invoked a complicated network of values, namely, justice, prudence, temperance, fortitude, and obedience, which corresponds to and to some extent partly overlaps with the moral virtues subsequently specified.[14] It has been suggested that the five fingers isolate the sense of touch among the five senses, since all the other senses are founded upon touch (*ST*, 1a 76.5), but why the poet should need to isolate the sense of touch in this way is far from evident. Perhaps the most interesting suggestion is that of Horgan who refers the five fingers to 'Gawain's knightly prowess in battle' (p.313) and cites the beginning of Psalm 143 which was included in the order of service for the ceremonial dubbing of a knight:

13. The original analysis of the five senses in terms of intemperance in my article, 'The Significance of the Pentangle Symbolism', pp. 774-75, cannot be justified.
14. R.H. Green, 'Gawain's Shield and the Quest for Perfection', *ELH*, 29 (1962), 121-39, in *Sir Gawain and Pearl: Critical Essays*, edited by R.J. Blanch (Bloomington and London, 1966), pp. 176-94 (p. 188).

Benedictus Dominus Deus meus,
Qui docet manus meas ad praelium,
Et digitos meos ad bellum. (Vulgate)

Blessed be the Lord my God, who teacheth my hands to fight, and my fingers to war. (Douay)

If we distinguish knightly prowess from the moral virtue of fortitude, as the subsequent account (644–50) compels us to do, then we may interpret it as strength, one of the bodily graces.[15] The poet does not otherwise specify any of the bodily graces in the pentangle passage, although a reference to Gawain's strength in 'his thik þrawen þyȝez' (579) precedes it and a reference to his handsomeness in 'Gawan gay' (667) immediately follows it. The third group of five is centred on the five wounds that Christ received on the cross, and these form the basis for the identification of the theological virtue of faith (*afyaunce,* 642), that is, of virtue infused by God as distinct from moral virtue acquired by repeated acts. More importance is attached to faith than to the senses and the bodily grace, since two lines and not merely one are devoted to it. That this is the case might seem obvious from the status of theological virtue, although it should be noted that the moral virtue of fortitude which follows is given yet more prominence. At least it can be said that the *Gawain*-poet's conception of a knight (like that of Chaucer) is a distinctively and centrally Christian conception. Indeed the crowning moral virtue of piety (654) can have no meaning unless it is linked to faith. The fourth group of five is based on the five joys of the Virgin Mary, and these are the source of Gawain's knightly courage (*forsnes,* 646). The attention that the poet devotes to elaborating this idea (644–50) is a measure of the importance of fortitude in the argument of his poem. Indeed the case could hardly be otherwise when the Beheading Game requires the knight to seek out his adversary to receive summary execution by the axe. Further it turns out that Gawain's courage will not in all respects be equal to the demands made upon him. Thus at the first blow of the axe he 'schranke a lytel with þe schulderes for þe scharp yrne' (2267). Gawain's courage should not for all that be underestimated, and the poem serves to test both its extent and its limitation. What needs to be observed at this point, however, is the correspondence between the degree of detail in the poet's account of the particular parts of the pentangle and their actual significance in the development of the argument of the poem.

15. See also J. Leyerle, 'The Game and Play of Hero', in *Concepts of the Hero in the Middle Ages and the Renaissance* (London, 1976), pp. 49-82 (p.57): 'The second pentad states that Gawain never failed in his *fyue fyngres* (641); this apparently puzzling strength is a reference to the five fingers bent together into a fist, a conventional indication of physical strength'.

It cannot be said, however, that there is a perfect congruity in the organization of the scheme of the pentangle on the one hand and its meaning as an expression of the perfection of the rational soul on the other. Thus the first and fifth groups of five have reference to five senses and five moral virtues respectively, whereas the third and fourth groups of five have reference to a single theological virtue and a single moral virtue respectively. It is perhaps because of this lack of complete coordination that there is a tendency to identify the pentangle's symbolism with the five moral virtues of the fifth group. Thus Brewer writes:

> In particular, Gawain's courtesy is associated with his virtue in the symbolic device of the pentangle in his shield. The five virtues attributed to him, separate yet inextricably connected like the points of the pentangle, are *franchise,* fellowship, cleanness, courtesy, pity (652–5). Really, all these virtues might be said to be subsumed, in one way or another, under courtesy.[16]

Similarly Silverstein refers to the fact that Gawain possesses 'in gold-fined purity the five virtues symbolized by the device on his shield' (pp. 9–10). Formulations such as these fall short of the precision of the poet's own analysis. Indeed if these formulations were consistently followed they would remove from the poem its moral core in the virtue of courage specified in the fourth group. At the same time it is perfectly proper to emphasise the importance of the fifth group, both because of its climactic position and the specification of each of the five elements composing the group. Not all scholars by any means are agreed on the justice of so straightforward a proposition, and Davis himself has written in direct refutation of it (p.95):

> Despite the importance given to this group of virtues by their climactic position, they do not seem to have been chosen by the poet with especially close regard to the adventure which follows, or to the particular qualities for which Gawain is later praised.

The disagreement arises not so much in respect of the general observation concerning the climactic position of the virtues, but concerning the detailed definition of the particular virtues themselves. Here we need to bear in mind not only lexical considerations, but also the distinction between general and particular in the organization of the pentangle stanzas from which our analysis has proceeded.

16. D.S. Brewer, 'Courtesy and the *Gawain*-Poet', in *Patterns of Love and Courtesy*, edited by J. Lawlor (London, 1966), p. 54.

The first of the five virtues, *fraunchyse* (652), is perhaps the least problematic of all of them, for everyone seems to be agreed that by it the poet intends to single out the virtue of magnanimity or generosity of spirit. Such generosity of spirit is displayed by Gawain in the repeated action of the daily exchange of winnings. On the first exchange Gawain professes not to have seen such meat gained in hunting in seven years (1381–82); on the second he professes never to have seen such a quantity of flesh on any boar (1629–32) and even goes so far as to feign horror at the size of the boar's head in order to praise the lord (1633–34). On the third day Gawain takes the initiative in the exchange of winnings. He is bound to think, like the hunters on the previous two days (1362–80 and 1615–28), that he has done well. If two kisses match the winning of the boar, it is hard to imagine how the host can improve on his performance in the hunting field in such a way as to match the three kisses won on the third day in the bedroom. The only possible course of action for a generous man on the third day is to intervene in order to spare the lord's embarrassment at the poor return for his efforts (1942–47). For Burrow, Gawain's intervention (1948–49) is an example of brusqueness, the sign of a bad conscience (*A Reading*, p. 111). But it is not explained why we should attribute brusqueness to a knight so courteous as Gawain. The narrative is controlled not by the states of mind of the characters in it, but by the imposed abstract idea, namely that of the pentangle in general, and here of generosity in particular. A narrative so shaped focuses not on bad consciences but on courtesy and generosity. The importance of generosity of spirit does not, however, rule out all implication of material generosity, for the one accompanies the other. Indeed material generosity *(largesse)* is a moral concept that subsequently becomes of importance in Gawain's bitter condemnation of himself (2379–81):

> For care of þy knokke cowardyse me taȝt
> To acorde me with couetyse, my kynde to forsake,
> Þat is larges and lewté þat longez to knyȝtez.

A lofty disregard for wealth remains throughout the Middle Ages a distinctive quality of those who are of free or noble birth. The fundamental link between nobility and generosity (already evident in the semantic history of *gentillesse)* is reflected by Caxton in his translation (c.1484) of a French version of Ramón Lull's *Le libre del orde de cauayleria* (116/6–9):

> Chyualrye and Fraunchyse accorden to gyder . . . the knyght must
> be free and franke.[17]

17. Reference is to *The Book of the Ordre of Chyualry: Translated and Printed by William Caxton,* edited by A.T.P. Byles, EETS (OS) 168 (London, 1926).

Chaucer himself uses the word *fredom* to denote the virtue of generosity in his portrait of the Knight in the *General Prologue* (*CT*, A 46), and also combines the notions of freedom and generosity in stressing the hospitality of the Franklin (*CT*, A 339–54). The *MED* glosses *fraunchis(e)* (2(a)) as: 'nobility of character, magnanimity; liberality, generosity; a noble or generous act'. Both senses of generosity are relevant here, and are to be found in the accompanying citations. It seems likely, therefore, that in his use of *fraunchyse* the *Gawain*-poet intends us to be aware of both spiritual and material generosity.

The meaning of *fela3schyp* (652) has also not detained readers of the poem for long, but again it is not so self-evident as it might at first appear. The obvious sense of the word is 'companionableness', and this is certainly appropriate in its context. The *MED* glosses *fela3schyp* (s.v. *felaushipe*, n.4) as 'the spirit that binds companions or friends together; charitable feeling for one's fellows; charity, amity, comraderie'. This meaning is displayed negatively in the sorrow felt by Gawain's companions at Camelot on his departure for what seems certain death (672–86) and positively in the warmth of the greeting that the host at Hautdesert extends to Gawain on Christmas Eve (981–94). But the moral quality that is distinctive of the relationship between companions and is the force that binds the companions together is that of loyalty, and this meaning is at least implicit in the poet's use of *fela3schyp* here. Such an implication would, of course, be especially evident in a chivalric context. The best illustration of the moral significance of *fela3schyp* is to be found in *The Knight's Tale* in the relationship of Perotheus and Theseus, for the Knight is here concerned to show by juxtaposition the infidelity of Palamon and Arcite to one another as a result of a disordered love (*CT*, A 1191–1200):

> A worthy duc that highte Perotheus,
> That felawe was unto duc Theseus
> Syn thilke day that they were children lite,
> Was come to Atthenes his felawe to visite,
> And for to pleye as he was wont to do;
> For in this world he loved no man so,
> And he loved hym als tendrely agayn.
> So wel they lovede, as olde bookes sayn,
> That whan that oon was deed, soothly to telle,
> His felawe wente and soughte hym doun in helle.

Thus the companionship of host and guest at Hautdesert results in the lord's proposal of a game between the two which leads (along with the exercise of other virtues) to a requirement of fidelity in the fulfilment of its terms (1083–1125). No one doubts the importance of fidelity in the moral argument of the poem, and hence it is fitting that it should be included in the poet's detailed specification of the virtues symbolized by the pentangle. It cannot be smuggled into the discussion solely by reference to *trawþe* (626), for as we have established that word bears the general sense of 'righteousness'.

Whereas some significant meanings in the *Gawain*-poet's use of *fraunchyse* and *felaȝschyp* have in the past been overlooked, the critical discussion on the moral implications of *clannes* (653) and *cortaysye* (653) has been if anything too elaborate. Davis in his note to lines 652–54 (p.95) observes that *clannes* 'in ME meant not simply "chastity" but "sinlessness, innocence" generally'.[18] But the meaning of *clannes* in Middle English is not at issue here; rather it is its meaning in this particular passage. As far as that is concerned it is evident that the sense of 'sinlessness' or 'innocence' is quite inappropriate. It is a specific and not a general meaning that is required by the immediate context, and there can be no doubt that the meaning which the poet intends is 'chastity'. The use of the word *clannes* in this specific manner is well attested in the fourteenth century. It is unambiguously used thus by Chaucer in *The Second Nun's Tale* (*CT*, G 159–60):

> And if that ye in clene love me gye,
> He wol yow loven as me, for youre clennesse.

It is this meaning that gives point to the linking of *clannes* with *cortaysye*, for the tension between the two moral concepts is explored at great length in the bedroom scenes at Hautdesert. Burrow wishes to stress (*A Reading*, p.48) that *clannes* does not necessarily imply celibacy. This is indeed true, but it does imply celibacy or rather virginity outside marriage. Burrow goes on to explain the poet's conception of *clannes* as follows (*A Reading*, p.48):

> The poet understood 'cleanness', I am sure, as the generally accepted condition of knightly love — a condition which ruled out the 'vnleful lust' of adultery as a matter of course, but not true-love or even 'love-talking' with one's hostess.

Much depends on what we understand by 'true-love' here, for Burrow is perhaps a little too anxious to assure us (*A Reading*, p.41) that the ideal represented by Gawain is not an ascetic ideal. There is, of course, no middle ground between adultery (*fin'amors*) and chastity (*amour courtois*); if by 'true-love' we understand a chaste love before marriage and by *luf-talkyng* (927) we understand that such chaste love is accompanied by courtesy, then Burrow's analysis can be accepted. Thus we can entertain the possibility of a

---

18. Compare *MED*, s.v. *clennesse* n. 2(a), where the glosses 'uprightness' and 'integrity' are also provided.

chaste love between a young man and another man's wife. The moral idealism of the pentangle passage certainly rules out any ambiguity in the poet's conception of *clannes*.

*Cortaysye* is, as we have seen, a word of considerable scope in the fourteenth century, and it is this aspect of the word that Davis chooses to stress in his note (p.95):

> *Cortaysye* was a word of great range and power at this time, embracing 'chivalrous' conduct of all kinds from courtly politeness to compassion and nobility of mind, and extending to divine grace.

But it is a specific and not a general meaning that is again required in the present context. This specific meaning is 'politeness', for the generosity that prompts such politeness has already been specified by *fraunchyse*. Dante uses *cortesia* in this sense in his illustration of the nobility of youth (*Conv.*, IV.26. 12–13):

> Ancora è necessario a questa etade essere cortese  . . . E questa cortesia mostra che avesse Enea questo altissimo poeta, nel sesto sopra detto, quando dice che Enea rege, per onorare lo corpo di Miseno morto, che era stato trombatore d'Ettore e poi s'era raccomandato a lui,  s'accinse e prese la scure ad aiutare tagliare le legne per lo fuoco che dovea ardere lo corpo morto, come era di loro costume.

> Further, it is needful to this period of life to be courteous . . . And this courtesy that most lofty poet shows Aeneas to have had in the above said sixth book, where he says that Aeneas, king as he was, to honour the corpse of the dead Misenus (who had been Hector's trumpeter, and had afterwards commended himself to him), girt himself and took the axe to help to hew the wood for the fire which was to burn the dead body, as was their custom.

Gawain is in medieval literature the very pattern of courtesy, and it is for this reason that he is invoked by Chaucer in *The Squire's Tale* (*CT*, F 89–97):

> This strange knyght, that cam thus sodeynly,
> Al armed, save his heed, ful richely,
> *Saleweth* kyng and queene and lordes alle,                                      greets
> *By ordre*, as they *seten* in the halle,                              in sequence; sat
> With so heigh reverence and obeisaunce,
> As wel in speche as in contenaunce,
> That Gawayn, with his olde curteisye,
> Though he were comen ayeyn out of Fairye,
> Ne koude hym nat amende with a word.

Gawain's courteous behaviour towards the wounded Erec, contrasted with the boorishness of Kay, is made much of by Chrétien in *Erec et Enide* (3907–4252). No better illustration of the *Gawain*-poet's conception of *cortaysye* can be found, however, than in his own representation of the manner in which Gawain takes up from Arthur the game proposed by the Green Knight (339–61).

The *Gawain*-poet would seem to attach a special significance to *pité* (654), the fifth and final virtue of the fifth and final group of five, and indeed he tells us that it 'passez alle poyntez' (654). Unfortunately the form *pité* is ambiguous in the late fourteenth century, and can stand for either 'pity' or 'piety'.[19] And indeed both compassion and piety are predicated of Gawain in a single sentence of the *Perlesvaus,* where it is said of him (4435–38 and p.129):

> Misire Gavains ne se partist ja d'ostel ou il geüst qu'il n'oïst messe ançois qu'il em partist, si la peüst avoir, ne onques ne trouva dame ne damoisele desconsellie dont il n'eüst pitié.

> Sir Gawain never left a house where he had found lodging without first hearing mass if it was being sung, and he never came across a lady or maiden in need but he took pity on her.

The first of these two meanings is in many ways an attractive one. The sense of 'compassion' fits easily into the social context of the fifth group of virtues, and points to a quality that is a familiar element of the ideal of chivalry in the late fourteenth century. The compassion of Theseus in *The Knight's Tale*, for example, is evident in his response to the distress of the company of ladies that greets him on his triumphant return to Athens (*CT*, A 952–58):

| | |
|---|---|
| This gentil duc doun from his courser *sterte* | leapt |
| With herte *pitous,* whan he herde hem speke. | compassionate |
| Hym thoughte that his herte wolde breke, | |
| Whan he saugh hem so *pitous* and so *maat,* | sad; dejected |
| That *whilom* weren of so greet *estaat*; | formerly; rank |
| And in his armes he hem alle up *hente,* | raised |
| And hem conforteth *in ful good entente.*[20] | kindly |

Again, at the very beginning of Spenser's Legend of Temperance, the knight Sir Guyon experiences pity, both false and true, in his encounters with Duessa and Amavia (*FQ*, II.1.14, and 42). Unsurprisingly a large number of

19.  Both *pity* and *piety* are derived ultimately from Latin *pietas*; see *OED's* note s.v. *pity*.
20.  See also *The Knight's Tale*, A 1748-61.

critics (perhaps the majority) have settled upon the meaning 'pity' for the final virtue of the fifth group; they include among the editors of the poem Davis, Waldron, Barron, and Silverstein (although not Gollancz). Nevertheless there are two serious and, I think, decisive objections to the interpretation of *pité* as 'compassion'. First, it is not at all clear why compassion 'passez alle poyntez', and second, nothing much (if anything at all) is said about Gawain's compassion, unlike that of Theseus or of Guyon.

Pity is sorrow for another's misfortune and can be either a passion or a moral virtue (*ST*, 2a 2ae 30.3):

> Dicendum quod misericordia importat dolorem de miseria aliena. Iste autem dolor potest nominare, uno quidem modo, motum appetitus sensitivi. Et secundum hoc misericordia passio est, et non virtus. Alio vero modo potest nominare motum appetitus intellectivi, secundum quod alicui displicet malum alterius. Hic autem motus potest esse secundum rationem regulatus; et potest secundum hunc motum ratione regulatum regulari motus inferioris appetitus . . . Et quia ratio virtutis humanae consistit in hoc quod motus animi ratione reguletur, ut ex superioribus patet, consequens est misericordiam esse virtutem.

> Mercy means pain over another's misfortune. In this context, however, pain can denote a movement of the sense appetite, in which case mercy is an emotion or feeling, not a virtue. Or it can denote a movement of the intellective appetite when one grieves at the sight of another's misfortune. A movement of this sort can be regulated by right reason and, thus regulated, can in turn regulate the movements of the lower appetite . . . But we have already seen that the essence of human virtue lies in regulating the soul's movements by reason, and so it follows that mercy is a virtue.

Pity is unambiguously identified by Aquinas as a moral virtue in his reply to the fourth argument of this article which raises the issue of its status as an intellectual, theological, or moral virtue, and further among the moral virtues whether it belongs to justice or to the virtues concerned with the passions (*ST*, 2a 2ae 30.3 *ad* 4):

> Ad quartum dicendum quod misericordia, secundum quod est virtus, est moralis virtus circa passiones existens; et reducitur ad illam medietatem quae dicitur nemesis, quia *ab eodem more procedunt*, ut in *Rhet.* dicitur.

> As a virtue, mercy is one of the moral virtues, with the emotions as its field of operation; and is to be resolved into the same 'mean' as indignation, because both of them, as Aristotle points out, in the *Rhetoric, stem from the same moral quality.*

Since justice is the highest of the cardinal virtues, it would seem to follow that mercy does not occupy a high place among the moral virtues. Nevertheless, in his consideration of the question of mercy as the highest of the virtues (*ST*, 2a 2ae 30.4) Aquinas examines its merit in relation to charity, concluding that charity must occupy the highest place as uniting man to God. But mercy is the greatest of the virtues which bear upon the relation of man to his neighbour (*ST*, 2a 2ae 30.4):

> Sed inter omnes virtutes quae ad proximum pertinent potissima est misericordia, sicut etiam est potioris actus; nam supplere defectum alterius, inquantum hujusmodi, est superioris et melioris.

> Of all the virtues which have to do with our neighbour, however, mercy is the greatest, even as its act also surpasses all others, for to relieve the wants of another is, as such, the function of someone higher and better.

In some sense, therefore, it might be argued that pity 'passez alle poyntez'.

But the moral argument is complicated and finally unconvincing. The case for piety as the highest of the moral virtues is by contrast straightforward and unambiguous, although it is complicated in a different way by the conflation of two distinct moral virtues, namely those of piety and religion. Piety in the strict sense is a specific kind of justice that consists in the payment of the debt that we owe to our parents and country for our upbringing (*ST*, 2a 2ae 101.3 *corp.* and *ad* 1). Piety is thus closely allied to religion, that is, the moral virtue of honouring our debt to God as creator. Since religion is a more comprehensive term than piety, it contains piety within it, and hence piety itself can come to be used for the worship of God (*ST*, 2a 2ae 101.1 *ad* 1):

> Ad primum ergo dicendum quod in majori includitur minus. Et ideo cultus qui Deo debetur, includit in se, sicut aliquid particulare, cultum qui debetur parentibus . . . Et ideo nomen pietatis etiam ad divinum cultum refertur.

> The greater takes in the less; thus the kind of homage owed to God already embraces as but a partial form of itself the kind owed to parents . . . . This is the explanation of the use of *pietas* to refer to homage towards God.

The term 'piety' will henceforth be used in the sense of the virtue of religion, that is , the prevailing modern sense of piety (*OED*, II.2). Now pity and piety come together in reference to the virtue of gentleness, the virtuous mean in respect of the emotion of anger (*ST*, 2a 2ae 157.4 *ad* 3):

Ad tertium dicendum quod misericordia et pietas conveniunt quidem cum mansuetudine et clementia inquantum concurrunt in eumdem effectum, qui est prohibere mala proximorum; differunt tamen quantum ad motivum. Pietas enim removet mala proximorum ex reverentia, quam habet ad aliquem superiorem, puta Deum vel parentem; misericordia vero removet mala proximorum ex hoc quod in eis aliquis contristatur inquantum aestimat ea ad se pertinere . . .

Mercy and piety coincide with gentleness and clemency in producing the same effect of warding off evils from our neighbour, nevertheless their motives are different. Piety does it out of reverence towards superiors, God and those from whom we draw life. Mercy does it because it grieves for another as though for oneself, for the fellow-feeling which counts as your own what affects another . . .

But piety is classified under justice, and furthermore is the highest of the virtues under justice (*ST*, 2a 2ae 81.6):

Dicendum quod ea quae sunt ad finem sortiuntur bonitatem ex ordine in finem, et ideo quanto sunt fini propinquiora tanto sunt meliora. Virtutes autem morales . . . sunt circa ea quae ordinantur in Deum sicut in finem. Religio autem magis de propinquo accedit ad Deum quam aliae virtutes morales, in quantum operatur ea quae directe et immediate ordinantur in honorem divinum. Et ideo religio praeeminet inter alias virtutes morales.

Means to an end receive their goodness from being directed to their end, and the nearer they are to the end the better they are. Now moral virtues are concerned with matters that are directed to God as their end. Moreover, religion approaches more closely to God than the other moral virtues because its actions are proximately and immediately directed to his honour. Hence, religion excels the other moral virtues.

In other words it is piety that 'passez alle poyntez', and this fact seems to have been recognized by *MED*'s gloss of *pite* as 'godliness, reverent and devout obedience to God, . . . piety' (4). Everything is to be gained from this unforced interpretation, since the issue of piety is a central issue of the poet's narrative. Thus Gawain is anxious to make his religious observances as Christmas approaches (748–62). The festival of Christmas is scrupulously observed at Bertilak's court (930–40), both with a fitting gravity (*soberly*, 940) and joyously (995–1000). Gawain attends mass on the subsequent days of the religious festival, in particular on the first two days of the Exchange of Winnings agreement (1309–11, and 1558). On the third and final day of that agreement, his last full day in this world as he supposes, Gawain conscientiously goes to confession (1876–84). Of course, the meaning of that confession scene has been (and perhaps still is) one of the most controversial features of the poem. But the nature of the controversy itself makes a powerful case for the importance of piety in the argument of the poem. Davis rejects the interpretation of *pité* as 'piety' because 'Gawain's piety has been fully shown in 642–50, and further emphasis on it would be otiose' (p.96). In so doing he inadvertently draws attention to the precision of the poet's moral and theological analysis. The five joys of Mary are introduced by the poet to account for Gawain's courage and not his piety (644–50). The five wounds of Christ are the object of Gawain's faith or belief (642–43); faith is a theological virtue (see *ST*, 1a 2ae 62.3) and not a moral virtue. Piety is not faith but the scrupulous observance of religious duties.

Although the pentangle stresses the interrelationship of virtues, not all possible virtues are specified by the *Gawain*-poet. Among the theological virtues, hope and charity are not mentioned. One can contrast Spenser's Red Cross Knight, upon whose shield the 'bloudie Crosse  . . . was also scor'd, /For soueraine hope, which in his helpe he had' (*FQ*, I.1.2). But unlike Red Cross, Gawain is not to be tested by despair (*FQ*, I, canto 9). Among the moral virtues, gentleness is not mentioned, but Gawain unlike Spenser's Guyon is not 'inflam'd with wrathfulnesse' (*FQ*,II.1.25) by the deceits of a Duessa and an Archimago. Clearly the selection of virtues in *Sir Gawain* is determined by the special nature of the tests that Gawain undergoes. These are wide-ranging moral and spiritual tests, and the virtues they demand correspond in part to those delimited by Dante in accordance with the ages of adolescence and youth (*Conv.*, IV.26.2):

> Dice adunque che sì come la nobile natura in adolescenza *ubidente, soave e vergognosa*, e adornatrice de la sua persona si mostra, così ne la gioventute si fa *temperata, forte*, amorosa, cortese e leale: le quali cinque cose paiono, e sono, necessarie a la nostra perfezione, in quanto avemo rispetto a noi medesimi.

> It says, then, that as the noble nature in adolescence shows itself to be obedient, sweet, and alive to shame, giving adornment to the person, so, in the prime of life, it is temperate, and brave, and loving, and courteous, and loyal, which five things appear and are necessary to our perfection in so far as has respect to ourselves.

It is evident that the specification of virtues in the pentangle passage has more in common with Dante's youth than adolescence. There is no necessary inconsistency with our earlier definition of Camelot in terms of adolescence, since (apart from the fluctuating age-limit of adolescence from twenty-five to thirty) there is no reason to suppose that the *Gawain*-poet has linked the virtues to the ages of man in the same way that Dante has done.

Righteousness or nobility in individual men cannot be defined essentially, for the rational soul is the form of man, that is, of the species. It can only be defined, therefore, by its effects, that is, in conduct or in Gawain's quest considered as a whole (*Conv.*, IV.16.9):

> Dico adunque che, con ciò sia cosa che in quelle cose che sono d'una spezie, sì come sono tutti li uomini, non si può per li principii essenziali la loro ottima perfezione diffinire, conviensi quella e diffinire e conoscere per li loro effetti.

> I say, then, that inasmuch as in those things which are of one species, as are all men, we cannot define their best perfection by essential principles, we must define and know it by the effects they manifest.

Gawain's acts, like all human acts, will be the products of so many free choices. But they can only be properly understood and evaluated in relation to the circumstances in which they are made. Thus Gawain's failure to hand over the girdle as a winning on the third day (a failure of which he is at the time entirely unaware) cannot be understood apart from the effect of the fear for his life in which he stands.

## III

The pentangle passage defines for us the human limits within which our imaginations are to operate. Two important conclusions at least emerge from a reading of it. The first is that human behaviour is a matter of considerable complexity, and that a man is called upon to reconcile the divergent claims that are made upon him at moral and spiritual levels. The second is that Gawain, embodying to the full the values of Camelot, is a perfect representative of Christian chivalry.

The second conclusion can be the source of some confusion in our reading of the poem. There is a danger of treating the pentangle symbolism with the wrong kind of rigour, and thus of supposing that Gawain's behaviour is subjected to a more critical scrutiny than the poet intends. It is necessary to clarify the nature of the claim that the poet makes on behalf of his hero. Dante has shown us the truth when he says that nobility is the perfection of each thing in accordance with the peculiarity of its nature. Here we need to recognize that the perfection of human nature is limited and imperfect, a paradox that is a necessary consequence of the doctrine of original sin, and implied perhaps by the association of the device of the pentangle with Solomon (625). Gawain's perfection does not require us to suppose that he is without sin and that moral behaviour is for him inevitable. Indeed the first supposition would be heretical and the second would offend against the very definition of moral behaviour, that is, of activity dependent upon a free and deliberate act of will. The poet does not make impossibly absolutist claims on Gawain's behalf by means of the pentangle symbolism, as even so sensitive a critic as Burrow assumes.[21] It is clear in fact that Gawain's perfection is relative and not absolute (654–55):

> . . . þyse pure fyue
> Were harder happed on þat haþel þen on any oþer.

And in this respect we can appreciate more fully the fitness of the pentangle as a geometrical symbol. There is indeed at times a tendency to overlook the distinction between the geometrical figure and its symbolic import, that is, the proper and transferred senses of the device. Thus moral error on Gawain's part leads readily to the conclusion of a disruption of the geometrical figure. Thus Burrow refers to a 'broken pentangle' (*A Reading*, p. 50), and Green claims that the 'pentangle is shattered' (p. 192) when Gawain accepts the girdle. But these inferences are by no means necessary. The pentangle takes its place in a geometrical series, and possesses a greater unity than either a triangle or a quadrangle. As such it is fitted to symbolize the greater complexity of the rational soul in comparison with that of the vegetative or sensitive

21. Compare the reference to 'the geometric absolutism of the pentangle passage' (*A Reading*, p.51), and the consequent observation that 'Gawain is not, as the poet claimed in the pentangle passage, "faultless" *absolutely*, like refined gold or a perfect pearl; but he is so *relatively*, in comparison with other men ("bi oþer gay kny3tez")' (*A Reading*, p.134). This is a common error of interpretation. Thus M. Thiébaux, 'Sir Gawain, the Fox Hunt, and Henry of Lancaster', *Neuphilologische Mitteilungen* (1970), 469-79 writes (p. 474): 'It is the fox hunt that is the most telling of the three, for its resolution reveals a Gawain not so faultless, not quite so perfect a knight as the Pentangle had seemed to betoken', and A. Henry, 'Temptation and Hunt in *Sir Gawain and the Green Knight*', *Medium Aevum*, 45 (1976), 187-99 comments that 'Gawain loses the right to wear the symbol of unflawed perfection' (p. 194). The same absolutist conclusions are arrived at in the book-length study of R.G. Arthur, *Medieval Sign Theory and Sir Gawain and the Green Knight* (Toronto, 1987). The 'spatial endlessness' of the pentangle is taken to signify God as '*Summa Veritas*' or 'Absolute Truth' (p. 46). But the same sign that is applied to God *simpliciter* can be applied to man *secundum quid* (p.73), so that by ascribing to Gawain a sign for absolute truth the poet is claiming that Gawain is in accord with truth, that is, in a state of faith; thus 'the shield labels Gawain as true in a relative sense, that is, faithful' (p. 87). In the course of the narrative, however, Gawain is seen to undergo a moral and spiritual decline; he 'is first displayed as humanly perfect and then shown to be, in reality, seriously flawed' (p. 141).

souls. But the geometrical unity of the pentangle is not a perfect unity, for it falls short of the simple unity of the circle. Now the figure of the circle is fitted to represent an absolute perfection, and indeed is so used by Boethius in the *De consolatione philosophiae* to represent the divine simplicity (Book III, Prosa 12, 160–62):

> Ne fooldist thou nat togidre by replicacioun of wordes a manere wondirful sercle or envirounynge of the simplicite devyne?

The pentangle is by comparison geometrically imperfect, and hence is fitted to represent a human excellence that is correspondingly imperfect. Not any kind of human imperfection is compatible with the nature of the pentangle, but only that degree which is compatible with the highest human excellence. Nevertheless, the figure of the pentangle comprehends symbolically the notion of human imperfection. The poet's claim in the pentangle passage, therefore, is not that Gawain is devoid of any human flaw, but that his behaviour is perfect of its kind. Samuel Johnson has expressed the idea with characteristic elegance:

> In narratives, where historical veracity has no place, I cannot discover why there should not be exhibited the most perfect idea of virtue; of virtue not angelical, nor above probability, for what we cannot credit we shall never imitate, but the highest and purest that humanity can reach, which, exercised in such trials as the various revolutions of things shall bring upon it, may, by conquering some calamities, and enduring others, teach us what we may hope, and what we can perform.[22]

Gawain's virtue is exercised in trials in the Beheading Game and the Exchange of Winnings, and these are trials that make the ultimate demand upon his very life. It is not to be denied that his courage and fidelity are found wanting in the course of them. But it does not follow that we should call into question the fitness of the pentangle as a symbol of his moral excellence, for as we have seen the symbol does not claim completeness of virtue. The claim is merely that the human excellence displayed by Gawain cannot be exceeded by any other mortal man. This is not in itself a small matter, but only in the course of the subsequent narrative can we see whether it is justified or not.

---

22. Reference is to Samuel Johnson, *The Rambler*, No.4 (March, 1750), edited by W.J. Bate and A.B. Strauss, 3 vols (New Haven and London, 1969), in *The Yale Edition of the Works of Samuel Johnson*, Volume III, p. 24.

# CHAPTER FIVE

# The Action of the Hunting and Bedroom Scenes

I

THE MORAL SERIOUSNESS of *Sir Gawain and the Green Knight* is clearly established by the pentangle passage, and in the light of its values commentators have addressed themselves to the judgments of Gawain's conduct made by the Green Knight (2331–68), Gawain himself (2369–88, 2406–38, and 2494–512), and Arthur and his court (2513–21). It is not a matter of dispute that the moral outcome is determined in the series of bedroom exchanges, framed by the hunting scenes, which take place in Fitt III between Gawain and the host's wife. Nevertheless the moral implication of these events, reinforced as it is by the poem's interlocking structure, has not prevented some readers from reducing the bedroom interchanges to the level of light comedy or even farce. Thus Barron believes that Gawain's 'elaborate and self-conscious piece of play acting' when he feigns surprise at the lady's presence in his room and crosses himself (1200–1203) provokes laughter and that 'though we may not be able to define the cause of our laughter, it must materially affect our relationship to the hero hereafter.'[1] On the other hand

---

1. Barron, *Trawthe and Treason* (1980), p. 12. A similar view is expressed by D. Mills, 'An Analysis of the Temptation Scenes in *Sir Gawain and the Green Knight*', *JEGP*, 67 (1968), 612-30, when he observes that Gawain's crossing himself 'is a gesture of comic surprise rather than a serious reminder of moral danger' (p. 613). More judicious is the opinion of C. Dean, 'The Temptation Scenes in *Sir Gawain and the Green Knight*', *Leeds Studies in English*, 5 (1971), 1-12 (p. 4): 'He makes the sign of the cross so that he might be þe sauer (1202). This action should probably not be considered very significant. Very likely it is nothing more than part of his pretence of waking up.' Dean is right to emphasise the naturalness of Gawain's action. It is what a pious knight would do on any morning. But the reason for that action is also significant, for it points to the ever-present reality of moral danger. And in the actual circumstances of the first bedroom scene the action has more than its usual significance, for Gawain is indeed in immediate moral danger. Thus B.S. Levy, 'Gawain's Spiritual Journey: *Imitatio Christi* in *Sir Gawain and the Green Knight*', *Annuale Mediaevale*, 6 (1965), 65-106, is surely right when he observes (p. 96): 'Nor is Gawain unaware of his vulnerability, for at the first approach of the lady, who attempts to distract him from his basic concern for his spiritual welfare, he carefully blesses himself to assure the safety of his soul.'

we do not laugh when Lancelot is tested by a lady in the *Perlesvaus* and also resorts to crossing himself as a means of defence (8401–3, and 8409–11, and p.223):

> Ele sailli sus isnelement e s'en vient eu vergier la ou Lanceloz gisoit. Ele le trova dormant, si s'asiét dejoste lui, si　le conmença a regarder en sospirant, . . . Ele aproche sa boche de la sieue e le besa au meuz e au plus bel q'el sot .iii. foiz, e Lanceloz s'esveilla tantost, si sailli sus e fist croiz sor lui; puis esgarda la damoisele.

> The lady jumped up and came to the orchard where Lancelot lay. She found him still asleep, and so she sat down at his side and　began　to gaze at him, sighing . . . She lowered her lips to his and kissed him three times as finely and as　sweetly as she could, and Lancelot woke up at once and leapt to his feet and crossed himself, and then saw the maiden.[2]

Clearly there is a difference of religious and moral sensibility here that makes it difficult for the modern reader to invest such actions with the seriousness that they deserve. In the same way Davenport compares the temptation of Gawain to fabliau, and observes that 'by choosing the wiles of a woman as the means by which Gawain's honour and self-command are tested, the poet indicates a basically comic view of Gawain's failure, and introduces a note of parody into the poem' (*The Art*, p.139). Such comparisons are essentially misconceived, and fail to give due moral weight to the values of chastity and courtesy. At the same time there is a violation of the poem's imaginative integrity as expressed in the idea of the pentangle.

It should indeed be axiomatic that the hunting and bedroom scenes are to be understood in relation to the poem's idea, for to repeat Aquinas (*ST*, 1a 15.2):

> Ratio autem alicujus totius haberi non potest, nisi habeantur propriae rationes eorum ex quibus totum constituitur; sicut aedificator speciem domus concipere non potest, nisi apud ipsum esset propria ratio cujus-libet partium ejus.

2.　B. J. Whiting, 'Gawain: His Reputation, His Courtesy and His Appearance in Chaucer's *Squire's Tale*', *Mediaeval Studies*, 9 (1947), 189-234 and printed in *Twentieth Century Interpretations* of *Sir Gawain and the Green Knight*, edited by D. Fox (Englewood Cliffs, New Jersey, 1968), pp. 73-78, records an example from Gerbert de Montreuil's *Continuation de Perceval* in which Gawain is saved from death by his piety in making the sign of the cross: 'Gawain, with a touch of happy, if not completely congruous, piety, makes the sign of the cross as he enters the bed, and the knife is more or less miraculously disclosed to him' (p. 197).

Now a plan governing a whole necessarily involves knowing what is special to the parts which make up the whole; just as an architect cannot plan a house without knowing what is special to each part of it.

The idea of the pentangle establishes two fundamental principles, namely that nobility is a complex unity made up of interrelated parts and that, relative to other men, Gawain stands for the highest perfection of human nobility. The organization of the hunting and bedroom scenes builds upon and reflects these principles. The bedroom scenes are set within the hunting scenes and linked to them by the Exchange of Winnings agreement. The Exchange of Winnings agreement in its turn is set within the Beheading Game, and these too are linked, for the outcome of the Beheading Game is dependent upon the outcome of the Exchange of Winnings agreement. By means of this complex, interlocking structure of events there is a comprehensive testing of Gawain's *trawþe*. Our point of departure is Gawain's physical, moral, and spiritual excellence. This being so, the traditional contrast between the health of the hunting field and the sinfulness of the bedroom has to be subordinated to our sense of that excellence.

Moreover, the poet has once more given us the means of measuring that excellence, for Gawain's actions at this point are to be judged by their conformity to the terms of the Exchange of Winnings agreement. As in any proper game, the rules are set out with the greatest possible clarity and precision. On Gawain's part there are four elements to be observed; first, he will remain in bed; second, he will get up in time for mass; third, he will go to his food; and fourth, he will be entertained by the companionship of the host's wife until the host himself returns (1096–99). We can see for ourselves how these conditions are fulfilled by Gawain on the three successive days. The appearance of the lady in Gawain's bedroom is not only a violation of the rules of courtesy, but also of the implied pattern of the Exchange of Winnings agreement itself. Nevertheless, although the appearance of the lady in Gawain's bedroom complicates the predicted pattern of action, it does not in fact succeed in dislocating it. For all the difficulties created by the lady's intervention, Gawain remains true to the pattern of action required of him by his host.

At the same time the lord plays his part to the full in the hunting field. He is true to his word in getting up early and going off to the hunt (1133–38), and he does not do so without a fitting display of courtesy and piety (1135). Once again the pattern is repeated on the following days (1412–16, and 1688–96). The lord is not a poacher (like the man in *The Parlement of the Thre Ages*), but a true sportsman who respects the laws and conventions of hunting. He observes the close season, and so does not interfere with the male deer (1154–57). Although a great multitude of deer is slain, the slaughter is controlled and not wanton, being of 'hyndez barayne' (1320) and 'of dos and of oþer dere' (1322). The lord is open and generous when it comes to the exchange of winnings itself. He does not disguise his delight as a sportsman in his achievement, but he does not exult to the discomfiture of a worthy opponent, for he conducts himself towards Gawain 'al godly in gomen' (1376). In all this we are reminded that the best games are those which are suffused with sportsmanship and in which the opponents are well matched. We can see that the values of the host are not essentially different from those of Gawain himself as they are set out in the pentangle passage. Indeed the equality of host and guest is revealed in the discriminating generosity that Gawain displays towards the host on each successive evening. The venison is the best that he has seen in seven years in the season of winter (1381–82); it is the biggest quantity of flesh that he has ever seen on a boar (1629–32); and the embarrassment of 'þis foule fox felle' (1944) is a matter to be passed over as quickly as possible (1948–49).

The notion of equality between Gawain and the lord is sustained in the actual exchanges of the winnings themselves on the three successive evenings. The importance of these exchanges is underlined by the public ceremony that attends them, for they do not take place until the whole court has been assembled (1372–75, and 1623–25). Even allowing for the differences of the third evening (and they are significant differences) the transaction remains a public transaction (1924–27). The lord's success on the first day is matched by the kiss that Gawain gives 'as comlyly as he couþe awyse' (1389). It is not hard for us to believe that it could be superior to the lord's winnings (1392–94), but it is right for Gawain not to respond to the lord's promptings on this score. It is not for him to reveal to the husband the impropriety of the wife. Gawain is not bound by any promise to declare the source of his winnings (1395–97), and by his generous acknowledgment of the lord's success in the deer hunt has already shown himself to be abiding by the spirit as well as the letter of the agreement. The awesome prize of the boar on the second day does not diminish but on the contrary reveals the true worth of the two kisses that Gawain in his turn delivers to the lord (1639–40). Gawain is justified in claiming equality here: 'Now ar we euen . . . / Of alle þe couenauntes þat we knyt' (1641–42). On the third day Gawain's three kisses (1936–37) seem to earn for him a great advantage, for they are, as the lord truly acknowledges them to be, 'suche prys þinges/ . . . suche þre cosses/so gode' (1945–47). Yet there remains an equality in this exchange too despite the superficial inequality, and it is an equality that is not entirely to Gawain's disadvantage. The lord is dissatisfied, but the fox did not get away from its pursuers. Indeed a ceremonial tribute or salute is paid to the fox as a fitting adversary (1916–17):

> Þe rich rurd þat þer watz raysed for Renaude saule
>         with lote.[3]

In the same way the worth of Gawain's three kisses is not wholly under-
mined by his failure in the matter of the girdle.

The equality that is explicit in the Exchange of Winnings enables us to
estimate the kisses that Gawain receives and exchanges at their true value. It
is impossible to accept the view put forward by Davenport (*The Art*, p. 139)
that they expose the hero to ridicule:

> The receiving and giving back of Gawain's gains, the kisses from the
> Lady, both expose him to ridicule: as receiver Gawain is a parody of
> the youthful, chivalrous lover as he lies in bed using his wits to fend off
> the importunities of the bold, provincial lady; as giver Gawain is made
> to look a ninny as he solemnly plants kisses on the Lord's teasing face.

Malory's Lancelot sees no dishonour, and presumably no foolishness, in
giving a kiss when he resists the temptation to love-making during his
imprisonment by Mellyagaunce (*The Book of Sir Launcelot and Queen
Guinevere*, 1136/18–27):

> So she cam to hym agayne the same day that the batayle shulde be and
> seyde,
>     'Sir Launcelot, bethynke you, for ye ar to hard-harted. And therefore,
> and ye wolde but onys kysse me, I shulde delyver you and your
> armoure, and the beste horse that was within sir Mellyagaunce stable.'
>     'As for to kysse you,' seyde sir Launcelot, 'I may do that and lese no
> worshyp. And wyte you well, and I undirstood there were ony
> disworshyp for to kysse you, I wold nat do hit.'
>     And than he kyssed hir.

Further, the kisses exchanged between Gawain and the lady can be seen to
correspond to a pattern of courtly decorum, as J. Nicholls has observed.[4] The

---

3.  It is necessary here to reject the description of J.D. Burnley, 'The Hunting Scenes in
    *Sir Gawain and the Green Knight*', *The Yearbook of English Studies*, 3 (1973), 1-9
    (p. 9): 'On the hunting field anxiety turns to panic and an unceremonious death
    which invites our contempt and, with memories of the previous heroic struggle, a
    deep sense of disappointment.' A contrast may be noted with the lack of success of
    the hunt in *The Book of the Duchess*, for here the hounds had 'on a defaute yfalle'
    (384), that is, they had fallen in error since they had been foiled by the hart. See D.
    Scott-MacNab, 'A Re-examination of Octovyen's Hunt in *The Book of the Duchess*',
    *Medium Aevum*, 56 (1987), 183-99 (pp. 191-92).
4.  J. Nicholls, *The Matter of Courtesy: Medieval Courtesy Books and the Gawain-Poet*
    (Woodbridge and Dover, New Hampshire, 1985): 'the seemingly erotic kisses are so

only kiss on the first day is that of farewell (1305–8); the two kisses on the second day are 'a delayed gesture of greeting' (1504–5)[5] and an act of farewell (1555–57); and the three kisses on the third day are of greeting (1757–58), pretended farewell after rejection in love (1794–96), and final leave-taking (1868–69). Above all the public exchange of the kisses thus received is a means of defining Gawain's moral excellence. The first kiss that Gawain bestows on the lord is given *comlyly* (1389), and this indicates the courtesy that is the dominant note of the first day's interchanges between Gawain and the lady. The same idea is present on the second day, for Gawain kisses the lord *hendely* (1639). The kisses that the lady gives Gawain on the third day are passionately delivered, for she exhausts every feminine art and feeling, and this is reflected by the vigour with which Gawain bestows the kisses in the Exchange of Winnings (1937):

> As sauerly and sadly as he hem sette couþe.

To win kisses so entirely pure and passionate from a lady so beautiful, determined, and clever in the circumstances that Gawain finds himself involves moral action of quite exceptional courtesy and chastity. It is this combination of virtues that sets Gawain apart from a hero like Yder, for Yder succeeds in preserving his chastity only by means of kicking his temptress in the belly (*Yder*, 370–80):

> E Yder respont brefment qu'il ment
> E qu'il n'a de s'amor ke fere;
> Ançois li loe ensus a treire
> E qu'el se gart qu'il ne la fiere.
> Quanques il puet se treit ariere,
> Mes ele se treit tot dis soentre.
> Yder la fiert del pié al ventre
> Si qu'el chei ariere enverse
> E qu'el en devint tote perse.
> Jo nel sai pas de ço reprendre
> Kar il ne se poeit defendre.

> Yder replied briefly that she was lying and that he was not interested in her love; instead he advised her to go away and to be careful that he did not strike her. He drew away from her as much as possible, but she

placed that they can also be seen as conventional gestures of greeting and farewell' (p. 133). See also his continuing discussion on p. 134, where the reference to Lancelot is cited (n. 56).

5.    The phrase is that of Nicholls, p. 134.

drew closer immediately. Yder kicked her in the belly so that she fell backwards and her colour drained away. I cannot criticize him for this as he was unable to defend himself in any other way.

*Yder* is a sophisticated romance, and the poet's defence of his hero's conduct is not simply to be dismissed. The cruelty of Yder's action is to be explained by the desperate peril he is in, for the virtue of chastity has to overcome powerful and almost irresistible desires. The courtesy that Gawain manages to display in such circumstances is in no respect worthy of laughter but only of the highest admiration.

The equality of host and guest is shown above all by the fellowship that they share. Thus the two 'laȝed, and made hem blyþe/Wyth lotez þat were to lowe' (1398–99) at the end of the first day, and this pattern of fellowship is repeated on the two succeeding days (1623–24, 1680–85, and 1952–59). The lord is not, however, merely Gawain's equal in an open competition, but is superior to him in his knowledge of the true significance of the events that are taking place. The lord is to be the judge of Gawain's conduct, and the poet anticipates for us the judgmental function of Fitt IV by giving to the lord on the evening of the second day of competition words that carry a special authority and resonance (1679): 'For I haf fraysted þe twys, and faythful I fynde þe'. These words are conceived by the poet in no more of a naturalistic spirit than those he has given to the wife (1283–87), but they are important in giving moral shape and weight to the events that he describes.

Thus the terms of the Exchange of Winnings agreement, the repeated actions, and the interlocking structure are the artistic means by which the poet develops and clarifies his meaning. These are the elements that we must pay attention to ourselves if we are not to disturb the subtle moral and imaginative balance of forces which he has thereby created.


## II


We must also take note of the primacy of another artistic principle, namely the priority of action to character. A character is to be perceived in the first place as the fitting agent of an action of some kind. This is not to say that character is unimportant, but only that it is secondary and unintelligible except in relation to the action. Although this may be a difficult principle for the modern reader to accept, it is a principle of great antiquity, most memorably asserted by Aristotle in the *Poetics* (6):

> Tragedy is essentially an imitation not of persons but of action and life, of happiness and misery. All human happiness or misery takes the form

of action; the end for which we live is a certain kind of activity, not a quality. Character gives us qualities, but it is in our actions — what we do — that we are happy or the reverse. In a play accordingly they do not act in order to portray the Characters; they include the Characters for the sake of the action.[6]

What is applied by Aristotle to tragedy is no less applicable to narrative poetry, and it is so applied by Tasso in the *Discorsi* (Book III) at the end of the sixteenth century (II, 228 and p. 67):

> . . . presupponendo che la favola sia il fine del poeta (come afferma Aristotele, e niuno ha sin qui negato) . . .

> . . . assuming the fable to be the goal of the poet (as Aristotle affirms, and no one has denied to this day) . . .

Once we begin to look to the relation between the hunting and bedroom scenes in *Sir Gawain* in terms of action rather than or as prior to character, that is, with character as fittingly subordinated to action, then much begins to make sense that would otherwise be obscure. It is by giving priority to character over action that Gollancz concludes that 'Gawain's conscience makes him unwilling to prolong discussion of the exchange' (p.124) on the third day, and it is for the same reason that he is followed by a critic so sensitive as Burrow (*A Reading*, p.111). It is to be noted that Burrow assumes that the courteous Gawain can act brusquely on occasion since he knows that even the most courteous people sometimes lapse from the highest standards of courtesy. But the *Gawain*-poet cannot present Gawain as discourteous other than by a specific violation of the idea of nobility in terms of which his narrative is organized. And if it were so that Gawain has been discourteous, the discourtesy would need to be brought before the Green Knight for judgment in the same way as the violation of fidelity through the concealment of the girdle. In the light of the principle of the primacy of action we may now turn directly to the corresponding patterns of action in the three sets of hunting scenes and bedroom scenes.

On the first day of hunting the deer are quick to sense danger; they try to escape to the high ground, but are driven back by the ring of beaters (1150–53). It is indeed in this way that they are eventually slaughtered at the

---

6.  Aristotle goes so far as to say that 'a tragedy is impossible without action, but there may be one without character' (*Poetics*, 6). This is a hard saying. What it means is that actions are carried out by agents, but by 'character' Aristotle understands moral choice, and human agents are not always seen in the act of making such choices. Characters are then seen to possess a moral, but not a poetic autonomy. See G.F. Else, *Aristotle's Poetics: the Argument* (Cambridge, Massachussetts, 1957), pp. 238-39.

low-lying hunting stations (1167–73). In the same way Gawain is quick to
sense danger (1182–83), and he too tries to get to safer ground, but is en-
circled in his bed by the determined purpose of the lady (1218–25). There is
no doubt, as Davis observes (p.107), a contrast between the noise of the hunt
(1158–66) and the stillness of the bedroom (1182–94). But stillness is not to
be taken for peace. Gawain is being hunted with the stealth that is necessary,
as we have seen, in a deer hunt (*PTA*, 40–42), and remains in deadly danger.
*The Master of Game* (pp.8–11) emphasizes the great joy of hunting, and
especially the hunting of the hart (see also p.29), and this emphasis is
strongly present in the *Gawain*-poet's account (1174–77):

> Þe lorde for blys abloy
> Ful oft con launce and ly3t,
> And drof þat day wyth joy
> Thus to þe derk ny3t.

Again, the joy of the chase is matched by the joy in the bedroom. The lady
exudes a surface gaiety and charm (1208–12) and Gawain responds in kind
(1213–17). Indeed, throughout this first interchange these qualities are
continually stressed (1245, 1247, 1248, and 1263). The issue of the first day
finally turns on a question of courtesy, for Gawain's reputation for courtesy
is challenged by the lady (1290–1304).[7] Here is another direct link with the

7.   Assumptions about Gawain's reputation for courtesy are often imported into
     interpretations of the poem, and these in their turn need to be challenged. Gawain is
     often identified in the later romances as sexually active and even lecherous, so that
     sexual innuendo is taken to be a predictable element in his conversation, and love-
     making the end towards which that conversation is directed. Thus Whiting, 'Gawain:
     His Reputation, His Courtesy and His Appearance in Chaucer's *Squire's Tale*',
     describes Gawain as the 'well-mannered wooer of almost any available girl' (p.
     203). This conception of Gawain has hardened into dogma, so that Spearing
     represents the hero of *Sir Gawain* in terms of a secular *cortaysye* defined as
     'thoughtfulness for others, refined manners, deference, the service of ladies, and
     elegant love-making' (*The Gawain-Poet*, p. 11). But the image of Gawain is by no
     means so clearcut in the medieval romances, and Whiting is obliged to counter the
     view that Gawain was originally a model of chastity (p. 203). Indeed, since we are
     dealing here with fictional creations not historical realities, as Whiting himself
     reminds us (p. 203), we can accommodate two or several traditions concerning the
     character of Gawain. There is no evidence, so far as I am aware, that Chrétien's
     Gawain was unchaste. The courtesy and chastity of Gawain are disparaged by the
     Maidens of the Tent in *Perlesvaus* much as they are by the lady in *Sir Gawain*
     (*Perlesvaus*, 1813-17, and p. 64):

     > 'Par Dieu, fet l'une a l'autre, se ce fust cil Gavains qui niés est le roi Artu, il
     > parlast a nos autrement, e trovissions en lui plus de deduit que en cestui; mes
     > cist est uns Gavains contrefez. Malement est enploiee l'onneurs q'on li a fete
     > en ceste tente'.

framing hunting scene, for the cutting up of the deer (1323–64) is entirely a matter of courtesy. First of all, the correct order must be observed, and this is underlined by the series of deictic adverbs, syþen (1330, 1332, 1339, 1354, and 1363) and þen(ne) (1333, 1337, 1340, 1353, 1356, and 1357). Secondly, skill is required, and this is emphasized by a series of evaluative adverbs and adverbial phrases focusing on the swiftness, deftness, and correctness of the procedure: *lystily* (1334), *grayþely* (1335), *radly* (1341, and 1343), *verayly* (1342), *by resoun* (1344), and *swyft* (1354). Thirdly, there is a mastery of the technical vocabulary, as for example in the use of *querré* (1324) and *asay* (1328). And fourthly, each huntsman gets the portion of the deer to which he is properly entitled (1358): 'Vche freke for his fee, as fallez for to haue'. Here is true courtesy in the behaviour that fully matches the occasion. Hunting is a proper activity for men of a medieval court, and the cutting up of the deer is a proper concern of huntsmen; hence ' þe *best* boȝed þerto with burnez innoghe' (1325). Moreover, the propriety of the hunt is observed from the beginning to the end by the accompaniment of the fitting sounds. The uncoupling of the hounds is signified by three long single notes, ' þre bare mote' (1141). The death of the deer and the return home are marked by a like formality; 'baldely þay blw prys' (1362) and 'strakande ful stoutly' (1364). The significance of this display of nobility is brought out by Malory in *The Book of Sir Tristram* (682/25–683/4):

> And every day sir Trystram wolde go ryde an-huntynge, for he was called that tyme the chyeff chacer of the worlde and the noblyst blower of an horne of all maner of mesures. For, as bookis reporte, of sir Trystram cam all the good termys of venery and of huntynge, and all the syses and mesures of all blowyng wyth an horne; and of hym we had fyrst all the termys of hawkynge, and whyche were bestis of chace

> 'In faith', said one, 'if this were Gawain, the nephew of King Arthur, he would speak to us differently, and we should find in him more entertainment than in this man: this Gawain is an impostor. The honour we have paid him here was ill-spent.'

(Compare also *Sir Gawain*, 1478-94, and see *Perlesvaus*, 6995-96 and p. 190, where Gawain is represented as not merely chaste, but also shy). Thus Gawain's courtly conversation in *Sir Gawain* does not necessarily presuppose any sexual element, as Nicholls (*The Matter of Courtesy*, p. 129) observes, drawing out in the process a comparison between the innocent talk of love in *Sir Gawain*, 1506-7 and at Theseus's feast in *The Knight's Tale* (CT, A 2203). The chaste tradition is essentially that within which the Gawain of *Sir Gawain* has been conceived and which the pentangle passage has made explicit, although the *Gawain*-poet is familiar with the alternative tradition and exploits the tension between the two in the bedroom scenes of Fitt III. For a recent discussion of the history of Gawain in medieval romance, emphasising the positive rather than the negative sides of his character, see J. Matthews, *Gawain: Knight of the Goddess* (Wellingborough, 1990).

and bestis of venery, and whyche were vermyns; and all the blastis that
longed to all maner of game: fyrste to the uncoupelynge, to the sekynge,
to the fyndynge, to the rechace, to the flyght, to the deth, and to strake;
and many other blastis and termys, that all maner jantylmen hath cause
to the worldes ende to prayse sir Trystram and to pray for his soule.
AMEN, SAYDE SIR THOMAS MALLEORRÉ.

Here we see the importance that is attached to the development and mastery
of the correct terms, and it is in relation to the correct terms that the bedroom
and hunting scenes of the first day are finally linked. For just as Gawain is
concerned 'lest he hade fayled in fourme of his castes' (1295), so the poet is
anxious to ensure that he has distinguished between the *avanters* (1342) and
the numbles proper (1347–48):

> And þat þay neme for þe noumbles bi nome, as I trowe,
>      bi kynde.

The second day's hunt is of sterner stuff, as is at once evident from the
uncoupling of the hounds 'among þo þornez' (1419). The course of the hunt
is no longer over hills and dales (1151–52), but over marshy ground amid
rough cliffs (1429–36). The boar is a ferocious adversary (1437–53, and
1571–80), and he makes even brave men flinch (1460–63, and 1573–76).
Similarly, there is a shift in tone between the first and second day's bedroom
scenes, for on the second day there is a greater directness in the confrontation
between the lady and Gawain. The lady comes to Gawain with a clear purpose (1472–76), but Gawain is now ready for her (1477). Further, the
analogy with the action of the hunt is once again clear. As the arrows bounce
off the boar (1454–59), so Gawain's words of greeting meet a swift reply
(1478): 'And ho hym ȝeldez aȝayn ful ȝerne of hir wordez', and the lady
undeterred returns to the attack (1479–80). The debate now turns not only on
the propriety of kissing (1481–94), a matter of courtesy, but also on the
admissibility of the use of force (1495–1500), a matter that bears on a knight's
courage. The combination of these two virtues in Gawain is seen in his initial
response to the lady's importunity whereby she seeks to elicit from him an
inappropriate forwardness in kissing (1492):

> 'Do way,' quoþ þat derf mon, 'my dere, þat speche.'

But the lady's argument, as Burrow has shown (*A Reading*, pp. 90–91), is
more subtle than it first appears. For a lady to refuse Gawain would be
churlish (1497) and, according to Andreas Capellanus, *De amore* (I.11), the
resistance of a peasant woman to amorous embraces is not to be overcome

'nisi modicae saltem coactionis medela praecedat ipsarum opportuna pudoris'.[8]
The underlying reality of the argument is acknowledged by Malory in the
account of the begetting of Torre by Pellinore on a maid, subsequently a
cowherd's wife (*The Tale of King Arthur*, 101/10–15):

> Anone the wyff was fette forth, which was a fayre houswyff. And there
> she answerde Merlion full womanly, and there she tolde the kynge and
> Merlion that whan she was a mayde and wente to mylke hir kyne, 'there
> mette with me a sterne knyght, and half be force he had my maydynhode.
> And at that tyme he begate my sonne Torre.'

Malory has here softened his French source, which represents Pellinore as
having entirely disregarded the maid's will, *u je vausisse ou non* (*Works*,
p.1326). Sidney's Cecropia shows no such faint-heartedness. She puts the
argument for violence to her son Amphialus, languishing in a hopeless love
for the heavenly Philoclea, with a brutal frankness (*Arcadia*, 1590; III.17.3):

> Tush, tush sonne (said *Cecropia*) if you say you love, but withall you
> feare; you feare lest you should offend; offend? & how know you, that
> you should offend? because she doth denie: denie? Now by my truth; if
> your sadnes would let me laugh, I could laugh hartily, to see that yet
> you are ignorant, that No, is no negative in a womans mouth. My sonne,
> beleeve me, a woman, speaking of women: a lovers modesty among us
> is much more praised, then liked  . . . above all, mark *Helen* daughter
> to *Jupiter*, who could never brooke her manerly-wooing *Menelaus*, but
> disdained his humblenes, & lothed his softnes. But so well she could
> like the force of enforcing *Paris*, that for him she could abide what
> might be abidden. But what? *Menelaus* takes hart; he recovers her by
> force; by force carries her home; by force injoies her; and she, who
> could never like him for serviceablenesse, ever after loved him for
> violence.[9]

Amphialus is interrupted by a messenger before he can answer these arguments. But Sidney knows that they require no answer. Their wickedness is
sufficiently vouched for by the wickedness of the one who delivers them. For
Gawain, too, there can be no compromise with such arguments even in a
qualified form (1498–1500):

8.  'Unless the remedy of at least some compulsion is first applied to take advantage of
    their modesty.' Reference is to the text and translation of P.G. Walsh, *Andreas
    Capellanus on Love* (London, 1982), pp. 222-23.
9.  Reference is to *The Prose Works of Sir Philip Sidney*, Volume I, *Arcadia*, 1590,
    edited by A. Feuillerat, reissued with minor corrections (Cambridge, 1969), p. 452.

> '3e, be God,' quoþ Gawayn, 'good is your speche,
> Bot þrete is vnþryuande in þede þer I lende,
> And vche gift þat is geuen not with goud wylle.'

The values of the pentangle forbid any possible use of force in winning a woman's love, whether lady or peasant, and Gawain's rebuttal of the lady's proposition is thus direct and forceful in itself. Gawain stands his ground here as does the boar against its adversary (see 1450–51, 1562–66, and 1582, and *The Master of Game*, p. 49), but at the same time he offers the lady no discourtesy (1501–7). The lady is obliged to retreat, and pretends in the process to be fearful of offending one who can take against such propositions in so decided a way (1508–9). She shifts her position now from that of teacher (1481–91) to that of pupil (1525–34). This is a stratagem that Gawain recognizes in his urbane reply (1535–39), and undermines by the effective use of the rhetorical device of *gradatio* (1540–45). Thus the lady's imposture is exposed and she is forced to break off the contest of the second day (1554–57). But for all the surface charm we are left in no doubt of the strenuousness of the moral struggle that has taken place (1549–50):

> Þus hym frayned þat fre, and fondet hym ofte,
> For to haf wonnen hym to wo3e, what-so scho þo3t ellez.

But, like the lord's killing of the boar (1583–96), Gawain's triumph on the second day is decisive (1551–53):

> Bot he defended hym so fayr þat no faut semed,
> Ne non euel on nawþer halue, nawþer þay wysten
>                  bot blysse.

On the third day the fox leads the huntsmen a merry dance, dodging and doubling back (1707–8), but when he thinks that he is safe he runs into more trouble (1709–14). He is forced into the open (1715–18), rebuked by the pursuing hounds (1719–25) and given no respite (1726–28). On the third day Gawain too is under attack from all sides. The lady now exploits her sexual charms to the full (1733–41), and rebukes the knight for sleeping in his bed (1742–47). This is doubly unfair, for Gawain is preoccupied by anxious fears of impending death (1748–54). He has to manoeuvre in this way and that to avoid the dangers that beset him, at once of unchastity, discourtesy, and infidelity (1770–75). He does not yield to unchastity either by admitting to a previous love (1788–91) or by acknowledging the lady's love in offering her a love-token (1805–7) or by accepting from her a love-token (1821–23). Nor has he been moved by the great value of the precious ring that she first offers

him (1817–20). His rejection of all the lady's blandishments and impor-
tunities is complete (1839–41):

> 'And þerfore, I pray yow, displese yow noȝt,
> And lettez be your bisinesse, for I bayþe hit yow neuer
>     to graunte.'

But, like Reynard before him, when he thinks that he has escaped from the
danger he finds himself in most deadly peril. The lady, like the *titleres* at
Reynard's tail (1726), presses relentlessly. Suddenly she shifts her ground,
and is prepared to vilify Gawain (1846–47) with a charge of covetousness of
which it is already apparent that he is free (1826–29). She appeals instead
(with unerring aim) to the knight's fears for his life (1849–54), and as he
struggles with the contending emotions of fear and relief (1855–58) she
prevails upon him to make that fateful promise which marks the limit of his
virtue (1863–65): 'þe leude hym acordez/ þat neuer wyȝe schulde hit wyt,
iwysse, bot þay twayne/for noȝte'. Thus Gawain is taken in the trap, for from
the contradiction of the promises thus made to the lady and the lord there is
no escape.


## III


The intricate and delicately balanced structure of *Sir Gawain* is nowhere
more evident than in the enclosing of the bedroom scenes within the hunting
scenes, and the parallel development of the action of the three days. The
repeated actions are not only significant in themselves, but also in the very
fact of being repeated. Each single action demands to be viewed in relation to
the larger pattern of which it is a part.[10] Now the question of the symbolic
value of the hunts ought not to be considered apart from the parallels that
exist between them in the progressive development of the fable. If one of the
hunts is symbolically significant, all three are likely to be symbolically

---

10. The general position is admirably stated by Burnley, *YES*, 3 (1973), p. 2: 'The co-
    occurrence of three seduction scenes with three hunting scenes has attracted the
    attention of every reader of the poem, and the almost unanimous desire to pair the
    scenes in some way can scarcely be ascribed to a universal aberration of sensibility.
    If, however, the scenes cannot be paired , then occurring as they do in a context of
    parallels, their evident deliberation must constitute a major flaw in an otherwise
    carefully constructed poem. The probability is, therefore, that a grand overall pattern
    is conceived in Fitt III whose moral significance unites in some way with the moral
    theme of the poem.' Unfortunately the ensuing discussion fails to do justice to the
    narrative details by means of which the respective hunting and bedroom scenes are
    linked.

significant; if two of the hunts are not symbolically significant, why should we assume that a third which is structurally parallel is symbolically divergent? Here is an aesthetic objection to Burrow's reading (*A Reading*, p. 98) in which he posits symbolic value on the third day only in violation of the poem's structure, and is led as a result to violate the moral significance of the poem by predicating cunning of Gawain (*A Reading*, p. 112). Our first principle, then, in respect of the poem's symbolism, is that we seek to identify a consistent symbolic relation between the hunting and bedroom scenes corresponding to the parallel narration of the events of the three days.

In the second place the symbolism of deer, boar, and fox is not to be pressed to the point of identity any more than the symbolism of the pentangle. To look for an identity between symbol and referent is to deny the very meaning of a symbol, which lies not in denotation but in suggestiveness. Judgment is always required of the reader in knowing how far and in what directions to press the potential significance of a symbol. To look for a symbolic identity between Gawain and the deer, boar, and fox respectively is an error of judgment, akin in many ways to that of those who insist upon reading allegorical works in terms of a one-for-one correspondence in the levels of meaning. In the present instance the judgmental error is based upon the elevation of character at the expense of fable, and the consequent imposition of a psychological frame of reference alien to the poet's exposition of his abstract, co-ordinating idea. If we are not to posit a deer-like timidity of Gawain on the first day, and a boar-like ferocity of him on the second day, by what imaginative logic are we to posit a fox-like cunning of him on the third day? Commentators who recoil from the ideas of timidity and ferocity as applied to Gawain should recoil also from the application to him of cunning, and for the same reason, namely its inaptness. The symbolism, as is only too evident in the case of the fox, has a moral value, but being moral it is generalized. We may contrast in this respect the symbol of the pentangle and its value of nobility or righteousness. The poet intends to apply this symbol directly to Gawain and he goes out of his way to do so, enforcing the relation with a syllogistic precision (623–35). The symbols of deer, boar, and fox are not fastened on Gawain in this way, and we must assume that the poet (no less than his modern readers) wishes to avoid the absurdity of doing so.

At the same time no reader can deny the attribution of cunning to the fox — 'so Reniarde watz wylé' (1728) — nor its relevance to the bedroom scene on the third day. It is a good point at which to examine the way in which the symbolism works. The fox is cunning, it is true, but no less cunning are the hounds that pursue him. And it is the cunning of the hounds that the poet first of all chooses to draw to our attention (1699–1700):

> Summe fel in þe fute þer þe fox bade,
> Traylez ofte a traueres bi traunt of her wyles.

It is clear that the symbolic value of cunning is diffused rather than concentrated; cunning is relevant to the fable at this point, not the cunning of any particular agent in it. The idea of cunning can be applied, therefore, with perfect consistency to the lady's actions. Thus of the fox it is said (1727):

> Ofte he watz runnen at, when he out *rayked*,

and shortly afterwards of the lady making her purposeful way to Gawain's bedroom (1735):

> Bot ros hir vp radly, *rayked* hir þeder.

The coincidence of terms here, linking the fox and the lady, is well designed by the poet to alert his audience to the moral significance of the events that he is about to describe. And again, whereas the fox is cunning, he can hardly be called cunning for seeking to avoid the blow from the hunter's sword. There is no living creature, cunning or simply prudent, that would not instinctively seek to save its life in this fashion.[11] But the notion of cunning has become so imprecisely generalized that Savage is able to characterize the death of the fox as follows:

> . . . the fox resorts to a bit of trickery, and that bit of trickery is the very cause of his undoing. The position of Gawain is the same: in his desire to avoid death from the impending blow, he resorts to trickery, and his recourse to duplicity proves the sole and only cause of his disgrace. Thus the two situations closely resemble one another.[12]

But the resemblance consists in the instinct for life itself. Gawain suddenly sees in the offer of the girdle the hope of escape from certain death, and in

11. A graphic instance of the animal instinct for life is given by Leonard Woolf, *The Journey Not the Arrival Matters: An Autobiography of the Years 1939-1969* (London, 1969), pp. 20-21:

   My bitch had five puppies and it was decided that she should be left with two to bring up and so it was for me to destroy three. In such circumstances it was an age-old custom to drown the day-old puppies in a pail of water. This I proceeded to do. Looked at casually, day-old puppies are little blind, squirming, undifferentiated objects or things. I put one of them in the bucket of water, and instantly an extraordinary, a terrible thing happened. This blind, amorphous thing began to fight desperately for its life, struggling, beating the water with its paws. I suddenly saw that it was an individual, that like me it was an 'I', that in its bucket of water it was experiencing what I would experience and fighting death, as I would fight death if I were drowning in the multitudinous seas.

12. H.L. Savage, 'The Significance of the Hunting Scenes in *Sir Gawain and the Green Knight*', *JEGP*, 27 (1928), 1-15 (p. 6).

grasping at that hope is undone by the lady's cunning (1859–63). If there is a direct moral comparison between Gawain and the fox it is with the fox as a thief, for the fox was 'ofte þef called' (1725) and Gawain in withholding the girdle from the lord is technically and objectively guilty of theft. The resemblance between Gawain and the fox can go no further, for the knight 'voyded of vche vylany' (634) is not to be characterized by cunning.[13] It is here above all that the reader needs to exercise some tact in not pressing an analogy beyond the bounds that a poet has devised for it.

Thus although the idea of cunning is obviously relevant to the action of the third day, it is limited and defined by that action and does not explain every part of that action. And in the same way, as we have seen, the caution of the deer and the fierceness of the boar are analogies that cannot be pressed beyond certain definite limits. Indeed, the moral issue of the third day is in fact for Gawain one of courage rather than cunning. The evidence for this is that the poet reminds us of Gawain's need for the help of the Virgin Mary (1768–69):

> Gret perile bitwene hem stod,
> Nif Maré of hir kny3t mynne.[14]

The immediate connection of the Virgin Mary is with the virtue of courage rather than chastity. This fact is established in the pentangle passage (644–50), and once again we must seek to do justice to the particularities of this poem (and especially to the matter belonging to its co-ordinating idea) rather than to more general considerations. Courage is necessary in the man who remains continent, for continence is nothing other than the resistance of evil passions, namely the desires and pleasures of touch. Moderation is above all most difficult in respect of these passions, and hence the virtue of temperance is principally concerned with them (Aquinas, *ST*, 2a 2ae 141.4). But since

13. The eloquence of Savage has undoubtedly been influential in the attribution of cunning to Gawain; compare also the beguiling formulation he makes in *JEGP*, 27 (1928), p. 5: 'On the third day, then, a false beast is roused in the forest, and a false man revealed in the castle; a sly fox is caught in the wood, a "sly fox" in the castle.' Not all critics, however, have been persuaded. L. Blenkner, OSB, 'The Three Hunts and Sir Gawain's Triple Fault', *American Benedictine Review*, 29 (1978), 227-46 notes that 'on the day of the fox, guileless Gawain is pointedly un-wily' (p. 239), and that 'there is . . . nothing tricky or devious in Gawain's acceptance of the girdle' (p. 243).

14. According to Davis (p. 121), following Hulbert and Knott, the intervention of Mary here constitutes yet another artistic blunder, for it interferes with the testing of Gawain at a crucial point. But the operation of human free will is a secondary cause concerned with contingent realities, and is dependent on the first cause which is God. The will cannot be the ultimate source of its own free acts (see Aquinas, *ST*, 1a 2ae 10.1 *ad* 1, and 10.4 *ad* 2).

temperance is the moderation of the desires and pleasures of touch, it is as a consequence also directed to the sorrows that result from the absence of such pleasures (*ST*, 2a 2ae 141.3). And it is in the endurance of these sorrows that the virtue of courage, or more particularly perseverance (*ST*, 2a 2ae 137.2 *ad* 1), is called for. It is hardly possible to overstate the courage that Gawain displays here, for he has at the same time to contend with fears for his life, and these fears undoubtedly make him more susceptible to the lady's charms. The reason is that the presence of strong emotion predisposes one to the arousal of other emotions. Thus a man moved by fear is more likely to be moved by love than a man who is not moved by fear.[15] Hence it is courage that Gawain shows when he responds decisively to the most powerful of the sexual temptations that the lady sets before him (1776):

'God schylde,' quoþ þe schalk, ' þat schal not befalle!'

And it is in respect of the virtue of courage that Gawain's moral fall corresponds to the fox's death. The fox in seeking to save his life from the blow of the hunter's sword retreats into the jaws of the pack of hounds (1898–1905). And Gawain, seeking to avoid death from the blow of the axe at the Green Chapel, falls into the trap cunningly laid for him by the lady (1855–67). No wonder he is later to rue upon the 'wyles of wymmen' (2415).

---

15. The relation of fear and love has been the subject of empirical testing. The experimental data are described by E. Berscheid and E. Walster in *Foundations of Interpersonal Attraction,* edited by T. L. Huston (New York and London, 1974), pp. 363-64. I owe this reference to Dr Margret Fine-Davis, Centre for Women's Studies, Trinity College, Dublin.

# CHAPTER SIX

# The Definition of Gawain's Sinfulness

## I

IN A POEM SO intricately constructed and coherently developed as *Sir Gawain* a single mistake in interpretation is liable to have far-reaching consequences. Such is the case in respect of the identification of *pité*, the final virtue of the fifth pentad, with its modern equivalent of 'pity', rather than with 'piety'. Tasso points to the importance of piety in the concept of chivalric perfection, and also perhaps to a reluctance to acknowledge it, when he writes that 'chi vuol formare l'idea d'un perfetto cavaliere, non so per qual cagione gli nieghi questa lode di pietà e di religione' (Mazzali, I, 193).[1] The issue of piety assumes central importance when we come to Gawain's confession of his sins immediately after the acceptance of the girdle (1876-84), and it is no surprise that this passage has become the centre of critical controversy.

Upon the hunting and bedroom scenes the poet has imposed the idea of righteousness as symbolized by the pentangle, and hence he illustrates among other virtues the virtue of piety. This is evident in the conduct of both Bertilak and Gawain. On three successive days Bertilak goes to mass before he sets off for the hunting-field (1135–36, 1414–16, and 1690):

> Ete a sop hastyly, when he hade herde masse,
> With bugle to bent-felde he buskez bylyue.

> So þat þe mete and þe masse watz metely delyuered,
> Þe douthe dressed to þe wod, er any day sprenged,
> to chace.

> After messe a morsel he and his men token.

On the first and second days Gawain also goes to mass (1309–11 and 1558), but on the third day he goes to confession (1876–84):

---

1. 'I do not know why anyone who wishes to form the idea of a perfect knight should deny him the commendation of piety and religion' (Cavalchini and Samuel, p. 39).

Syþen cheuely to þe chapel choses he þe waye,
Preuély aproched to a prest, and prayed hym þere
Þat he wolde lyste his lyf and lern hym better
How his sawle schulde be saued when he schuld seye heþen.
Þere he schrof hym schyrly and schewed his mysdedez,
Of þe more and þe mynne, and merci besechez,
And of absolucioun he on þe segge calles;
And he asoyled hym surely and sette hym so clene
As domezday schulde haf ben di3t on þe morn.[2]

The difference in Gawain's action on the third day is explained by the fact that he is in imminent danger of death. The poet significantly calls our attention to Gawain's anxious thoughts about the blow at the Green Chapel when the lady first enters his bedroom on this fateful third day (1750–54). Gawain's response to his justified fears of death is entirely proper, for in the Middle Ages the Church required a public confession of sins by those in expectation of death (*ST*, 3a *Suppl.*, 6.5):

> Et quia ea quae sunt de necessitate salutis, tenetur homo in hac vita implere, ideo si periculum mortis immineat, etiam per se loquendo, obligatur aliquis ad confessionem faciendam tunc . . .

> Moreover, since man is bound to fulfil in this life those things that are necessary for salvation, therefore, if he be in danger of death, he is bound, even absolutely, then and there to make his confession . . .[3]

It is necessary that sacramental confession should be made to a priest (*Suppl.*, 8.1). If circumstances make such a confession impossible, confession can in the hour of need be made to a layman (*Suppl.*, 8.2):

> . . . et ita etiam minister poenitentiae, cui confessio est facienda ex officio, est sacerdos; sed in necessitate etiam laicus vicem sacerdotis supplet, ut ei confessio fieri possit.

---

2.    On this passage compare *The Parlement of the Thre Ages*, 645-48:

> Ite ostendite vos sacerdotibus,
> To schryue 3ow full schirle, and schewe 3ow to prestis.
> Et ecce omnia munda sunt vobis,
> And 3e þat wronge wroghte schall worthen full clene.

3.    Reference is to *Divi Thomae Aquinatis Summa Theologica*, second edition (Rome, 1894), Volume V, *Tertiae Partis Supplementum*, translated by Fathers of the English Dominican Province (London, 1917).

In like manner the minister of Penance, to whom, in virtue of his office, confession should be made, is a priest; but in a case of necessity even a layman may take the place of a priest, and hear a person's confession.

The common occurrence of such a need accounts for the spread in the fifteenth century of the Latin treatises known generically as the *Ars Moriendi*, and also for its translation into English as *The Book of the Craft of Dying*. At the end of the century Caxton reflects the continuing importance of deathbed confession by his publication of two related treatises, *The Art and Craft to Know Well to Die* (1490) and the *Ars Moriendi* (?1491).[4] A central part of all these versions is the interrogation of the dying man; indeed *The Book of the Craft of Dying* and *The Art and Craft to Know Well to Die* contain two sets of interrogations, drawn respectively from St Anselm's *Admonitio Morienti* and Gerson's *Opusculum Tripertitum*.[5] If circumstances are such as to make public confession of any kind impossible, whether to priest or layman, true contrition with the intention of making confession is sufficient (*Suppl.*, 2.3 *sed contra* and 6.1):

> Nullum peccatum dimittitur, nisi quis justificetur: sed ad justificationem requiritur contritio . . .

> . . . no sin is forgiven a man unless he be justified. But justification requires contrition . . .

> Et ideo ad culpae remissionem et actualis, et originalis requiritur sacramentum Ecclesiae, vel actu susceptum, vel saltem voto, quando articulus necessitatis, non contemptus, sacramentum excludit . . .

> Wherefore for the remission of both actual and original sin, a sacrament of the Church is necessary, received either actually, or at least in desire, when a man fails to receive the sacrament actually, through an unavoidable obstacle, and not through contempt.

There is no question at this time of justification by faith alone. Gawain therefore fulfils a religious obligation when he makes a complete confession of his sins on the eve of his departure from Bertilak's castle. In his confession, therefore, we have an outstanding example of his piety. But it is no more than we should expect in a knight so aptly symbolized by the device of the pentangle on his shield and coat armour. Thus we see at this point in the

4.  Texts of the three English translations are made available in my unpublished doctoral thesis, 'A Critical Edition of Caxton's *The Art and Craft to Know Well to Die* and *Ars Moriendi* together with the Antecedent Manuscript Material', 2 vols (University of Oxford, 1973).
5.  See Morgan, 'A Critical Edition', II, 129-31.

narrative an importance attached to piety that corresponds to the importance claimed for it in the pentangle passage. It is indeed central to the poet's moral and spiritual exposition.

Moral acts are the products of free and deliberate movements of the will, and their corresponding habits or virtues presuppose such freedom and deliberation. An act that is grudging cannot for that reason be described as morally good. Virtue requires not only that we do what is good, but that we do it by reason of its goodness. The mark of a virtuous act, therefore, is that it is performed promptly and with pleasure (*ST*, 1a 2ae 107.4). Gawain's attendance at mass and at confession amounts to more than a religious formality. They are the moral acts of the virtue of piety, and so the poet observes of them that they are performed with promptness and pleasure (1309–11, 1558, and 1872–76):

> And he ryches hym to ryse and rapes hym sone,
> Clepes to his chamberlayn, choses his wede,
> Boȝez forth, quen he watz boun, blyþely to masse.

> Then ruþes hym þe renk and ryses to þe masse.

> When ho watz gon, Sir Gawayn gerez hym sone,
> Rises and riches hym in araye noble,
> Lays vp þe luf-lace þe lady hym raȝt,
> Hid hit ful holdely, þer he hit eft fonde.
> Syþen cheuely to þe chapel choses he þe waye . . .

Such promptness on Gawain's part has reference to more than the habit of virtue in general, but is the special mark of the act of devotion, the internal act of the virtue of religion, that is, in our sense, piety (*ST*,2a 2ae 82.1):

> Unde devotio nihil aliud esse videtur quam *voluntas quaedam prompte tradendi se ad ea quae pertinent ad Dei famulatum*. Unde dicitur (Exodus, 35.20), quod *multitudo filiorum Israel obtulit mente promptissima atque devota primitias Domino.*

> Devotion, therefore, is nothing other than the will to give oneself promptly to those things that pertain to the service of God. Hence, it is written, *everyone offered first fruits to God with a most prompt and ready heart.*

The importance of promptness in carrying out religious observances is signified in the words that Gawain uses in his anxious prayer to God and the Virgin Mary on Christmas Eve (753–58):

> And þerfore sykyng he sayde, 'I beseche þe, lorde,
> And Mary, þat is myldest moder so dere,
> Of sum herber þer *heȝly* I myȝt here masse,
> Ande þy matynez to-morne, mekely I ask,
> And þerto *prestly* I pray my pater and aue
>            and crede.'

A fundamental moral principle, derived from Aristotle's *Ethics*, is that the virtues are interconnected. The principle is explained by Aristotle in terms of the possession of the virtue of prudence (*Ethics*, VI.13):

> But in this way we may also refute the dialectical argument whereby it might be contended that the virtues exist in separation from each other; the same man, it might be said, is not best equipped by nature for all the virtues, so that he will have already acquired one when he has not yet acquired another. This is possible in respect of the natural virtues, but not in respect of those in respect of which a man is called without qualification good; for with the presence of the one quality, practical wisdom (i.e. prudence), will be given all the virtues.[6]

It is this conception of the virtues as interconnected, as we have seen, that the symbolism of the pentangle is above all designed to express. Piety as a virtue, therefore, is connected with other moral virtues, and indeed it is introduced by the poet immediately in conjunction with four other virtues — generosity, fidelity, chastity, and modesty — as constituting a fifth group of fives (651–55). If Gawain's confession to the priest is an act of piety, it cannot be taken to imply the simultaneous commission of sin. And here we confront a seemingly intractable moral difficulty, namely the reconciliation of the fact of piety with the fact of infidelity. The poet has shown with a characteristic moral precision that on the third day Gawain is brought through fear for his life to fall short in fidelity. The moral situation is accurately stated by the Green Knight himself in the judgment scene of Fitt IV (2366–68):

> Bot here yow lakked a lyttel, sir, and lewté yow wonted;
> Bot þat watz for no wylyde werke, ne wowyng nauþer,
> Bot for ȝe lufed your lyf; þe lasse I yow blame.

By pledging to the lady that he will conceal the girdle from her lord, Gawain has entered into two mutually incompatible agreements, for by the Exchange

---

6.  Reference to the *Ethica Nicomachea* is to the translation of W.D. Ross, revised by
    J.O. Urmson, in *The Works of Aristotle*, edited by W.D. Ross, Volume IX (Oxford,
    1975).

of Winnings agreement he is already obliged to hand over all his gains to the lord (and the girdle is undeniably such a gain). If Gawain confesses his sin of infidelity, he will undoubtedly be required to make restitution by way of satisfaction. And yet there is no suggestion in the poem of any attempt to do so.

Those scholars who recognize in Gawain's confession of his sins an act of piety are led as a result to deny the gravity of the act of withholding the girdle in the Exchange of Winnings agreement (the resultant infidelity of the fidelity to the promise to the lady to conceal the girdle). According to Davis (p. 123) the withholding of the girdle is not to be considered a sin at all:

> The poet evidently did not regard the retention of the girdle as one of Gawain's 'mysdedez, þe more and þe mynne', which required to be confessed.

T. P. Dunning likewise finds no special moral difficulty to be posed here, and reduces Gawain's retention of the girdle to nothing more than a social solecism:

> To 'orthodox imaginative men of the fourteenth century', the situation would seem clear enough: the girdle, as the lady assured Gawain, was not of any great material value (1847– 8); the bargain with his host was, as Professor Smithers calls it, 'sportive' (M.Æ. xxxii (1963), 175); Gawain's resolve to retain the girdle was a yielding to superstition to which even the best of Christians are sometimes prone, but he certainly did not construe this resolve as a sin, worthy of being mentioned in confession. It was, however, a social solecism, as the Green Knight will rub in later (though he excuses him) . . . [7]

But this is a trivialisation of the moral issues of the poem, and Burrow is right to object to it as such (*A Reading*, p. 106):

> . . . notice that the particular 'chivalric virtue' in question here, fidelity to the pledged word, shares its name with the whole Christian-chivalric complex to which it belongs — both are 'trawþe'. Are we to believe that Gawain's 'untrawþe' (narrow chivalric sense) involves no more than a marginal disturbance of his (broad sense) 'trawþe'? Surely not. If Gawain's integrity, his virtue, is 'trawþe' (and the poet chose the word), then 'untrawþe' is to be looked to. It is not, *prima facie* at least, a trivial matter.

7.   T.P. Dunning, Review of J.A. Burrow, *A Reading of Sir Gawain and the Green Knight* (London, 1965), *RES*, NS, 18 (1967), 58-60 (p. 59).

The interconnection of the virtues, and in the present case the linking of *fela₃schyp* and *pité* in the same group of five virtues, does not admit of the moral reduction of infidelity to a social solecism.

Those scholars who see in Gawain's retention of the girdle in the Exchange of Winnings agreement the sin of infidelity are led in contradiction of the poet's explicit words (1876–84) to call into question the piety of his confession. The confession is to be seen rather as a false confession, an act of impiety. Gollancz tells us (p.123) that 'though the poet does not notice it, Gawain makes a sacrilegious confession', and Burrow claims (*A Reading*, p.109) that Gawain's confession 'must be seen as invalid — not a remedy, but a symptom of his fall from grace'. In both these cases there is a failure to appreciate the seriousness of the moral offence. There is a hierarchy of sins as well as of virtues, and the gravest of sins are those committed directly against God (*ST*, la 2ae 73.3):

> . . . peccatum quod est circa ipsam substantiam hominis, sicut homicidium est gravius peccato quod est circa res exteriores, sicut furtum; et adhuc est gravius peccatum quod immediate contra Deum committitur, sicut infidelitas, blasphemia et hujusmodi. Et in ordine quorumlibet horum peccatorum, unum peccatum est gravius altero secundum quod est circa aliquid principalius vel minus principale.

> . . . sins which affect the very being of a man such as homicide are worse than sins which affect an exterior good, e.g. theft; and more serious still are those sins which are immediately against God, as infidelity, blasphemy, etc. And in each of these basic areas of sin, one sin will be worse than another if its object is more important than that of another.

The response of pious Moslems to the blasphemy of Salman Rushdie's *Satanic Verses* may indicate to uncomprehending modern readers the horror that would have been felt by a medieval Christian at a sacrilegious confession. The *Gawain*-poet is lucid and subtle in his moral analysis. It is unthinkable that he would fail to detect an act of theft or of murder on the part of his hero, and it is even less likely that he would have failed to detect an act of sacrilege. The assumption of a false confession implicitly devalues the meaning of piety, and this is evident in Burrow's own reconstruction of Gawain's act as an act of piety (*A Reading*, p.105):

> So Gawain approaches his priest, not because he has just imperilled his soul by agreeing to hide the girdle, but because he thinks he is to die next morning. He simply takes a convenient opportunity to do what any Christian should do when in peril of death. It is a routine visit.

Here piety is robbed of its essential meaning as a moral act, for the exercise of virtue can never be merely a routine matter. But if Gawain were guilty of impiety his sin would cry out for recognition. This is not only because of its intrinsic seriousness. The poem as a whole is ordered to the idea of righteousness as it is defined in the pentangle passage, and an act of impiety would be the violation of a virtue that is given exceptional emphasis as the final virtue of the final group of virtues. But in the judgment scene of Fitt IV, where cowardice, covetousness, and infidelity are mentioned and indeed insisted upon (2366–68, 2373–75, 2378–84, and 2505–12), there is no mention of an act of sacrilege.

The only possible position that does justice to the moral argument of the poem is one that recognizes the retention of the girdle as involving an act of infidelity and the confession in the face of imminent death as an act of piety. Gawain's infidelity and piety can be reconciled on the assumption that Gawain, unlike the reader of the poem, is blind to the moral implications of his act when he makes his promise to the lady to conceal the girdle from her lord. And the moral situation that the poet describes is such as to make this an entirely reasonable assumption. Indeed self-knowledge in a sinner is always difficult to achieve; as the psalm (18.13) has it:

Delicta quis intelligit? Ab occultis meis munda me.

Who can understand sins? from my secret ones cleanse me, O Lord.

The need for self-knowledge in the penitent sinner is symbolized by the first of the three steps at the entrance to Purgatory proper in *Purgatorio*, IX.94–96:

Là ne venimmo; e lo scaglion primaio
  bianco marmo era sì pulito e terso
  ch'io mi specchiai in esso qual io paio.

We came on then, and the first step was white marble so smooth and clear that I mirrored myself in it in my true likeness.[8]

---

8.  See P. Armour, *The Door of Purgatory: A Study of Multiple Symbolism in Dante's Purgatorio* (Oxford, 1983). Armour rejects the sacramental interpretation of the three steps as representing contrition, confession, and satisfaction in favour of the moral interpretation by which the three steps represent self-knowledge, the sorrow of contrition, and shame (pp. 1-34). Accordingly, the fictional Dante's own experience of the penitential process begins with the self-knowledge that leads to shame (*Purg.*, XXX. 76-78):

Li occhi mi cadder giù nel chiaro fonte;
  ma, veggendomi in esso, i trassi all'erba,
  tanta vergogna mi gravò la fronte.

My eyes fell down to the clear fount, but, seeing myself in it, I drew them back to the grass, so great shame weighed on my brow.

Sin, then, is characteristically the product not of knowledge, but of ignorance. This is the opinion of Socrates, and as Aquinas observes it contains a measure of the truth (*ST*, la 2ae 77.2):

> In quo quidem aliqualiter recte sapiebat. Quia cum voluntas sit boni vel apparentis boni, nunquam voluntas in malum moveretur nisi id quod non est bonum aliqualiter rationi bonum appareret: et propter hoc voluntas nunquam in malum tenderet, nisi cum aliqua ignorantia vel errore rationis. Unde dicitur *Prov., Errant qui operantur malum.*

> There is something to be said for this opinion. Since the object of the will is the good, or at least the apparent good, the will is never attracted by evil unless it appears to have an aspect of good about it, so that the will never chooses evil except by reason of ignorance or error. Thus it says in *Proverbs, Do not those who plot evil go astray?*

But Aristotle shows in the *Ethics* that it is possible for a man to do what he knows is not good for him. Here Aristotle distinguishes between knowledge possessed and exercised, and knowledge that is possessed but not exercised. Man sins through ignorance by failing to exercise the knowledge that he possesses of what is good for him (*Ethics*, VII. 3):

> But (a), since we use the word 'know' in two senses (for both  the man who has knowledge but is not using it and he who is using it are said to know), it *will* make a difference whether, when a man does what he should not, he has the knowledge but is not exercising it, or *is* exercising it; for the latter seems strange, but not the former.

Aquinas distinguishes three kinds of sin, in so far as there is a defect of reason (sin of ignorance), a defect of the sensitive appetite (sin of passion), and a defect of the will (sin of malice). Although the sin of ignorance is the term specifically applied to acts in which there is a defect of reason, all three kinds of sinful act involve ignorance of some sort (*ST*, la 2ae 78.1 ad l):

> Ad primum ergo dicendum quod ignorantia quandoque quidem excludit scientiam qua aliquis simpliciter scit hoc esse malum quod agitur: et tunc dicitur ex ignorantia peccare. Quandoque autem excludit scientiam qua homo scit hoc nunc esse malum: sicut cum ex passione peccatur. Quandoque autem excludit scientiam qua aliquis scit hoc malum non sustinendum esse propter consecutionem illius boni, scit tamen simpliciter hoc esse malum: et sic dicitur ignorare qui ex certa malitia peccat.

Sinning out of ignorance means total unawareness that a thing is evil. Sometimes ignorance involves only temporary unawareness that a given thing is here and now evil, and this is what happens when a man sins under the impact of emotion. Sometimes, however, a man fails to consider that the loss suffered is not worth the gain even though he knows full well that the loss is itself evil, and in this case ignorance is compatible with resolute malice.

Gawain's piety in confession is irreconcilable with his act of infidelity only on the assumption of a sin of malice in which the simple knowledge of evil is present.[9] But the poet has made it clear that Gawain's sin stems from passion. Not only does the poet show us the hero tormented by fears on the third day of the Exchange of Winnings agreement (1750–54), but he explains also Gawain's motive in accepting the lady's offer of the girdle (1855–58):

> Þen kest þe kny3t, and hit come to his hert
> Hit were a juel for þe jopardé þat hym iugged were:
> When he acheued to þe chapel his chek for to fech,
> My3t he haf slypped to be vnslayn, þe sle3t were noble.

Gawain's sin is a sin of passion, and the ignorance which characterizes it is ignorance of the particular knowledge that can and should be derived from universal knowledge. Passion can prevent a man from drawing a correct conclusion from universal knowledge, but instead can direct his attention to a universal idea that is consistent with it. The Aristotelian argument is formulated by Aquinas as follows (*ST*, 1a 2ae 77.2 *ad* 4):

> Unde Philosophus dicit in *Ethic.*, quod syllogismus incontinentis habet quatuor propositiones, duas universales: quarum una est rationis, puta *nullam fornicationem esse committendam*; alia est passionis, puta *delectationem esse sectandam*. Passio igitur ligat rationem ne assumat et concludat sub prima; unde, ea durante, assumit et concludit sub secunda.

> Thus Aristotle writes that the incontinent man forms a syllogism from four propositions of which two are universal, e.g. one from reason that says *fornication is to be avoided*; and another from emotion that says

9. In his reconstruction of Gawain's confession in 'The Two Confession Scenes in *Sir Gawain and the Green Knight*', *Modern Philology*, 57 (1959), 73-79, Burrow explicitly attributes to Gawain a deliberation in his sinning: 'He goes to confession, rather than to Mass, because he realizes that he has sinned in agreeing to conceal the gift of the girdle from Bertilak, against his promise; but, though, presumably, he confesses this, he neither makes restitution . . . by returning the girdle nor resolves to sin no more' (p. 75).

*pleasure is to be sought after*. Accordingly, emotion hinders reason lest it draw a conclusion from the former and at the same time moves one to conclude from the latter.

This reasoning can be directly applied to Gawain's case. The first universal proposition of which Gawain has knowledge is that all winnings are to be exchanged. But he fails to draw from it the particular proposition that the girdle is a winning to be exchanged because he is hindered from doing so by fear. The second universal proposition of which he has knowledge is that a device that would preserve his life would be worthy of possession. Gawain is inclined towards this universal proposition by fear and so, being unhindered by fear in respect of it, draws from it the correct conclusion, namely that the girdle is such a device and hence worthy to be possessed. The lady cunningly exploits Gawain's temporary moral disarray, and represents the retention of the girdle as an act of virtue, namely the keeping of a pledge.

We cannot say, therefore, that Gawain goes to confession in a state of knowledge. Rather he goes in ignorance of the particular knowledge that it is unlawful for him to retain possession of the girdle. But confession is an act of virtue in so far as it is a true profession of that which a man has on his conscience (*Suppl.*, 7.2):

> Haec autem conditio ad virtutem pertinet, ut aliquis ore confiteatur, quod corde tenet; et ideo confessio est bonum ex genere, et est actus virtutis.

> Now to express in words what one has in one's thoughts is a condition of virtue; and, consequently, confession is a good thing generically, and is an act of virtue.

Now a true profession of a sin of which one is ignorant is not possible. Moreover, a complete account of one's sins will always be difficult because of the pervasive reality of sin, and many sins will have been simply forgotten. But forgetfulness does not necessarily imply a lack of sincerity in confession (*Suppl.*, 10.5 *ad* 4):

> . . . sed oblivio de actu peccati habet ignorantiam facti, et ideo excusat a peccato fictionis in confessione, quod fructum absolutionis, et confessionis impedit.

> Now forgetfulness of an act of sin comes under the head of ignorance of fact, wherefore it excuses from the sin of insincerity in confession, which is an obstacle to the fruit of absolution and confession.

A general confession is sufficient for mortal sins that have been forgotten (*Suppl.*, 10.5 *sed contra*):

. . . sed ille qui confitetur omnia peccata, quae scit, accedit ad Deum, quantum potest: plus autem ab eo requiri non potest; ergo non confundetur, ut repulsam patiatur, sed veniam consequetur.

Now he who confesses all the sins of which he is conscious, approaches to God as much as he can: nor can more be required of him. Therefore he will not be confounded by being repelled, but will be forgiven.

Thus provision is made for general confession in a treatise such as *The Book of the Craft of Dying*. The third interrogation of the Gersonian set ends as follows (*BCD*, 34/8–10):

Desirest thou also in thyn hert to haue verray knowynge of alle (the) offenses that thou hast doo ayenst God and foryete, to haue special repentaunce of hem alle?

The *Gawain*-poet leads us to understand that Gawain makes a sincere confession. He does what is possible for one who is ignorant of the particular knowledge that defines his sin. He must, therefore, have made a general as well as a particular confession of his sins.[10]

Passion does not excuse from sin altogether, unless it rules out entirely the voluntariness of an act, as in those who become mad through love or fear. But Gawain is not so moved by fear as to have lost the use of reason altogether (1866–67):

He þonkked hir oft ful swyþe,
Ful þro with hert and þoȝt.

10. Spearing justly observes that 'it is difficult not to feel that if we were to understand that Gawain was deliberately concealing what he knew to be a sin then the poet would have given us some insight into his consciousness at this point, in order to make the matter clear' (p. 225). The observation is developed by Davenport in such a way as to show the positive moral import it has for Gawain's conduct: 'the poet most significantly chooses to withdraw knowledge of Gawain's inner mind in the scenes immediately after his acceptance of the green belt, so that we are shown his going to confession, his mirth, and the last exchange of winnings, from outside. These acts exist in the poem as a performance of virtue, a completely convincing appearance of truth' (p. 189). The uncertain knowledge of sin in the sinner seeking expurgation is expressed by Agatha to Harry in T.S. Eliot's *The Family Reunion*, Part II, Scene II:

It is possible that you have not known what sin
You shall expiate, or whose, or why. It is certain
That the knowledge of it must precede the expiation.
It is possible that sin may strain and struggle
In its dark instinctive birth, to come to consciousness
And so find expurgation.

Ignorance of the moral status of the act of retaining the girdle does not therefore excuse from sin (*ST*, 1a 2ae 77.7 *ad* 2):

> Ad secundum dicendum quod ignorantia particularis quae totaliter excusat, est ignorantia circumstantiae quam quidem quis scire non potest, . . . Sed passio causat ignorantiam juris in particulari, dum impedit applicationem communis scientiae ad particularem actum. Quam quidem passionem ratio repellere potest . . .

> The ignorance of concrete fact which totally excuses from sin . . . is ignorance of a circumstance which could not possibly be foreseen. A highly emotional state causes one to be unaware of the particular application of a general principle, which is a detail of law rather than of fact. A reasonable man can and should withstand the influence of such emotions . . .

But passion does diminish the sinfulness of an act if it precedes that act (*ST*, 1a 2ae 77.6):

> Si igitur accipiatur passio secundum quod praecedit actum peccati, sic necesse est quod diminuat peccatum.

> When emotion precedes sin, it necessarily diminishes sinfulness.

Thus Gawain's sin in retaining the girdle is a mortal sin generically, but becomes venial through the weakness that results from the fear of death. It is to be classified as venial from the cause.[11] This is the position adopted by the Green Knight himself in the judgment scene of Fitt IV (2367–68):

> Bot þat watz for no wylyde werke, ne wowyng nauþer,
> Bot for ȝe lufed your lyf; þe lasse I yow blame.

---

11.  This conclusion is in accordance with that arrived at independently by other scholars. Thus Levy, 'Gawain's Spiritual Journey' comments that 'from a strictly theological point of view, Gawain's "sin" would have to be considered venial, for Gawain was caught in a dilemma, and his choice was thus not entirely voluntary' (p. l02, n. 54). P. J. C. Field, 'A Rereading of *Sir Gawain and the Green Knight*', *Studies in Philology*, 68 (l971), 255-69 concludes that 'breaking a secular promise over a possibly trivial matter in extenuating circumstances is a much less serious fault than committing adultery with no such excuse' and that the juxtaposition of the two temptations 'seems to put Gawain's lapse into perspective, and to place it firmly as a venial sin' (p. 269). Similarly L. Blenkner, OSB, ' The Three Hunts and Sir Gawain's Triple Fault', *American Benedictine Review*, 29 (l978), 227-46 comments that 'the hero does not deliberately sin; he tacitly consents to keep the girdle, but because he is ignorant he is not aware it is sin, and so his act of iniquity is a venial sin' (p. 231, n.5).

The ease and lucidity with which the *Gawain*-poet expresses a complex moral argument in a continuous narrative are made possible by an assumed foundation of Scholastic moral philosophy on which such an argument rests. Misinterpretation can result when the modern critic is unfamiliar with this philosophical foundation, as in the case of the confession scene. We need also at this point to consider some fundamental Scholastic principles about the goodness of human acts, for these have a direct bearing upon the poet's definition of Gawain's sinfulness.

There are two related activities involved in the creation of a human act. There is the interior act of the will, that is, the very act of willing elicited by the will itself, and there is the exterior act, that is, the determination of the will by its interior act results in the exterior act commanded by the will. Both the interior act of will and the exterior act have their proper objects. The proper object of the interior act of will is the end, and the proper object of the exterior act is the object itself with which it is engaged (*ST*, 1a 2ae 18.6):

> In actu autem voluntario invenitur duplex actus, scilicet actus interior voluntatis, et actus exterior; et uterque horum actuum habet suum objectum. Finis autem proprie est objectum interioris actus voluntarii, id autem circa quod est actio exterior est objectum ejus. Sicut igitur actus exterior accipit speciem ab objecto circa quod est, ita actus interior voluntatis accipit speciem a fine sicut a proprio objecto.

> Now we find a double activity here, namely the will's own internal activity and its externalized activity; and each of these has its objective. Strictly speaking the end intended is the objective for the will's internal act, while the objective for the external act is what it is engaged with. As the external act gets its specific character from the objective with which it is concerned so the internal gets its specific character from the end intended, this being its proper objective.

In accordance with this distinction an act can be said to be willed formally in relation to its end, and materially in relation to its object (*ST*, la 2ae 18.6):

> Et ideo actus humani species formaliter consideratur secundum finem, materialiter autem secundum objectum exterioris actus. Unde Philosophus dicit in *Ethic.*, quod ille qui furatur ut committat adulterium est per se loquendo magis adulter quam fur.

> Hence the specific character of human acts is assessed as to its form by the end intended and as to its matter by the objective of the external

deed. That is why Aristotle observes that *he who steals in order to commit adultery is directly more adulterer than thief.*

It is to be noted, therefore, that the sinner is responsible for both the formal and material sinfulness of an act, and this distinction becomes important in Gawain's specification of his own sinfulness in Fitt IV. In the poet's analysis of Gawain's conduct we need to be aware both of its formal and material dimensions. But we should not in the process elevate the intention of the agent above the objective nature of the act. The goodness in an exterior act derives from its object, and is not a function of the will. Theft, for example, as the taking of another's property is wrong in itself, independently of the intention of the agent. To suppose otherwise is to argue for a mere subjective basis for good and evil, and Aquinas is not willing to allow moral activity to be reduced in this way (*ST*, 1a 2ae 18.2):

> Et ideo sicut prima bonitas rei naturalis attenditur ex sua forma, quae dat speciem ei, ita et prima bonitas actus moralis attenditur ex objecto convenienti . . .

> Hence as the basic goodness of a natural thing is provided by its form, which makes it the kind of thing it is, so also the basic goodness of a moral act is provided by the befitting objective on which it is set . . .

Armed with these distinctions we may proceed to a further examination of Gawain's conduct in the crucial scenes of Fitts III and IV. And we shall see that the poet's representation of the conduct is characteristically lucid and precise.

Gawain's acceptance of the girdle offered to him by the lady is the last in a series of acts that progressively define his moral condition. Gawain values his courtesy even to the point of public misrepresentation of it (1658–63), but courtesy stops short of yielding to the sins of unchastity and infidelity (1770–75). Indeed Gawain is not prepared to acquiesce in the lady's suggestion that he has rejected her because of his love for another (1779–84). To do so would be to call into question the virtue of chastity, for chastity is in itself a sufficient ground for rejection of the lady's advances, irrespective of any other moral consideration whatsoever. This is perhaps not an attractive moral argument in our own age, but chastity as a virtue pursued for its own sake is rare at any time, as we may gather from the words of Spenser's Squire of Dames (*FQ*, III. 7.60):

> Safe her, I neuer any woman found,
>     That chastity did for it selfe embrace,
>     But were for other causes firme and sound;

> Either for want of handsome time and place,
> Or else for feare of shame and fowle disgrace.

It is the purpose of the *Gawain*-poet here to show that Gawain is firm and sound for the virtue of chastity itself. This is the point of the invocation of the apostle St John, for St John was revered as an example of celibacy (1788–91):

> Þe knyʒt sayde, 'Be sayn Jon,'
> And smeþely con he smyle,
> 'In fayth I welde riʒt non,
> Ne non wil welde þe quile'.

Chastity does not imply the absence of feeling but the control of feeling. The very demonstration of the virtue of chastity has involved the exertion of a great moral effort on Gawain's part, aided by the grace he receives from the Virgin Mary (1768–69), and it is softened by a consideration for the lady's own feelings in the expression of a gentle and compassionate smile (1789). The lady represents herself as a true unrequited lover, and so destined to a life of bitter unrelieved sorrow (1794–95). But she cannot by this stratagem induce Gawain to give her a gift as a keepsake, since such a keepsake would cast doubt upon the chasteness of his love for her and would be in itself dishonourable (1805–7). It is not by chance that the lady specifies Gawain's glove as a keepsake, for the glove has a possible sexual significance (1799–1800):

> Gif me sumquat of þy gifte, þi gloue if hit were,
> Þat I may mynne on þe, mon, my mournyng to lassen.

Criseyde's betrayal of Troilus is thus significantly prefaced by the giving of her glove to Diomede (*TC*, V. 1012–13):

> And after this, the sothe for to seyn,
> Hire glove he took, of which he was ful feyn. [12]

Gawain turns the discussion away from the gift of a glove, which he recognizes as a dishonourable act (1806–7), towards an apology for his inability to give an expensive gift that would truly be worthy of her (1808–9):

> And I am here an erande in erdez vncouþe,
> And haue no men wyth no malez with menskful þingez.

12. See the comment of C. Wood, *The Elements of Chaucer's Troilus* (Durham, N. C., 1984), pp. 102 and 187, n.6.

The distinction that he makes here is between an implicit acknowledgment of love and the explicit offering of a gift that any guest would consider fitting for his hostess.[13] But the lady is undeterred, and offers Gawain a gift in her own right, but Gawain rejects it, for the same argument that prevents him from offering a gift also prevents him from accepting one (1822–23). The lady then affects to believe that it is the costliness of the ring and not its symbolic import that has led Gawain to reject it (1826–29). She succeeds only in provoking the most emphatic rejection of an offer that it is possible for a poet to contrive (1836–38):

> And he nay þat he nolde neghe in no wyse
> Nauþer golde ne garysoun, er God hym grace sende
> To acheue to þe chaunce þat he hade chosen þere.[14]

There can be no doubt that in the scene between Gawain and the lady up to this point the poet intends us to see his hero in the most admirable light. He is zealous in the defence of his chastity, and resolute also in the defence of the rights of his host by turning aside from the sin of adultery. He laments his present incapacity to be generous (1808–12), but is unmoved by covetousness of the precious ring that the lady offers him as her gift (1817–20). And all the time he strives to maintain his reputation for courtesy, save in so far as courtesy in itself becomes prejudicial to acts of virtue.

It is by successive acts of virtue that the poet proceeds to the one sinful act by which Gawain's human imperfection is defined. The lady now shows her quality in entirely shifting the ground of her attack, for by doing so she is able to attribute to Gawain a covetousness that is the product only of her own suggestion (1846–47):

> 'Now forsake ȝe þis silke,' sayde þe burde þenne,
> 'For hit is symple in hitself? And so hit wel semez.'

She now takes advantage of a complication in the moral environment that results from the enclosing of the Exchange of Winnings agreement within the Beheading Game, for Gawain is beset by fears of impending death from the return blow. The poet has carefully drawn our attention to these fears at the

13. The distinction is not perceived by Spearing, and accordingly he misrepresents Gawain's words and intentions. Gawain's 'praise of the lady's efforts becomes positively patronizing' and '*his* honour is obviously in his mind too' (p. 211).

14. D. Burnley, *The Language of Chaucer* (London, 1989) describes such an accumulation of negatives in the phrase 'negative support', and explains it by the fact that 'each negating item is mutually supportive of the others in clarifying the total negative character of the clause' (p. 60). The purpose of such multiple negation is to add intensity to the utterance.

beginning of this third moral confrontation between Gawain and the lady (1750–54):

> In dreʒ droupyng of dreme draueled þat noble,
> As mon þat watz in mornyng of mony þro þoʒtes,
> How þat destiné schulde þat day dele hym his wyrde
> At þe grene chapel, when he þe gome metes,
> And bihoues his buffet abide withoute debate more.

And it is to these fears that the lady successfully appeals. She puts it to Gawain that by accepting the girdle he will preserve his life (1851–54); it is a proposition to which his fears readily lead him to assent (1855–58). Once she has secured her advantage, the lady does not fail to press it home. She begs the knight not only to accept the girdle, but faithfully to conceal it from her lord (1862–63). The knight agrees to do so (1863–65):

> . . . þe leude hym acordez
> Þat neuer wyʒe schulde hit wyt, iwysse, bot þay twayne
> for noʒte.

And we see that he is indeed faithful to his word, for he 'hid hit ful holdely' (1875). But he is by now compromised, for no knight can maintain faith between two irreconcilable pledges.

The poet's clarity in his representation of these moral issues in the temptations is reinforced throughout the rest of the narrative, so that we need be in no doubt as to what are Gawain's motives for his actions and what are not his motives. We may proceed to specify these motives in terms of covetousness, fidelity, and fear. First of all it is clear that Gawain is not motivated by covetousness, for he rejects the ring 'worth wele ful hoge' (1820) offered to him by the lady. Further, the poet reminds us that Gawain was not attracted to the girdle because of its costliness when he fastens it round his waist over his surcoat before setting out for the Green Chapel (2037–39):

> Bot wered not þis ilk wyʒe for wele þis gordel,
> For pryde of þe pendauntez, þaʒ polyst þay were,
> And þaʒ þe glyterande golde glent vpon endez.

Moreover, in his judgment of Gawain's conduct, the Green Knight too recognizes that covetousness was not a motive (2367):

> Bot þat watz for no wylyde werke, . . .

Secondly, it is clear that Gawain is moved by a deep regard for the pledged word, and shares the knightly perspective of an Arveragus that 'trouthe is the hyeste thyng that man may kepe' (*CT*, F 1479). His fidelity to his pledged word in honouring the Exchange of Winnings agreement is evident on the first two days (1385–97, and 1637–43), and also, up to a not insignificant point, on the third day as well (1932–41). He is faithful too in honouring the appointment at the Green Chapel in accordance with the terms of the Beheading Game, and his good faith in so doing is acknowledged by the Green Knight (2237–41). He is careful not to compromise his pledge to the Green Knight in the Beheading Game in accepting fresh obligations on the third day of the Exchange of Winnings agreement (1670–85). Even in concealing the girdle, as we have seen, Gawain is faithful to a pledge (1874–75). Thirdly, there can be no doubt that Gawain yields to the lady's importunity in pressing upon him the girdle because he recognizes its value as a means of saving his life (1851–61). The poet reminds us that the reason why Gawain wears the girdle over his coat armour in setting out for the final journey to the Green Chapel is (2040–42):

> . . . for to sauen hymself, when suffer hym byhoued,
> To byde bale withoute dabate of bronde hym to were
>           oþer knyffe.

The Green Knight himself identifies the motive of fear when he observes in his judgment that Gawain was moved to accept the girdle 'for ȝe lufed your lyf' (2368). Gawain in his turn has the honesty to recognize the justice of this description of his own conduct (2379–80):

> For care of þy knokke cowardyse me taȝt
> To acorde me with couetyse, my kynde to forsake.

Gawain's intention in accepting and retaining the girdle, the end or proper object of his interior act of will, is to save his life; formally, therefore, his sin is a sin of cowardice. Gawain's act of retaining the girdle is a sin materially in two respects. First of all it is materially a sin of covetousness. Gawain accuses himself of covetousness in retaining the girdle on three separate occasions (2374, 2380–81, and 2507–8). The threefold self-accusation of the sin of covetousness obliges us to consider it seriously, even though it is plainly at odds with Gawain's expressed motives. Covetousness cannot here be understood in the wide sense of the inordinate desire of any temporal good whatsoever, that is, as *cupiditas* in opposition to *caritas*,[15] for this would be to suggest a more radical failure in respect of the virtues of the pentangle than the poet's own exposition allows. And as Burrow rightly

---

15. As argued by D. F. Hills, 'Gawain's Fault in *Sir Gawain and the Green Knight*, *RES*, NS, 14 (1963), 124–31.

points out in his reply to Hills,[16] covetousness is opposed by Gawain not to *caritas* but to *larges* (2381), that is, generosity.[17] Covetousness is to be understood in the specific sense of the inordinate desire for riches, and its relevance here is to be explained by the specific classifications of this sin in the Middle Ages. Thus in the *Ancrene Wisse* we read:

> Edhalden cwide, fundles, oþer lane, . . . nis hit spece of ʒisceung & anes cunnes þeofðe?
>
> . . . withholding what has been promised, found, or borrowed, . . . is not this a species of covetousness and a kind of theft?[18]

By retaining the girdle, which properly belongs to the lord by virtue of the Exchange of Winnings agreement, Gawain is thus guilty of covetousness. Secondly, if we look at the act of retaining the girdle from a different but related point of view, we shall see it as a material failure on Gawain's part to keep faith with the lord in the Exchange of Winnings on the third day. And it is in these terms that the Green Knight puts it to Gawain (2354–57):

> Trwe mon trwe restore,
> Þenne þar mon drede no waþe.
> At þe þrid þou fayled þore,
> And þerfor þat tappe ta þe.

The dual significance of Gawain's act in respect of its material sinfulness reflects the central significance of the interconnectedness of the pentangle virtues, and in particular of the link between *fraunchyse* and *felaʒschyp* (652).

The poet's moral analysis is as lucid as it is subtle. Fear for life has led Gawain to the acceptance of the girdle into his permanent possession, and hence to the breaking of his faith with his host in the Exchange of Winnings agreement. The facts of the case and their moral significance are not in doubt, and they are confirmed for us, if confirmation were at all to be needed, by the Green Knight's subsequent rehearsal of them (2366–68). Nevertheless, at the same time as we specify Gawain's sins we cannot but also admire his moral excellence. The material covetousness in retaining the girdle must be set beside the formal generosity that Gawain displays in his acknowledgment of

16. J. A. Burrow, ' "Cupiditas" in *Sir Gawain and the Green Knight*: A Reply to D. F. Hills', *RES*, NS, 15(1964), 56.
17. Burrow explains Gawain's covetousness by invoking the distinction between the formal and material nature of a moral act (*A Reading*, pp. 135-36). It will be apparent that I find his exposition at this point entirely convincing.
18. The passage is quoted by Davis, p.128. The translation is that of M.B. Salu, *The Ancrene Riwle* (London, 1955), p. 93.

his host's winnings. Further, a single sinful act is not in itself sufficient to destroy the habit of virtue, for the habit of virtue is acquired by repeated acts, not by a single good act (*ST*, 1a 2ae 71.4 *sed contra*). Hence Gawain continues to perform virtuous acts after he has wrongfully taken the girdle into his possession with the intention of concealing it from the lord, and ironically displays his virtue by proceeding at once to carry out that intention.

# CHAPTER SEVEN

# The Judgment of Gawain's Conduct

Thou in thyself art perfect, and in thee
Is no deficience found; not so is Man,
But in degree  . . . (Milton)

I

IN PLEDGING TO THE lady that he will 'lelly layne fro hir lorde' (1863) the
girdle, Gawain has been led through her cunning (1846–50) and his own fear
for his life (1851–58) to compromise himself, for by the Exchange of
Winnings he is obliged to hand over the girdle as a winning to the lord. The
poet makes us aware of the compromise when he describes how Gawain
does in fact conceal the girdle (1872–75):

> When ho watz gon, Sir Gawayn gerez hym sone,
> Rises and riches hym in araye noble,
> Lays vp þe luf-lace þe lady hym raȝt,
> Hid hit ful holdely, þer he hit eft fonde.

This is indeed the act of a man who is habitually faithful to his pledged word,
but it is also by the same token  an act of infidelity.  Gawain's faithful infidelity is also suggested by the 'bleaunt of blwe' (1928) in which he is dressed
for the Exchange of Winnings on the third day, for blue is the colour of fidelity.
That is why Criseyde bids Pandarus take a ring with a blue stone to Troilus to
assure him of her continuing faithfulness (*TC*, III.885).

It is important to recognize that what the poet is concerned to represent
here is moral contradiction and not moral turpitude. Gawain is not simply
unfaithful in the Exchange of Winnings agreement on the third day. The three
kisses that he hands over have been hard won and are highly esteemed
(1936–37):

> Þen acoles he þe knyȝt and kysses hym þryes,
> As sauerly and sadly as he hem sette couþe.

It is this combination of moral excellence and sinfulness that is illustrated in
the juxtaposition of the pentangle and the girdle at the beginning of Fitt IV. In

this second arming scene the poet follows the systematic and orderly method of description that is recommended by the rhetoricians and is characterized by his own practice. But according to the logic of the poet's descriptive method the putting on of the surcoat and the wrapping about of the girdle will be separated by the girding on of the sword. The poet displays considerable syntactic ingenuity, as Burrow has explained (*A Reading*, p.115), in avoiding this natural effect of his own method (2025–36):

> Whyle þe wlonkest wedes he warp on hymseluen —
> His cote wyth þe conysaunce of þe clere werkez
> Ennurned vpon veluet, vertuus stonez
> Aboute beten and bounden, enbrauded semez,
> And fayre furred withinne wyth fayre pelures —
> ȝet laft he not þe lace, þe ladiez gifte,
> Þat forgat not Gawayn for gode of hymseluen.
> Bi he hade belted þe bronde vpon his balȝe haunchez,
> Þenn dressed he his drurye double hym aboute,
> Swyþe sweþled vmbe his swange swetely þat knyȝt
> Þe gordel of þe grene silke, þat gay wel bisemed,
> Vpon þat ryol red cloþe þat ryche watz to schewe.

The pentangle is a symbol of human perfection, and the girdle is the sign of Gawain's imperfection. But the girdle is not opposed to the pentangle, and does not take the place of the pentangle (Burrow, *A Reading*, p.116). It renders explicit the element of sinfulness that is implicit in the definition of human perfection. In one hardened by a sin of malice the wearing of the girdle might be taken for an act of shameless ostentation. But virtuous knights are not given to ostentation of any kind, as we see from Chaucer's portrait of his knight (*CT*, A 73–78). And no more is Gawain. It is the lesser sinfulness of sin preceded by passion of which Gawain is guilty (2037–40):

> Bot wered not þis ilk wyȝe for wele þis gordel,
> For pryde of þe pendauntez, þaȝ polyst þay were,
> And þaȝ þe glyterande golde glent vpon endez,
> Bot for to sauen hymself, when suffer hym byhoued.

The guide assigned by Bertilak to lead Gawain to the Green Chapel is no less a tempter than the lady, and the poet makes his function in the poem no less evident to the reader. First of all the relationship between lord and servant is reversed when the servant commands the lord to stop (2089–90). Although his language is formally correct in the use of the plural form of address (*yow*, 2091, etc., and *ȝe*, 2092, etc.), his manner is patronising in the assumption of superior wisdom that his words contain (2096):

Wolde ȝe worch bi my wytte, ȝe worþed þe better.

He knows what is in the moral interest of Gawain better than does Gawain himself. Secondly his language becomes overtly contemptuous and abusive towards Gawain after his temptation has been resisted. The polite plurals give way to the condescending singulars, most improperly used of a servant to his master (2140–42):

> 'Mary!' quoþ þat oþer mon, 'now þou so much spellez,
> Þat þou wylt þyn awen nye nyme to þyseluen,
> And þe lyst lese þy lyf, þe lette I ne kepe.'

Gawain has fallen short in fidelity through fear for life. The testing of Gawain by the guide is designed to take the moral issue one stage further, for Gawain is not simply a coward who abandons his pledged word when beset by fears. Indeed the guide's asseveration 'Mary!' (2140) is an implicit acknowledgment of Gawain's courage, for in the pentangle passage Gawain's courage is seen as being derived from the image of the Virgin Mary depicted on the inner side of his shield (648–50).

The guide assures Gawain of the formidable size (2098–2102) and merciless nature (2103–9) of his adversary. The keeping of his pledge in the Beheading Game involves the certainty of death (2111–13):

> Com ȝe þere, ȝe be kylled, may þe knyȝt rede,
> Trawe ȝe me þat trwely, þaȝ ȝe had twenty lyues
>                 to spende.

These are truths that we ourselves can easily vouch for, and there is no need for Gawain to misbelieve the truth of the guide's words. The guide promises to conceal Gawain's guilt in words that are specifically intended to recall the loss of fidelity in the concealment of the girdle (2124–25):

> . . . I schal lelly yow layne, and lance neuer tale
> Þat euer ȝe fondet to fle for freke þat I wyst.

But the temptation here is less insidiously stated. Indeed the moral issues are straightforward for Gawain (although hardly the less difficult for that), and Gawain responds honourably towards them. We are confirmed in our belief in the lesser imperfection of Gawain's sin. When the simple knowledge of evil is present Gawain does not hesitate to reject the course of cowardice and infidelity (2129–31):

Bot helde þou hit neuer so holde, and I here passed,
Founded for ferde for to fle, in fourme þat þou tellez,
I were a kny3t kowarde, I my3t not be excused.

The poet therefore asserts Gawain's excellence in terms of those very virtues
in which he has fallen short. And this fact is further acknowledged by the
guide himself when he takes his departure (2149–51). It is also clear that in
the midst of the dangers that confront him, Gawain's confidence rests
securely in God (2136–39):

Þa3e he be a sturn knape
To sti3tel, and stad with staue,
Ful wel con Dry3tyn schape
His seruauntez for to saue.

This is a point important enough for the poet to return to it in the wheel at the
end of the following stanza (2156–59):

'Bi Goddez self,' quoþ Gawayn,
'I wyl nauþer grete ne grone;
To Goddez wylle I am ful bayn,
And to hym I haf me tone.'

Thus the poet also asserts the excellence of Gawain's faith, or rather (as with
his courage and fidelity) reasserts it, for faith is one of the virtues explicitly
set out in the account of the pentangle as a symbol (642–43).[1]

1.    The explicit statement of Gawain's faith here rules out any interpretation of the
      wearing of the girdle as an act of superstition (such as that of N. Jacobs, 'Gawain's
      False Confession', *English Studies*, 51 (1970), 433-35, whereby we learn that
      'Gawain's reliance on sorcery rather than the mercy of God is culpable both as pride
      in the form of presumption and as sloth in the form of infirm faith' (p. 433)). The
      wearing of charms is superstitious and unlawful if they bear inscriptions that involve
      demons or if confidence is placed in the form of the inscriptions or the manner in
      which they are worn (*ST*, 2a 2ae 96.4). If the girdle is such a charm the wearing of it
      would be a contradiction of Gawain's piety, for superstition is a vice opposed to the
      virtue of religion (*ST*, 2a 2ae 92.1). It would also be a contradiction of his faith, for
      piety presupposes faith as being an outward confession of faith (*ST*, 2a 2ae 94.1 *ad*
      1). But the wearing of charms is not superstitious if they derive their power from
      God and the saints (*ST*, 2a 2ae 96.4 *ad* 3):

      Ad tertium dicendum quod eadem ratio est de portatione reliquiarum. Quia si
      portentur ex fiducia Dei et sanctorum quorum sunt reliquiae, non erit illicitum: si
      autem circa hoc attenderetur aliquid aliud vanum, puta quod vas esset triangulare,
      aut aliquid aliud hujusmodi quod non pertineret ad reverentiam Dei et sanctorum,
      esset superstitiosum et illicitum.

In the description of Gawain's solitary journey on the final stage of his quest to the Green Chapel (2160–2238), the poet reminds us insistently of the perils of the situation in which the hero now finds himself. He describes the desolation and seeming hostility of the place itself; the rough rocks that graze the skies (2166–67); the water boiling in the stream (2172–74); and the grass-covered mound with its devilish associations (2178–96). The suggestion of menace is at once confirmed by the description of the hideous noise of grinding (2199–2204 and 2219–20) and of the size and sharpness of the Green Knight's axe (2223–25):

> A denez ax nwe dyȝt, þe dynt with to ȝelde,
> With a borelych bytte bende by þe halme,
> Fyled in a fylor, fowre fote large.

The poet focuses entirely on the fearsome qualities of this weapon. There is no occasion here, as there was in the description of that other axe on the first meeting in Arthur's hall (see 214–20), to dwell on the fine craftsmanship of which it is a product. There is no comfort either to be found for Gawain in the mood of the man who wields this evil weapon. He strides forward to the meeting with the hero 'bremly broþe' (2233). The poet has thus superbly concentrated his effects, and, what is more, has presented them to us from Gawain's point of view (2163, 2167 and 2169–70):

> And  þenne he wayted hym aboute, and wylde hit hym þoȝt.

> Þe skwez of þe scowtes skayned hym þoȝt.

This same consideration applies in the wearing of relics. If it is out of confidence in God and the saints, whose relics they are, this is not wrong. But if account were taken of some irrelevance, for instance, that the locket is triangular and the like, which has no bearing on the reverence due to God and the saints, it would be superstitious and wrong.

The lawful use of charms is also acknowledged in Chaucer's *Parson's Tale* after a vehement denunciation of superstitious practices (*CT*, I 607):

Charmes for woundes or maladie of men or of beestes, if they taken any effect, it may be peraventure that God suffreth it, for folk sholden yeve the moore feith and reverence to his name.

Now the source of the qualities attributed by the lady to the girdle is not specified (1849-54). Since Gawain is not accused of superstition we are entitled to believe that its power is derived from God. Further, when Gawain fastens the girdle twice around his waist (2030-36) the action is not carried out in any special manner that might suggest an act of superstition. We may draw a clear contrast with Chaucer's presentation of superstition in his *Franklin's Tale*, where the resort to astrological magic is condemned in unambiguous terms as 'supersticious cursednesse' (*CT*, F 1272). Gawain's act of acceptance of the girdle is followed by the confession of his sins (1876-79) and this act constitutes, as we have seen, the clearest demonstration of his piety.

And ofte chaunged his cher þe chapel to seche:
He seȝ non suche in no syde, and selly hym þoȝt.

We are made sharply aware of the dangers that he confronts and the fears that
they inspire, and as a result we are bound not only to recognize his great
fidelity (2237–38), but also the courage that such fidelity requires of him.

In the account of the blows that Gawain receives at the hands of the Green
Knight (2239–2330) the poet reveals yet again a precision in his moral
analysis. Gawain's physical response indicates at one and the same time the
extent and limitations of his courage. We are led to admire the courage with
which he presents himself for his death and controls his fears (2255–58).
Such conduct entirely justifies the poet's description of him as one 'þat doȝty
watz euer' (2264). But it is at this very point that the great courage of the
knight fails him, for he flinches as the blow descends (2265–67):

Bot Gawayn on þat giserne glyfte hym bysyde,
As hit com glydande adoun on glode hym to schende,
And schranke a lytel with þe schulderes for þe scharp yrne.

This relative failure of nerve corresponds to the partial failure in the Exchange
of Winnings agreement, and it brings down on Gawain's head the sternest of
recriminations (2268–79). Such recrimination stands in need of explanation
when we compare this incident with a similar incident in *Perlesvaus*. Here
Lancelot is compelled to enter into a Beheading Game at the Waste City, and
he too flinches when he comes to receive the return blow. But no criticism is
offered him for doing so *(Perlesvaus,* 6695–700 and p.183). The reason is
that the fact that Lancelot has presented himself for the return blow in the
first place speaks volumes for his outstanding courage and fidelity. Indeed
the author records that at least twenty knights before Lancelot had failed to
keep their promise because of a lack of courage *(Perlesvaus,* 6714–23 and
pp.183–84). The Green Knight's rebuke of Gawain for flinching is deliberately
overdone, for there is a calculated exaggeration of Gawain's offence on the
poet's part. The rebuke underlines and does not diminish the reality of
Gawain's courage. And Gawain is justly enabled to say in his own defence
that it does not lie in his power to restore his own head after the manner of
the Green Knight himself (2280–83). There is a suggestion here of an unfair-
ness in the rules of the game as it applies to the two contestants. Before the
second blow is offered Gawain gives his word to receive it without flinching
(2284–87). This pledge enables the poet to set before us once again the
admirable combination of fidelity and courage in his hero, for Gawain is as
good as his word (2292–94):

Gawayn grayþely hit bydez, and glent with no membre,
Bot stode stylle as þe ston, oþer a stubbe auþer
Þat raþeled is in roché grounde with rotez a hundreth.

The poet shows once again that Gawain does not yield to his fears when he
has a direct knowledge of their moral consequences. As in the testing by the
guide Gawain's reputation for fidelity is restored, so here his reputation for
courage is restored. The good knight offers no resistance on the occasion of
the third blow until the blow itself has been struck, even though he has the
expectation only of death (2305–8):

Þenne tas he hym stryþe to stryke,
And frounsez boþe lyppe and browe;
No meruayle þaȝ hym myslyke
Þat hoped of no rescowe.

By means of this narrative of the beheading the poet has realised in Gawain
the classic definition of courage, namely, firmness of mind in the face of the
fears aroused by the dangers of death (*ST*, 2a 2ae 123.4). The manner in
which Gawain receives the three blows aimed at him enables us to see his
fidelity and especially his courage in their proper perspective. There is no
need for us to minimize the seriousness of Gawain's failing, for the sinfulness of the human condition is not something that the poet wishes lightly to
accommodate. But at the same time we can appreciate the great moral excellence of Gawain. The poet intends us to share in the Green Knight's unfeigned
admiration of the courage of the man, and underlines it by rhetorical amplification (2331–35):

The haþel heldet hym fro, and on his ax rested,
Sette þe schaft vpon schore, and to þe scharp lened,
And loked to þe leude þat on þe launde ȝede,
How þat doȝty, dredles, deruely þer stondez
Armed, ful aȝlez: in hert hit hym lykez.[2]

We have been led to see that in this life authentic courage in its noblest
manifestations co-exists with the weakness of man's fallen nature.

2.  Spearing takes a very different view of this scene (p. 190): 'That pleasure of the
    Green Knight's is not entirely flattering to Gawain. He is pleased with him, from the
    same standpoint of superiority that might enable one to be pleased with a small boy
    or a pet dog that showed fighting spirit.' These analogies cannot be accepted, for
    they unduly diminish the person of the hero. It is true, of course, that the Green
    Knight possesses the superiority of knowledge and Gawain the vulnerability of
    ignorance. But the gap between the two is that of equable judge and penitent sinner,
    and this is how it subsequently comes to be expressed. And there is nothing childish
    (in the pejorative sense) about the penitent sinner.

We must not as readers withhold from Gawain the admiration that is due to his virtuous conduct in the quest that he has undertaken. But we must recognize at the same time that he is blind to his sins in failing to hand over the girdle to the lord in the Exchange of Winnings agreement, and that such sins are properly to be cleansed by satisfaction. The poet duly proceeds to these matters in the meeting between Gawain and the Green Knight at the Green Chapel. The penitential significance of this meeting cannot escape the attention of any reader of the poem, and it has in many respects been satisfactorily explained by Burrow (*A Reading*, pp. 127–33). But the second or quasi-confession stands in relation to the first not as valid to invalid, but as the completion of a moral process.

The Green Knight occupies the role of confessor, and Gawain that of penitent sinner. It is not possible to hide one's sins from the supreme judge, as the fictional Dante learns when he comes to make his confession before Beatrice (*Purg.*, XXXI.37–39):

> Ed ella: 'Se tacessi o se negassi
>    ciò che confessi, non fora men nota
>    la colpa tua: da tal giudice sassi!

> And she: 'Hadst thou kept silence or denied what thou confessest, thy fault would be not less plain, by such a judge is it known.'

Similarly the Green Knight is the judge who understands the hidden causes of things, and hence gives a true report of Gawain's motives and measures the extent of his sin (2366–68):

> Bot here yow lakked a lyttel, sir, and lewté  yow wonted;
> Bot þat watz for no wylyde werke, ne wowyng nauþer,
> Bot for ȝe lufed your lyf;  þe lasse I yow blame.

The importance of the Green Knight's function as judge explains why so much is made of his jovial nature. Bertilak is a jovial type in the full medieval sense; he is not only merry and companionable (908–9, 936–37, 981–87, 1086–87, and 1174–77), he is also generous (988–90, and 1156–57) and courteous (833–37, 1002, and 1029–36). It is Jove who dispenses justice, and justice is to be dispensed with equanimity. The authority of Bertilak is characterized by that lack of harshness of spirit or gentleness that disposes to mercy (2336–38):

> Þenn he melez muryly wyth a much steuen,
> And wyth a rynkande rurde he to þe renk sayde:
> 'Bolde burne, on þis bent be not so gryndel.'

He thus resembles as judge the merciful and patient Lord who rebukes Jonah for his foolish lack of patience (*Patience*, 524–25):

> Be noȝt so gryndel, god-man, bot go forth þy wayes,
> Be preue and be pacient in payne and in joye.

The third blow that the Green Knight delivers is not seen in any way as an act of mercy, however, but as an act of satisfaction for sin, that is, a due punishment (2389, and 2393–94):

> Thenn loȝe þat oþer leude and luflyly sayde . . .
> 'I halde þe polysed of þat plyȝt, and pured as clene
> As þou hadez neuer forfeted syþen þou watz fyrst borne.'

Satisfaction for sin is an act of justice , and it is defined as (*Suppl.*, 12.3):

> . . . illatae injuriae recompensatio secundum justitiae aequalitatem.
>
> . . . *compensation for an inflicted injury according to the equality of justice.*

Man cannot make satisfaction in the sense of quantitative equality, that is, he cannot do anything that equals the goodness of divine grace, but he can do so in the sense of proportionate equality. By the justice of satisfaction, therefore, is to be understood a strict measure in accord with proportionate equality (*Suppl.*, 8.7 *sed contra*, and 13.1 *sed contra*):

> Isaiae 27: *In mensura contra mensuram, cum abjecta fuerit, judicabis eam*; ergo quantitas judicii punitionis peccati est secundum quantitatem culpae.
>    Praeterea. Homo reducitur ad aequalitatem justitiae per poenitentiam inflictam: sed hoc non esset, si quantitas culpae, et poenae non sibi responderent; ergo unum alteri respondet.
>
> . . . It is written (Isa. xxvii.8): *In measure against measure, when it shall be cast off, thou shalt judge it*. Therefore the quantity of punishment adjudicated for sin answers the degree of fault.
>    Further, man is reduced to the equality of justice by the punishment inflicted on him. But this would not be so if the quantity of the fault and of the punishment did not mutually correspond. Therefore one answers to the other.
>
> Satisfactio est, cum poena culpae aequatur; quia justitia est idem, quod contrapassum, ut Pythagorici dixerunt . . .

. . . there is due satisfaction when the punishment balances the fault, since *justice is the same as counterpassion*, as the Pythagoreans said (Aristotle, *Ethic*. v).

It is in accordance with the principle of *contrappasso* or fitting retribution that Dante assigns punishment to the impenitent sinners in hell. Thus the spirits consumed by lust, that is, those who in their lives set the disturbance of passions above the order of reason, are driven weeping and wailing before the unrelenting tempest (*Inf*., V. 28–51). And in the same way the impiety of diviners in claiming to forecast future events is punished by the denial of ordinary forward vision (*Inf*., XX.10–15). But the example of fitting retribution that comes closest, potentially and implicitly at any rate, to *Sir Gawain* is that of Bertran de Born whose head is severed for the fomenting of the rebellion of Henry against his father Henry II of England (*Inf*., XXVIII. 112–42). Bertran explains the meaning behind this terrible punishment as follows (*Inf*., XXVIII. 139–42):

'Perch'io parti' così giunte persone,
    partito porto il mio cerebro, lasso!,
        dal suo principio ch'è in questo troncone.
Così s'osserva in me lo contrapasso.'

'Because I parted those so joined I carry my brain, alas, parted from its root in this trunk; thus is observed in me the   retribution.'

The principle of fitting retribution is the principle of measure that is at work in *Sir Gawain*, and it accounts for the contrivance of three blows of the axe to match Gawain's conduct on the three days of the Exchange of Winnings agreement (2352–53, and 2356–57):

For boþe two here I  þe bede bot two bare myntes
            boute scaþe . . .
At  þe  þrid  þou fayled  þore,
And  þerfor  þat tappe ta  þe.

It is the same principle that explains the poet's earlier comparison between the girdle and the axe. When describing the massive blade of the Green Knight's axe — it is four feet wide — the poet is led to observe, somewhat oddly it seems to a modern reader, that (2226):

Hit watz no lasse bi þat lace þat lemed ful bryȝt.[3]

3.    Davis (p. 126) takes *lace* (2226) to refer to a 'thong' wrapped  about the shaft of the axe in the manner of that described in the first fitt (217-18). But it is hard to see what point there can be in such a reference. The identification of the lace  with the lady's

The girdle is the measure of Gawain's sin, and the axe the instrument of punishment for that sin. The concerns of the final fitt, then, are those of justice simply, and not of justice and mercy.[4] Gawain receives at the hands of the Green Knight what is strictly due to his virtue. There need be no doubt that if he had fallen gravely short in his quest he would, like Bertran de Born, have lost his head, for the *Gawain*-poet is no less morally realistic than Dante. Sin involves a disturbance of the order of justice, and that order can only be restored by the virtue of penitence. When Gawain's sin is disclosed to him, he shows himself to be excellent in the moral virtue of penitence no less than in the theological and moral virtues set forth under the symbol of the pentangle. This is not to argue for a gap in the scheme of the pentangle, but for a necessary implication of that imperfection which is contained in the pentangle. Gawain's behaviour from here onwards follows in detail the requirements of penitential practice, and it has been the failure of critics to set his conduct in a penitential context that has accounted for some notably unsympathetic and even hostile misinterpretations of it. I shall indicate in the notes to the discussion that follows the points at which these misinterpretations need to be corrected.

The virtue of penitence is to be classified as a part of justice (*ST*, 3a 85.3). It is the right reason whereby one chooses to grieve for past sins that merit such grief, and in proportion to the nature of those sins, for there is also a mean of virtue in relation to the sorrow of repentance (*ST*, 3a 85.1). Hence penitence is a specific virtue concerned with the destruction of past sins (*ST*, 3a 85.2):

> Manifestum est autem quod in poenitentia invenitur specialis ratio actus laudabilis, scilicet operari ad destructionem peccati praeteriti, inquantum est Dei offensa, quod non pertinet ad rationem alterius virtutis. Unde necesse est ponere quod poenitentia est specialis virtus.

> Now it is clear that with penitence there is an act of special value, namely of working towards the destruction of past sin as an offence against God, and this belongs to the specific function of no other virtue. Hence we conclude that penitence is a special virtue.

The habit of the virtue of penitence is expressed in the three related acts of contrition, confession, and satisfaction.[5] The nature of the relationship between

---

girdle was first made by S. Malarkey and J. B. Toelken, 'Gawain and the Green Girdle', *JEGP*, 63 (1964), 14-20 and printed by D.R. Howard and C. Zacher, *Critical Studies of Sir Gawain and the Green Knight* (Notre Dame, Indiana, 1968), pp. 236-44, and is further supported by Waldron in his note to 2225f. (p. 125).

4. Burrow's discussion of justice and mercy (*A Reading*, pp. 137-40) is not here relevant, and results from the erroneous assumption of an invalid confession.

5. The acts of penitence are not related to the virtue as parts but as effects (*ST*, 3a 90.1 *ad* 2). On contrition, confession, and satisfaction as acts of virtue, see *Suppl.*, 1.2, 7.2, and 12.2.

them is plainly to be seen in the standard definition of contrition as (*Suppl.*, 1.1 *arg*.1):

> . . . dolor pro peccatis assumptus, cum proposito confitendi, et satisfaciendi.
>
> *. . . an assumed sorrow for sins, together with the purpose of confessing them and of making satisfaction for them.*

The conditions of all three are fulfilled in the conduct of Gawain.

Contrition involves a great disturbance of soul, for it is nothing less than a crushing of the heart. Such a disturbance results from the fact of being torn from one's own previous judgment of one's acts. Thus the fictional Dante is broken like a cross-bow under too great a strain before Beatrice's accusations (*Purg.*, XXXI.16–21):

> Come balestro frange, quando scocca
>     da troppa tesa, la sua corda e l'arco,
>     e con men foga l'asta il segno tocca,
> sì scoppia' io sott'esso grave carco,
>     fuori sgorgando lacrime e sospiri,
>     e la voce allentò per lo suo varco.
>
> As a cross–bow shot with too great strain breaks the cord and bow and the shaft touches the mark with less force, so I broke down under that heavy charge, pouring forth tears and sighs, and my voice failed in its passage.

In the same way Gawain is overwhelmed by his new-found sense of sin, and takes a long time to absorb the shock of the Green Knight's disclosure. He has to come to terms with the reversal of his judgment that he has been faithful to the lord in the Exchange of Winnings agreement and to the Green Knight in the Beheading Game. The realisation of his moral sinfulness in retaining the girdle fills him with shame (2369–72):

> Þat oþer stif mon in study stod a gret whyle,
> So agreued for greme he gryed withinne;
> Alle  þe blode of his brest blende in his face,
> Þat al he schrank for schome  þat  þe schalk talked.

This is without doubt Gawain's first realisation of his sin, and indeed shame answers to the first recognition of sin, for shame is a reaction to a shameful deed as present (*ST*, 3a 85.1 *ad* 2). Since penitence is not merely a passion, but a virtue, true contrition requires a willed displeasure for the sin committed (*Suppl.*, 3.1):

> . . . in contritione est *duplex* dolor: *unus* est in ipsa voluntate, qui est essentialiter ipsa contritio, quae nihil aliud est, quam displicentia praeteriti peccati. Et talis dolor in contritione excedit omnes alios dolores, quia quantum aliquid placet, tantum contrarium ejus displicet: finis autem ultimus super omnia placet, cum omnia propter ipsum desiderentur; et ideo peccatum, quod a fine ultimo avertit, super omnia displicere debet.

> . . . there is a twofold sorrow in contrition: one is in the will, and is the very essence of contrition, being nothing else than displeasure at past sin, and this sorrow, in contrition, surpasses all other sorrows. For the more pleasing a thing is, the more displeasing is its contrary. Now the last end is above all things pleasing: wherefore sin, which turns us away from the last end, should be, above all things, displeasing.

The importance of willed displeasure for sin is also stressed in a treatise such as *The Book of the Craft of Dying* (47/11–48/3):

> . . . therfor to euery suche man that is in suche caas and is come to hys last ende (it) is to be counceiled besily that he laboure wiþ reson of hys mynde after hys power to haue ordinat 7 verray repentaunce, that is to menynge, not withstondynge þe sorwe 7 greuaunce of (hys) siknesse 7 drede that he hath of hasty deth, that he vse reson asmoche as he may, and enforce hym self to haue wilfully ful displesynge of alle synne for the due ende 7 (a) parfyt entent, that is for God . . . [6]

Gawain's response to the Green Knight's disclosure of his sin is not one of uncontrolled self-disgust, for that would be to add one sin of passion to another, but one of willed displeasure. The poet makes this distinction clear when he states that Gawain remained in silent thought for a long time before speaking (2369). Gawain's willed displeasure at his sins is repeatedly emphasised by the poet, for it is so essential to his future spiritual welfare. He repudiates his cowardice and covetousness (2374):

> 'Corsed worth cowarddyse and couetyse boþe!'

He repudiates also the girdle as a sign of the breaking of faith (2378):

> 'Lo! þer þe falssyng, foule mot hit falle!'

And he condemns the infidelity itself and the loss of righteousness that is its necessary consequence (2382–84):

6. The author of the Latin *Ars Moriendi* is here following Duns Scotus, *Quaestiones in Lib. IV Sententiarum, Distinctio XX*; see Morgan, 'A Critical Edition', Volume II, pp. 136-37.

> Now am I fawty and falce, and ferde haf ben euer
> Of trecherye and vntrawþe: boþe bityde sorȝe
>              and care![7]

It is important to recognize also that Gawain's action in removing the girdle and flinging it fiercely to the lord (2376–77) is not an impetuous gesture, but the expression of a proper alienation from sin. In order to make this distinction clear the poet has set Gawain's action in a carefully ordered sequence of events; it not only follows upon a period of silent thought and inward mortification (2369–72) but is placed between the penitent's two judgments of his sin (2373–75, and 2379–84). These judgments are considered judgments, as is suggested by their very compatibility, and they answer to one of the conditions that is essential to a proper confession of sin, namely that it should be the product of knowledge (*Suppl.*, 9.4):

> . . . prima (sc. conditio) est, ut aliquis *sit sciens*; et quantum ad hoc confessio dicitur esse *discreta*, secundum quod in actu omnis virtutis prudentia requiritur: est autem haec discretio, ut majora peccata cum majori pondere confiteatur.

> The first (sc. condition) is knowledge, in respect of which confession is said to be *discreet*, inasmuch as prudence is required in every act of virtue: and this discretion consists in giving greater weight to greater sins.

It is necessary to stress the prudence that Gawain displays here, since prudence is not an obvious mark of Gawain's judgment of his own sinfulness for a modern reader unacquainted with penitential practice and Scholastic moral philosophy.[8] But the amplification of the judgment and the repetition of the same specific moral terms are intended as an implication of Gawain's prudence (2374–75, and 2379–81):

7.   The spiritual outlook of Gawain's detestation of his sins is reflected in the words of the preacher at the retreat at Belvedere in Joyce's *Portrait of the Artist*. The distinction between mortal and venial sin is here of little comfort, for 'even venial sin is of such a foul and hideous nature that even if the omnipotent Creator could end all the evil and misery in the world, the wars, the diseases, the robberies, the crimes, the deaths, the murders, on condition that He allowed a single venial sin to pass unpunished, a single venial sin, a lie, an angry look, a moment of wilful sloth, He , the great omnipotent God, could not do so because sin, be it in thought or deed, is a transgression of His law and God would not be God if He did not punish the transgressor'. See J. Joyce, *A Portrait of the Artist as a Young Man*, Granada Publishing Limited (London, 1977), p. 122. The *Portrait* was first published in 1916.
8.   Spearing writes of Gawain's response to his sin: 'Certainly he does not take a balanced view of his situation. At one moment, before the Green Knight explains things to him, his conscience is apparently quite clear . . . At the next moment, having learned the truth, he is accusing himself of every sin he can think of' (p. 227).

'Corsed worth cowarddyse and couetyse boþe!
In yow is vylany and vyse þat vertue disstryez . . .

For care of þy knokke cowardyse me taȝt
To acorde me with couetyse, my kynde to forsake,
Þat is larges and lewté þat longez to knyȝtez.'

In the language of Scholastic moral philosophy Gawain is saying that his sinful act is formally one of cowardice, and materially one of covetousness and infidelity. It will be seen that Gawain's own judgment corresponds to that of the Green Knight, and that both are in accord with the poet's representation of his conduct in the Exchange of Winnings agreement.

There is, however, a difference in emphasis or rather in perspective between Gawain's judgment and that of the Green Knight. The Green Knight addresses himself to the essential significance of Gawain's act and focuses as a result on Gawain's intention. And, *per se loquendo*, Gawain's act is one of cowardice, not of covetousness nor of infidelity. But the Green Knight does not disregard the proper object of Gawain's exterior act, namely his infidelity, for he stands in a twofold relation of faith to Gawain as a result of the Beheading Game and the Exchange of Winnings agreement. The Green Knight does indeed find fault with Gawain for the material sin (2366):

Bot here yow lakked a lyttel, sir, and lewté yow wonted.

But he finds in the passion of fear a mitigating circumstance; he blames Gawain, but he blames him the less as a result of it (2368). This is a judgment strictly in conformity with the principles of Scholastic morality; it is not indulgent, but even-handed.[9] Gawain's own situation is necessarily very different from that of the Green Knight. He is to be judged by the standards appropriate not to a confessor but to a penitent sinner. And here we need to note that it is not enough for a penitent's statement of his sins to be accurate; it must be also explicit, simple, and complete (*Suppl.*, 9.4):

Sed ex propria ratione hujusmodi actus, qui est confessio, habet quod sit manifestativa. Quae quidem manifestatio per quatuor impediri potest:

9.  Benson describes the Green Knight's attitude as one of 'indulgent forgiveness' (p. 247) and Spearing comments that 'the Green Knight is eventually more lenient towards Gawain's failing than Gawain himself is' (p. 31). But equanimity is not indulgence nor leniency. The reason why the Green Knight's judgment is light is not due to any absence of moral rigour on his part, but rather to the presence of moral virtue on Gawain's part. Thus it is only after Gawain has made his confession and done satisfaction for his sin in retaining the girdle that the Green Knight addresses him as 'Sir Gawayn' (2396). See V. L. Weiss, 'The Medieval Knighting Ceremony in *Sir Gawain and the Green Knight*', *Chaucer Review*, 12 (1978), 183-89 (p. 185).

primo per falsitatem; et quantum ad hoc dicitur *fidelis*, idest vera: secundo per obscuritatem verborum; et contra hoc dicitur *nuda,* ut non involvat obscuritatem verborum: tertio per verborum multiplicationem; et propter hoc dicitur *simplex*, ut scilicet non recitet in confessione, nisi quod ad quantitatem peccati pertinet: quarto, ut non subtrahatur aliquid de his, quae manifestanda sunt, et contra hoc dicitur *integra.*

By reason of its very nature, viz. confession, this act is one of mani-festation: which manifestation can be hindered by four things: first by falsehood, and in this respect confession is said to be *faithful*, i.e. true. Secondly, by the use of vague words, and against this confession is said to be *open*, so as not to be wrapped up in vague words; thirdly, by *multiplicity* of words, in which respect it is said to be *simple,* indicating that the penitent should relate only such matters as affect the gravity of the sin; fourthly none of those things should be suppressed which should be made known, and in this respect confession should be *entire*.[10]

Hence Gawain specifies his covetousness as well as his infidelity. But the Green Knight does not say that Gawain is not guilty of covetousness, he says that he was not motivated by it — a very different matter. And as we have seen, the covetousness has the same moral status as the infidelity; it is a sin materially, but not formally.

In discussing Gawain's detestation of his sins we have moved imperceptibly to his confession of them. This is inevitably the case when the penitent's assumed sorrow for his sins directly involves an intention to correct them. But confession is explicit in Beatrice's words to the fictional Dante in the earthly paradise (*Purg.*, XXXI. 5–6):

'dì, dì se questo è vero: a tanta accusa
tua confession conviene esser congiunta.'

'say, say if this is true; to such an accusation thy confession must
needs be joined.'

The distinctness of the act of confession as an essential act of the virtue of penitence is rendered explicit in two ways by the *Gawain*-poet, first of all subjectively in Gawain's words to the Green Knight (2385–86):

10.  The importance of completeness in confession is a matter that has already been raised in connection with Gawain's confession on the eve of his departure for the Green Chapel. The ubiquity of sin is impressed upon the gloomy spirits of Stephen Daedalus at the beginning of the retreat at Belvedere. He is led to reflect that at the final judgment 'every sin would then come forth from its lurking place, the most rebellious against the divine will and the most degrading to our poor corrupt nature, the tiniest imperfection and the most heinous atrocity' (*Portrait*, p. 104). It is the ubiquity of sin that explains the need for completeness in confession.

> I biknowe yow, kny3t, here stylle,
> Al fawty is my fare,

and second objectively in the Green Knight's acceptance of Gawain's confession as complete (2391):

> Þou art confessed so clene, beknowen of Þy mysses.[11]

Moreover, in his representation of Gawain's subsequent conduct the poet continually underlines its penitential fitness in respect of confession. Now confession is, as we have seen, an act of the special virtue of penitence, and as such it must meet certain specific conditions. First of all it must be full of shame in so far as it expresses the sinner's horror at the shamefulness of his sin (*Suppl.*, 9.4):

> Quae quidem primo initium sumit in horrore turpitudinis peccati; et quantum ad hoc confessio debet esse *verecunda*, ut scilicet non se jactet de peccatis propter aliquam saeculi vanitatem admixtam.

> First of all it takes its origin in the horror which one conceives for the shamefulness of sin, and in this respect confession should be *full of shame*, so as not to be a boastful account of one's sins, by reason of some worldly vanity accompanying it.

The sense of shame is still with Gawain when he comes to tell the court at Camelot of his sin (2501–4):

> He tened quen he schulde telle,
> He groned for gref and grame;
> Þe blod in his face con melle,
> When he hit schulde schewe, for schame.

There is nothing morbid in all of this, not at least if we judge it (as we surely must) from within the value system of medieval penitential literature.[12] The

---

11. Davis glosses *confessed so clene* as 'made clean by confession' (p. 173). But *clene* probably means here 'completely' (see *MED*, s.v.*clene* adv. 3. (a)); it is used in the phrase *clene-shriven* to mean 'fully shrived', as in a 1500 *Treat. G Battle* 431: Heme that were clene-shryvene off alle here synnes. Compare also *MED* s.v. *clene* adj. 6. (a) 'complete', under which is supplied an example from a 1470 Malory, *Wks.* 886/10: I mervayle . . . how ye durste take uppon you . . . the hyghe Order of Knyghthode . . . withoute clene confession.
12. D. Pearsall, *Old English and Middle English Poetry*, The Routledge History of English Poetry, Volume I (London, 1977) believes that 'the paragon of romance-heroes' is reduced 'to hysterical self-accusation and sour self-contempt' (p. 174).

sense of shame is nothing less than what is proper to the reality of sin. Any moral danger that may be perceived in this situation is not the indulgence of shame but the avoidance of shame. Langland sees the friars as the agents who undermine the salvific purpose of penance (*PPl*, B XX.281–85):

> For persons and parissh preestes, that sholde the peple shryve,
> Ben curatours called to knowe and to hele,
> Alle that ben hir parisshens penaunces enjoigne,
> And ben ashamed in hir shrift; ac shame maketh hem wende
> And fleen to the freres . . .

Meed the Maid has no difficulty in finding an accommodating friar (*PPl*, B III. 43–44):

> Thanne Mede for hire mysdedes to that man kneled,
> And shrof hire of hire sherewednesse — shamelees, I trowe,

and by the sound of it Chaucer's Friar is no less accommodating, for 'ful swetely herde he confessioun' (*CT*, A 221). The second specific condition of confession is that it should be tearful in spirit, that is, that it should be an expression of regret for the past sin (*Suppl.*, 9.4):

> Secundo progreditur ad dolorem de peccato commisso; et quantum ad hoc dicitur esse *lacrymabilis*.

> Then it goes on to deplore the sin committed, and in this respect it is said to be *tearful*.

Hence the confession of the fictional Dante to Beatrice is characterized by tearfulness (*Purg.*, XXXI. 34–36):

> Piangendo dissi: 'Le presenti cose
>   col falso lor piacer volser miei passi,
>   tosto che 'l vostro viso si nascose.'

> . . . weeping, I said: 'Present things with their false pleasure turned my steps as soon as your face was hid.'

It is evident that Gawain too retains a sense of the injury that his sin has done him, and still deplores it on his arrival at Camelot (2505–8):

> 'Lo! lorde,' quoþ þe leude, and þe lace hondeled,
> 'Þis is þe bende of þis blame I bere in my nek,
> Þis is þe laþe and þe losse þat I laȝt haue
> Of couardise and couetyse þat I haf caȝt þare.'

The third specific condition of confession is that it should be humble (*Suppl.*, 9.4):

> Tertio in abjectione sui terminatur; et quantum ad hoc debet esse *humilis*, ut se miserum confiteatur, et infirmum.

> Thirdly, it culminates in self-abjection, and in this respect it should be *humble*, so that one confesses one's misery and weakness.

The fictional Dante's humble abjection in his confession is shown in the image of him as a child, ashamed and silent, with eyes on the ground (*Purg.*, XXXI. 64–67):

> Quali i fanciulli, vergognando, muti
>   con li occhi a terra stannosi, ascoltando
>   e sè riconoscendo e ripentuti,
> tal mi stav'io . . .

> As children ashamed stand dumb with eyes on the ground, listening and acknowledging their fault and repentant, so I stood there . . .

The nourishment of such humility is Gawain's expressed motive for the acceptance of the girdle from the Green Knight himself (2437–38):

> And þus, quen pryde schal me pryk for prowes of armes,
> Þe loke to þis luf-lace schal leþe my hert.[13]

Such behaviour stands clearly defined when set against that of someone like the Wife of Bath, who displays the sin of pride in both its inward and outward forms (*CT*, A 449–57). She does not lament the reality of human imperfection, but rather rejoices in it (*CT*, D 105–12):

---

13. Spearing expresses a sense of unease about Gawain's conduct in this respect (p. 230): 'There is something noble about his determination to wear the token of his failing publicly, but there is something a little absurd too . . . he will punish himself openly in his reputation, by wearing something that will call other people's attention as well as his own to his imperfection. And yet, without judging him unsympathetically, may we not feel that there are still traces of pride in the feeling that one's own imperfection deserves such ostentatious treatment.' But the text focuses not on the effect that the wearing of the girdle has on others but on the effect it has on Gawain himself (2433-35):

> Bot in syngne of my surfet I schal se hit ofte,
> When I ride in renoun, remorde to myseluen
> Þe faut and þe fayntyse of þe flesche crabbed.

The issue here is not of reputation, but of humility. Spearing is not an unsympathetic reader of the poem, but his judgment of Gawain's conduct is deeply unsympathetic. The reason is that he has not fully understood the penitential ideas that the poet is here seeking to express.

Virginitee is greet perfeccion,
And continence eek with devocion,
But Crist, that of perfeccion is welle,
Bad nat every wight he sholde go selle
Al that he hadde, and gyve it to the poore,
And in swich wise folwe hym and his foore.
He spak to hem that wolde lyve parfitly;
And lordynges, by youre leve, that am nat I.

It has already been observed that the act of confession by its very nature as the manifestation of sin should be true, explicit, simple, and complete. Gawain's declaration of his sins to the court fulfils these conditions no less admirably than his earlier declaration of them to the Green Knight. And here we might justly commend the moral courage of one who is not deflected by shame from making so full a confession of his sins. Such courage in confession belongs to the general condition of virtue, as Aquinas also explains (*Suppl.*, 9.4):

> Quarta (sc. conditio) est, ut immobiliter operetur; et quantum ad hoc dicitur, quod debet esse *fortis*, ut scilicet propter verecundiam veritas non dimittatur.

> The fourth condition is that one should act immovably, and in this respect it is said that confession should be *courageous*, viz. that the truth should not be forsaken through shame.

As a truly contrite and fully confessed sinner, Gawain is willing to make satisfaction for his sin (2387–88):

> Letez me ouertake your wylle
> And efte I schal be ware.

But the Green Knight makes it clear that Gawain has done satisfaction for his sin by receiving the nick on the neck from the third blow of the axe (2392):

> And hatz þe penaunce apert of þe poynt of myn egge.

As a result it can be said that he has received absolution for his sin (2393–94):

> I halde þe polysed of þat plyȝt, and pured as clene
> As þou hadez neuer forfeted syþen þou watz fyrst borne.

His subsequent behaviour is therefore to be understood as that of one made whole again by penance.

It is very easy to misinterpret the matter which directly follows upon the second confession scene and which presents Gawain's leave-taking of Bertilak. The poet is all too readily seen by some modern readers as lapsing into a characteristically medieval anti-feminism, and Gawain as a result is held to show bad grace in blaming his failure in the quest not on his own weakness but on the deceit of women.[14] But it is impossible to attribute such conduct either to one whose virtue is symbolized by the pentangle or to one who has been made whole by penance.

It has to be said that Gawain is indeed the victim of deceit, for the cunning of the lady is amply evident in the bedroom scene of the third day, and it is symbolically confirmed by the analogy of the fox-hunt. But the argument that Gawain is a victim of such cunning is not in its turn to be pressed unreasonably. Gawain is certainly aware of his own responsibility as he is aware of feminine deceit (2414–15):

> Bot hit is no ferly þaȝ a fole madde,
> And þurȝ wyles of wymmen be wonen to sorȝe.

And no one is more severe in judgment on Gawain than Gawain himself (2374–84). Moreover, as we have seen, Gawain's severity is a due severity. When Gawain concludes that (2427–28):

> Þaȝ I be now bigyled,
> Me þink me burde be excused,

he does not literally mean that he should in fact be excused his sin, for that would be inconsistent with all that he has said before. Rather we must attribute to him the rueful good humour of one whose guilt for sin has now been removed.

The reference that Gawain now makes to Adam, Solomon, Sampson, and David (2416–19) is designed by the poet to draw attention once again to the central theme, namely that the highest human excellence is flawed. No human attainment is superior to that of these men, and yet all of them fell short (2422–24):

14. Such a perspective is endorsed with copious illustration in Arthur's *Medieval Sign Theory*, pp. 134-41. Gawain's words of farewell to Bertilak (2411-28) are seen to be not only discourteous, but also sinful in so far as they constitute an attempt by Gawain 'to excuse himself from responsibility for his own lapse' (p. 141). A better way forward is suggested by P.J. Lucas, 'Gawain's Anti-Feminism', *Notes and Queries*, NS,15 (1968), 324-25 when he comments that 'there is in these lines a semi-humorous mocking of the embarrassment that would be Gawain's on meeting the lady again' (p. 325).

> For þes wer forne þe freest, þat folȝed alle þe sele
> Exellently of alle þyse oþer, vnder heuenryche
>  þat mused.

Chaucer's Parson draws the same lesson from the same examples (*CT*, I 955):

> Ful ofte tyme I rede that no man truste in his owene perfeccioun, but he
> be stronger than Sampson, and hoolier than David, and wiser than
> Salomon.

And herein we may appreciate the special fitness of the association between Solomon and the pentangle (625–26), for the pentangle is a symbol that at one and the same time expresses human excellence and imperfection.

   In judging Gawain's conduct at this point we need to remember that he has already taken his leave of Bertilak and the ladies before setting out for the Green Chapel (1975–82), and has done so in such a warm and loving manner that he could hardly improve upon it even if he were to return to Hautdesert as Bertilak suggests (2400–2406). What may be construed as Gawain's bad grace in taking his final leave of Bertilak and the ladies is in fact another fine display of good manners. Considerable social tact is exercised by Gawain here, for he can hardly deny that these three have been responsible for his bitter self-knowledge of imperfection. Thus he courteously removes his helmet and wishes his host well, using the polite plural form of address (2407–10):

> 'Nay, for soþe,' quoþ þe segge, and sesed hys helme,
> And hatz hit of hendely, and þe haþel þonkkez,
> 'I haf soiorned sadly; sele yow bytyde,
> And he ȝelde hit yow ȝare þat ȝarkkez al menskes!'

And no less courteously does he commend himself to the ladies (2411–13):

> And comaundez me to þat cortays, your comlych fere,
> Boþe þat on and þat oþer, myn honoured ladyez,
> Þat þus hor knyȝt wyth hor kest han koyntly bigyled.[15]

15. Spearing comments that 'when he goes on to speak of the two ladies . . . his courtesy gives way to a raw sarcasm' (p. 223). Again there is a contradiction here of the idea represented by the pentangle, and there is no reason to see why it should be contradicted in this way. I owe my initial understanding of Gawain's courteous leave-taking to Waldron's note to 2425-28. Waldron draws attention to 'the almost jocular tone of this stanza . . . In spite of the reader's first impressions, Gawain's chivalry and social tact are most in evidence here: in order to avoid directly implicating Bertilak's wife in his condemnation of himself he falls back on the ecclesiastical commonplace of the "eternal Eve" ' (p. 134).

He remains their servant, and his gesture is more than an empty formality. He is even able to look with some ironic humour on the way in which he has been deceived. But these ironic possibilities have been hard earned in terms of the knowledge of himself that he has gained on the quest.

When Gawain returns to Arthur's court he does so as one made whole through penance, so that the stain of sin has been made clean. And it is the recognition of this fact that makes possible the joyful welcome of the court. But to understand the conduct of Gawain and the court on the knight's return it is necessary to set the responses of each in a proper perspective in relation to the virtue of penitence.

Although the sensible sorrow that accompanies contrition can be immoderate (*Suppl.*, 3.2), contrition itself lasts for the whole of the present life, even though satisfaction may have a temporal limitation (*Suppl*, 4.1):

> . . . in contritione . . . est *duplex* dolor: *unus* rationis, qui est detestatio peccati a se commissi: *alius* sensitivae partis, qui ex isto consequitur. Et quantum ad utrumque contritionis tempus est totius vitae praesentis status.

> . . . there is a twofold sorrow in contrition: one is in the reason, and is detestation of the sin committed; the other is in the sensitive part, and results from the former: and as regards both, the time for contrition is the whole of the present state of life.

Thus when Gawain returns to Camelot the slight wound in his neck is healed (2484), but his sorrow for his sins (2501–4) and his displeasure for them (2505–l0) remain unimpaired. The motive of sorrow persists because of the knowledge of the harm that has been done by sin (*Suppl.*, 4.1 *ad* l):

> . . . manet autem dolori, qui non solum de culpa est, inquantum habet turpitudinem, sed etiam inquantum habet nocumentum annexum.

> . . . but there does remain a motive of sorrow, which is for the guilt, not only as being something disgraceful, but also as having a hurt connected with it.

This harm is the obstruction that has been placed in the way of man and his salvation (*Suppl.*, 4.1):

> Quamdiu enim est aliquis in statu viae, detestatur incommoda, quibus a perventione ad terminum viae retardatur, vel impeditur; unde, cum per peccatum praeteritum vitae nostrae cursus in Deum retardetur, quia tempus illud, quod erat deputatum ad currendum, recuperari non potest, oportet quod semper in vitae hujus tempore status contritionis maneat, quantum ad peccati detestationem.

For as long as one is a wayfarer, one detests the obstacles which retard or hinder one from reaching the end of the way. Wherefore, since past sin retards the course of our life towards God (because the time which was given to us for that course cannot be recovered), it follows that the state of contrition remains during the whole of this lifetime, as regards the detestation of sin.

And this harm too Gawain acknowledges (2511–12):

> For mon may hyden his harme, bot vnhap ne may hit,
> For þer hit onez is tachched twynne wil hit neuer.[16]

There is no lack of spiritual or moral discernment on the part of the court in the welcome that it extends to Gawain. The best of knights returns in safety from a quest which has seemed to hold out only the certainty of death (see 672–86). The virtues symbolized by the pentangle he wears on shield and coat armour have been triumphantly vindicated, while the imperfection that accompanies them has been made good by satisfaction and absolution. And as Aquinas also explains, when the guilt is removed, so too is the shame (*Suppl.*, 4.1 *ad* 1):

> . . . erubescentia respicit peccatum, solum inquantum habet turpitudinem; et ideo postquam peccatum quantum ad culpam remissum est, non manet pudori locus.

> Shame regards sin only as a disgraceful act; wherefore after sin has been taken away as to its guilt, there is no further motive for shame.

Gawain has made a shameful confession of his sin to the court in his account of his adventures, and this is indeed an efficacious act.[17] But now the moment

---

16. See also *The Parson's Tale* (*CT*, I 304): 'Forther over, contricioun moste be continueel, . . .' Spearing misrepresents the point in stating that Gawain declares himself to be 'permanently stained with sin' (p. 221). Gawain is permanently affected with sorrow for sin. A similar misrepresentation is to be found in Arthur's conclusion that Gawain is unsuccessful in his attempt 'to make the green girdle a sign for endless *untrawþ* . . . because his views are doctrinally erroneous' (*Medieval Sign Theory*, p. 157). It is the critic, not the poet, nor the character, who is in error on the question of doctrine.

17. Compare once more the words of Beatrice in answer to the fictional Dante's confession (*Purg.*, XXXI. 40-42):

> Ma quando scoppia della propria gota
> l'accusa del peccato, in nostra corte
> rivolge sè contra 'l taglio la rota.

> . . . but when from a man's own cheek breaks forth condemnation of his sin, in our court the wheel turns back against the edge.

for shame has passed. The court shares its humanity with Gawain, and Gawain is its representative, the nephew of their king (2464–66). The only fitting response of such a court is to comfort the knight who has survived so profound a spiritual and moral examination, and to receive him back joyfully into their midst (2513–14):

> Þe kyng comfortez þe kny3t, and alle þe court als
> La3en loude þerat . . .

It is another sign of the fitness of the court's response (its courtesy in the strict sense) that it should wish to associate itself with the knight's imperfection (2514–18):

> . . . and luflyly acorden
> Þat lordes and ladis þat longed to þe Table,
> Vche burne of þe broþerhede, a bauderyk schulde haue,
> A bende abelef hym aboute of a bry3t grene,
> And þat, for sake of þat segge, in swete to were.

But the girdle, as a measure of Gawain's sin, is by the same token a measure of human excellence, and its fitness as such is acknowledged by the Green Knight (2398–99):

> . . . and þis a pure token
> Of þe chaunce of þe grene chapel at cheualrous kny3tez.

The girdle is the symbol of human virtue as it is proved in the quest of the Green Chapel, and as Aristotle observes (*Ethics*, IV.3) honour is the reward that is due to virtue. Since the adventure of the Green Chapel is one of the most marvellous adventures concerning Arthur (27–29) and since Arthur is by repute the noblest of the kings of Britain (25–26), the honour that is won for the court by Gawain's conduct is spread abroad and so becomes renown. At the end of the poem as at the beginning Gawain and the court are united in the renown of the Round Table (2519–21):

> For þat watz acorded þe renoun of þe Rounde Table,
> And he honoured þat hit hade euermore after,
> As hit is breued in þe best boke of romaunce.

The romance of *Sir Gawain and the Green Knight* justly takes its place, therefore, among 'þe Brutus bokez' (2523) as a witness of the nobility of England in the days of King Arthur.

# Index